BEST CANADIAN STORIES 2025

EDITED BY STEVEN W. BEATTIE

Biblioasis
Windsor, Ontario

FIRST EDITION
ISBN 978-1-77196-634-4 (Trade Paper)
ISBN 978-1-77196-635-1 (eBook)

Guest edited by Steven W. Beattie
Copyedited by John Sweet
Typeset by Vanessa Stauffer
Series designed by Ingrid Paulson

Published with the generous assistance of the Canada Council for the Arts, which last year invested $153 million to bring the arts to Canadians throughout the country, and the financial support of the Government of Canada. Biblioasis also acknowledges the support of the Ontario Arts Council (OAC), an agency of the Government of Ontario, which last year funded 1,709 individual artists and 1,078 organizations in 204 communities across Ontario, for a total of $52.1 million, and the contribution of the Government of Ontario through the Ontario Book Publishing Tax Credit and Ontario Creates.

PRINTED AND BOUND IN CANADA

CONTENTS

Steven W. Beattie

INTRODUCTION

What makes for a good short story? It's a deceptively simple question, innocuous-seeming even. But the form is so capacious, so mutable, so inherently welcoming of different approaches, styles, techniques, and voices, that a determination of quality becomes evanescent, like trying to bottle sunshine. Perhaps this is one reason so many writers default to metaphor in trying to explain it—bottling sunshine or, in the case of A.L. Kennedy, comparing a story's compressed force to lethal weaponry: "A story is small," Kennedy said, "in the way a bullet is small."

Indeed, a short story's defining property—that it is short— would seem to make it the ideal form for our distracted, attention-deficit age. Why, then, do we constantly hear from publishers that stories don't sell and from readers that they don't care for the form? Kennedy was on to something when she compared a story to a bullet. The image implies density and velocity, a potent combination in such a compact form. Stories derive their power from concision and concentration, which paradoxically requires more in the way of attention from both reader and writer. Stories are demanding; they cannot be consumed passively.

One of the most pernicious myths about short stories is that they are a stepping stone to novels. Debut writers will regularly get signed to a publisher with a collection of short fiction on the understanding that their next book will be a work of full-length fiction. The unspoken assumption here is that short fiction constitutes apprentice work, something a writer engages in to hone style, craft, and voice in preparation for the more sophisticated work of longer-form imaginative writing.

This is, to put it simply, nonsense. Surely such a sublime miniaturist as Cynthia Flood (whose brilliant collections such as *The Animals in Their Elements* and *Red Girl Rat Boy* aren't nearly as well known as they should be) is no less sophisticated a practitioner for painting on a smaller canvas. Other writers who have found praise for their novels (John Updike and Stephen King come immediately to mind) are actually better when working in the short form, where there is less temptation to expound at outrageous length or descend into self-indulgence on the page. Lisa Moore's novels gain attention from readers, critics, and award juries, but if you want to experience her in her most potent, undiluted form, look to her short fiction.

All of which is fine as a defence of the form but gets us no further in our inquiry as to what constitutes the essence of a successful short story. Some of this has to do with short fiction's protean nature. It is so changeable, so accommodating to different styles and approaches, that it actively resists containment. Even speaking of *the* short story seems reductive; the definite article tries unsuccessfully to tame a literary genre that is defiant in its refusal to be nailed down, so variable that any strict rubric about its properties or effects will almost by necessity end up lacking.

Some writers find it easier to define a short story by talking about what it is not. Flannery O'Connor, one of the twentieth-century masters of the form, tapped into her Catholic upbringing by offering a litany of things a story isn't: "Everybody thinks he knows what a story is. But if you ask a beginning student to write a story, you're liable to get almost anything—a reminiscence, an episode, an opinion, an anecdote, anything under the sun but a story." To this list I would add the following: a story is not a sermon; it is not a polemic or a jeremiad; it is not a sociological examination of race or class or gender; it is not a moral lesson. These things have their place, and indeed a story might contain aspects of any of them, but short fiction differs in its essence from other types of prose work.

Fine, one might reasonably object, but knowing what a story is not, what exactly *is* it?

O'Connor suggested that a story contains a complete dramatic action, and this is a pretty good starting point. Beyond that, Joyce Carol Oates, another American short fiction master, emphasizes a story's concision, which is inextricably tied into its formal presentation. "My personal definition of the form," Oates writes, "is that it represents a concentration of imagination, and not an expansion." Clark Blaise, one of this country's most accomplished short story writers, goes even further when he notes, "Most novels are watery, diluted, and bloated, and they do not have anything like the richness of a short story."

A story's richness is paradoxical, arising as it does out of a rigorous concatenation of focus, of subject, and of language.

Unlike novels, which are free to ramble, to meander, to indulge in subplots and large casts of characters and expansive vistas of time or geography, short stories zoom in, examining moments and incidents as if in extreme close-up. As such, the short story is an extraordinarily unforgiving form, leaving the writer nowhere to hide. Every word, every gesture, every movement is on display and open to intense scrutiny.

In this, the comparison with novels is perhaps deceptive. Both are imaginative prose works, but that, more or less, is where the similarities end. In their compression, their linguistic precision, their ruthless paring away of anything extraneous, short stories in fact share a closer affinity with a different genre altogether: poetry. Precise and evocative language, a telescoping of incident into brief moments without recourse to what went before or what comes after, an almost fanatical devotion to the work's effect on the level of the line as opposed to the paragraph or the page: all of these are attributes shared by short fiction and verse. The Canadian poet Zachariah Wells was not wrong when he referred wryly to a short story as a poem with an unhealthy affinity for the right-hand margin.

Beyond this, what makes not just a short story but a *good* short story, let alone one of the best of the year? Here we are on slippery ground. Qualitative demarcations such as "good" or "best" are subjective and will change depending upon who is making the determination. One reader might prize character above all else; another might look for stories steeped in atmosphere or far-off settings; yet another might gravitate toward a plot with a surprising twist on the final page. For my own part, it's tempting to suggest that recognizing a good short story is tantamount to US Supreme Court Justice Potter Stewart's test for obscenity: I know it when I see it.

This, of course, is unsatisfactory. But especially when dealing with a form so open to experimentation and play—what short fiction writer Diane Schoemperlen referred to as "jazzing around"—it's tricky to nail down precisely what works and what doesn't. The short form opens itself to such variety in structure, syntax, and approach it seems finally irreducible to a set of rigid rules or intransigent first principles. O'Connor again: "It's always wrong of course to say that you can't do this or you can't do that in fiction. You can do anything you can get away with, but nobody has ever gotten away with much."

After reading a year's worth of short stories published in magazines and literary journals, both in print and online, what stands out is the breadth of writing and the ways authors are working consciously to innovate within an established form. The epiphanic story epitomized by Chekhov and Joyce is only one template for these writers to expand upon; it bears little resemblance, for example, to the chronological leaps found in Caitlin Galway's "Heatstroke" or the frank surrealism of Cody Caetano's "Miigwetch Rex." The set-up for Mark Anthony Jarman's "That Petrol Emotion"—the driver of a car inadvertently hitting a young boy—superficially resembles Raymond Carver's "A Small, Good Thing," but there the comparison ends: Jarman's language is the prose equivalent of fusion jazz, with its proliferating alliteration and percussive tempo changes, a clear contrast to Carver's extreme minimalism. Then compare Jarman's prose to the long, flowing, subordinate-clause-laden sentences in Glenna Turnbull's "Because We Buy Oat Milk."

Each of these writers exemplifies a distinct approach to their material, but they share with the others compiled in these pages a strong narrative spine: they have not forgotten the importance of *story* in their attention to technique. The centrality of story may seem so obvious as to require no elucidation; perhaps the very obviousness of this aspect of short fiction is what allows it so frequently to go missing in work by writers who would much rather provide a subtle meditation on the ills of our society or a quiet slice of life in which nothing ever *happens*. No doubt there are successful stories that elevate mood over incident or examine stasis and quietude via small gestures and subtle shifts in language or psychology. Chris Bailey's "We've Cherished Nothing" is a precisely observed excavation of masculinity told from the prism of two PEI lobster fishers who do little more than talk; this too can be as captivating as any fast-paced actioner. But it never loses sight of its crucial narrative line.

Another element uniting these stories is an avoidance of overt self-seriousness. There is too often a prejudice among writers and readers alike that something humorous can't also be serious in intent; coming from a country whose two principal artistic achievements are short fiction and comedy, this seems at the very least paradoxical. This is one reason Liz Stewart and Lynn Coady are such a welcome breath of cool air. Their stories evince a quality that is fabulously rare in my reading: they are funny. Stewart's tale of a woman's misadventure involving a sex toy is one of the few laugh-till-it-hurts experiences I've had in recent memory. As for Coady, just wait for the moment in which she reveals the first words inadvertently captured on the reel-to-reel tape recorder her protagonist's father has acquired. Elsewhere, Kawai Shen tilts in the direction of racial identity in an insouciant manner that elicits a bark of laughter: "Her first impression of Ryan was that he was, incontrovertibly, a white male." It's the adverb that really sells it.

On its own, of course, humour is insufficient; it has to be in the service of something larger. What situates the stories in this volume, in my view, as among the "best" of the year is what the late postmodernist John Barth referred to as "passionate virtuosity." Examining the parallels in the writing of Italo Calvino and Jorge Luis Borges, Barth defined passionate virtuosity as a combination of "algebra" and "fire," with algebra standing for technical ability and fire for emotional resonance. As Barth pointed out, balance is essential in this regard. Too much technique without emotion is deadening; too much emotion absent technique is dully sentimental. The best stories contain both in proper measure.

Consider, for example, Kate Cayley's "A Day," which transports its reader to a divided Berlin during the reign of the Stasi in East Germany. Note the carefully evocative setting, which is described almost elliptically by indicating the narrator's youthful observations about the Berlin Wall, on the Communist east side "looped with razor wire, the concrete unblemished," while on the democratic west it is "[c]overed in blaring graffiti" and "seemed almost cheerful." The close attention to detail without recourse to bald exposition, while also remaining embedded in her first-person narrator's childhood impressions—her mixture of fear, excitement, and uncertainty—allows Cayley to imbue her story with the vibrancy of its historical setting while also maintaining a cool, ironic distance. This is what Barth meant about algebra and fire in combination.

Vibrancy is a good word to describe the core quality of the stories collected here. For all their variances in style, subject, and structure, each one feels alive on the page. These are stories that heave and seethe, yearn and ache. They are complete and internally integral; not one element can be elided without intrinsically damaging the story in question. "A story is a way to say something that can't be said any other way," claimed O'Connor, "and it takes every word in the story to say what the meaning is." She went on to offer one piece of advice that I have long taken to heart when it comes to reading and assessing short stories: "When anybody asks what a story is about, the only proper thing is to tell him to read the story."

So there it is. Go read the stories.

Mark Anthony Jarman

THAT PETROL EMOTION

Swans sail the canal as my car speeds the stone bridge, swans in the mirror while I zip around a lorry stopped at a shop, its flashers blinking robotically. Bono shilling his book on the radio, annoying me no end; will Bono ever stop talking about himself? Past the lorry, by the GAA clubhouse, a red-headed boy steps out, one foot on the sidewalk and one foot in the road, that borderline, the leg and the blow, all in a split second. Why did he step out? The boy rises, soundless shoes toward the clouds.

Bono speaks, the lad lands on his head, and I am made media villain. Dublin news reports a female driver stopped, undid her seat belt, but she did not get out of the car. Putting the car into gear, she drove away, leaving Danny the redhead on the walk.

It's true, I did undo my seat belt, a mortified moment to consider that blow, the world I drove into. A childhood, the hood of a car, summer waning to a fall. I was about to get out, but the plucky ginger stood up and walked back to his friend. Danny seemed right as rain and that was my hope. Just a bruise.

*

Later the complications, his head balloons, the injury bloody and infected. For the love of God, how was I to know? Danny's giant balloon head floats into the university hospital, floats into emergency surgery, his head floats onto the front page in full scary colour. Oh the cruel blow and ugly swelling! And what kind of horrible woman caused this? *Will she not turn herself in?*

I hear them in the polite pubs and cafés of Clontarf and Howth. Gardaí say they may know the make of the car and are "satisfied" it was a silver vehicle driven by a woman with blond hair. Well, that's half of Clontarf right there. Why the word "satisfied"?

Bono prattling on about himself. On *Top of the Pops* he was a twat with a mullet and now he thinks he's Pope of Ireland. I'm tired of bloody U2, I'd rather hear Feargal Sharkey and the Undertones belt out "Teenage Kicks."

On the same talk show Danny's mother asks, Now, why doesn't she turn herself in?

I could talk to a priest, whisper a word at confession, *I am the silver car,* but I no longer know the priests. We moved out to Clontarf from Usher's Island, fell away from the Church, and St Bridget's shut its door and became Sweet Thunder Discotheque.

I could have a word with the garda I know over in Raheny, see what to do. Martin's great *craic,* likes a pint with the lads, but he's being investigated by the corruption people to see if he's tied to this Hatch gang all after murdering each other's uncles and cousins. Martin has enough on his plate. For the moment it's just wait and hope.

My husband Declan is going through a rough patch. In an antique shop on the quays (lovely red doors) Declan found a handful of letters from Charles Dickens, the older Dickens writing to a youthful lover.

Declan knew these letters were rare and the shop said they were verified. Declan set to make a neat profit at Fonsie Mealy's auction house, enough to pay off the loan for the kitchen, maybe a holiday let in sunny Spain.

Then this expert Dr Litvack in Belfast, doesn't he write Fonsie Mealy's, says the letters are forgeries, says the signature is *clearly* wrong and they cannot be sold. What seemed good turned bad and Declan doesn't know which way to turn. It's not like stealing a mobile or waving a carving knife; he borrowed good money for the rare old letters and now all become shite.

And Declan's dad's in hospital, a stroke, must learn to walk again. In his hospital room a man grabbed his da's feet, trying to pull him out of bed. Mad! Declan's going to have to call the guards on him. A small grey-haired man shouting, pulling his feet, man doesn't have a clue. Going to have to put the guards on that man. So I can't tell Declan about Danny, not this minute.

Swans look so peaceful, gliding on the happy current. Now a car is handy, says Declan, but bikes are the best invention, we should have stopped inventing things after bikes. Declan says Mr Henry Ford created a monster. But such a happy occasion when we parked our first car in the front yard. A car! Now we're catching up to our cousins in Boston.

When the Celtic Tiger roared, we borrowed money from the bank, cut down the holly hedge, put in a sunroom, got another loan, bought a new water heater. Never had such money before and bankers calling asking do we want more. Soon three cars are parked in our tiny yard and everyone in the neighbourhood the same. I'd say we all went a bit mad.

On our cul-de-sac cars park right up on the sidewalk, straddling kerbs, and children out in the road. Nowhere to park and nowhere to play. And just look at all the headlights at night, long lines caught on Howth Road, horns honking like we're hotheaded Italians, flashing the finger and taking forever to come home from a cursing city. Yes, we have caught up with the Americans.

Dublin always a mood, a quiet kind of walking magic; I wonder if the magic's gone along with the quiet lanes. No leprechauns or pots of gold, just stolen mobiles and sex workers; lunatics shout at every corner and refugees from every broken country line up for the nightly soup kitchen right under the GPO's stately pillars.

Once the Irish had to sail abroad in coffin ships; now everyone comes to Ireland. Dublin full of Africans and Romanians, thousands of Romanians. We've been *invaded*. The government hands them money, so they are happy to come here. The Romanians walk into stores and fill their bags and walk straight out. The shops are short of staff from Covid and they can't stop them!

Shop wages are a pittance and dear dirty Dublin is very dear now. My niece Anna grew up right in this neighbourhood, but now she can't afford to buy here. So who is after buying up all our houses if it's not us? Real estate is mysterious, but it seems we've been taken over, we're being bought and sold. Young Anna feels betrayed. Good thing we bought the semi-detached when we did, or we'd be outside looking in, like the cheeky little fox at the end of our garden.

The radio talks of that poor sheep farmer in County Kerry. Home for a meal, happy to steer into his yard, home again, home again, jiggety jig, and doesn't he run his tires through a pile of noisy leaves. His young daughter hiding in the leaves to surprise him. The sirens come moaning to his farm and the man is never the same, never wants to hear those sounds again, never wants to get behind the wheel again.

It may sound dotty, but sometimes I feel that my car has always been here, forever, even before cars were invented, before they rolled off the boat. Our cars waited while we built cities for them, dreamed of their heat.

On the car radio Danny's mother says to do the right thing, surrender yourself to gardaí. But my own dear mother warned us, Do not stop for anyone, you just drive you.

I do hope Danny is all right. This will be on my mind a long, long time. Danny's sister on the talk show calling me a cow. Now does that help anything? I'd say they're enjoying it so, the whole lot of them. Nothing I do will change anything. I didn't mean to add a giant orb to his forehead. Why did the lad step out?

The shape waited inside Danny and I found it, teased it out for the media to venerate. Mind you, the other children quite enjoy Danny's head, his alien-from-outer-space look is popular, a new mask just in time for Halloween.

Bubble-head Danny a celebrity and so together we enter the newspaper pages, we join that poor immigrant woman stabbed on the quay below Heuston Station, join the addicts on O'Connell Street. Addicts stare on every street; where did they all hide before now? A paper cup for coins on the sidewalk, nodding off in front of every Spar, and once their mother's darling baby.

Was it fun at first? Can't they just stop? Can't people smarten up when they are harming themselves? I know I'm no better, so no need to give me a lecture. At school in Cornmarket we were taught that Cuchulain, in his rage and grief, fought the tide, the rolling sea, but it was no use to fight the tide.

The nuns and Jesuits spoke of history; now we ride radials that cost more than most rent, our sensors whisper suggestions: *petrol is low, turn at the next left, baby it's cold outside.*

And German cars just keep getting better. I float in a pulsing car, sixteen valves working in waking dreams of internal combustion. Without a car we simply can't cope.

This is the age of confession. I refuse to join. Once the trees are fallen over, does a gale feel regret? Someone stepped in the road by the GAA clubhouse, someone's car came at the same moment. I remember no sound or impact, the machine simply had its way. That is the extent of my confession.

Never used to see a fox in the city. In Queen Anne Park the sea wind blows off Bull Island and those long, lovely rows of headstrong oaks roar above silent scooters as ghost birds call from the mist. These new noiseless scooters must run on hope.

Declan fries up our eggs and blood sausage before we visit the hospital to see about the demented man pulling Da's legs out of bed. What if we walk past Danny's family and his balloon head? We sip our black tea and Declan says soon enough robots will take care of all the unpleasant tasks in the hospital, bots will play chess with Da and have friendly chit-chats about the weather. And friendly bots will drive us here and there in our cars, saving us so much palaver.

Clea Young

////////////

NEST

Don't mess with Marley was a common phrase in the housing co-operative where I was mercifully offered a unit, after several years on the wait-list, the summer my son, River, turned two. Marley didn't mix with the other parents, those supervising their children in the communal courtyard in varying degrees, depending on their child's age. I was out there most evenings and weekends—basically whenever River wanted to play with the other children—but I quickly learned the parent of a seven-year-old might duck inside to get dinner started or throw on a load of laundry. In a way I became an informal overseer of all the kids because I *had* to be out there; there was no turning your back on a two-year-old.

It would be more accurate to say, *Don't mess with Hunter and Koda,* Marley's boys. They were eight and ten, and had finally arrived at the top of the food chain. I observed that kids of a certain age—usually eleven or twelve, or those entering puberty— didn't play anymore, opting instead to cocoon with their video games and iPhones indoors. I'd watch them slink back and forth between the nearby 7-Eleven, clutching giant Slurpee cups. Sometimes I'd address them just to make them speak, to remind them they could. But that summer, Hunter and Koda hadn't yet aged out of the courtyard antics. They were full throttle with the water balloons and Nerf guns. They wanted action and they usually got it because, frankly, they brought it: an energy that accelerated the intensity of play and eventually tipped it over into argument and dissolution. Their presence put parents on edge. If things became unruly, it was understood that whoever had witnessed the trouble would step in and correct the behaviour. Not exactly discipline the children so much as act as referee to their play, and when those boys entered the mix, calling a time out was inevitable. Marley, though, didn't tolerate orders, not even gentle entreaties of her boys to chill out, if they didn't come from her. And somehow, without ever being present, she heard everything.

Marley's reputation was all gossip until one Saturday afternoon in July. I was outside, climbing up and down a set of concrete stairs, spotting River and shielding him from the limbs of the more sure-footed children flying past. There was some business with bamboo that I was peripherally aware of, children pulling it from the earth and javelin-tossing the stalks across the courtyard. Parents were trying to halt the destruction, threatening to take away privileges like screen time and dessert, none of which had any effect, though the bamboo harvest did eventually stop.

The conversation among the adults quickly turned back to what was on everyone's minds: the fugitive boys from Port Alberni, on Vancouver Island. They were teenagers, actually. At first they were just missing, then, within a matter of days, reports confirmed they'd ferried to the Mainland and were suspected murderers travelling north. The news cycle exploded with experts lecturing on alienated boys, violent video games, gender roles, and mental health. We traded sound bites and regurgitated facts about the teenagers' home lives, their parents and community. We speculated on where they'd turn up—relieved that tips from the public suggested they were moving away from British Columbia—and, most of all, why? Why had two childhood friends run off on a killing spree? None among us voiced our real concern, but we all wondered: Could it happen to us? Could our boys turn out like that?

"Dad?" Logan, a tremulous child with long hair and a hysterical fear of squirrels, vied for his father's attention.

"It's always the mothers who get blamed when boys go rogue," said Colleen, my immediate neighbour.

"This goes beyond rogue," said Jake, Logan's father. "It's psychotic."

"You watch," Colleen said. "Their mothers will be burned at the stake."

"Dad," Logan pleaded.

"What?" Jake snapped.

Logan pointed to the playhouse, a wooden gazebo with ferns sprouting from the roof. "They're going to stab us," he said quietly.

Apparently Hunter and Koda were filing the bamboo into spears to use on the other, less resourceful children. Jake left us to investigate.

"Whoa, whoa, whoa," I heard him say to the boys, crouched with Swiss Army knives in hand. "I'm calling a stop work order on this."

That's when Marley appeared, striding out of the shadows. "Watch your tone," she said. I almost let River fall headlong down the stairs. I grabbed his arm, but the yank startled and possibly hurt him and he started to wail.

Marley was tall and slender, lean in a way most mothers I knew were not, or no longer. Also stylish with an asymmetrical bob dyed platinum blond.

"You deal with your kids, I'll deal with mine," she said, arms triangulated like wings with hands on her hips. I thought of a katydid, camouflaged one moment, the most striking creature the next. River squawked and writhed in my arms, desperate to begin his obsessive stair-climbing again.

"It's okay, you're okay," I chanted, trying to quiet him so that I could hear what came next.

"This is what kids are supposed to do," Marley continued. "What you're seeing here is natural development." She was calm, composed, but everything about her was taut, trigger ready. I couldn't look away.

"I'm all for development," Jake said, "as long as it doesn't come at the expense of an eyeball." There was an attempt at light-ness in his voice, a desire to defuse.

Ignoring him, Marley said to her boys, "Keep it up." From what I could tell they'd never stopped, had barely even registered the altercation over their accumulating arsenal. Marley turned and legged it in her frayed denim shorts back to her place, but not before her eyes landed on me, holding River nearly upside down in my arms.

"Sometimes you have to let them fall," she said, not unkindly. And then she was gone.

"I do," I sputtered to no one. But did I? And why should I? Was she implying I should let River launch himself down ten concrete steps? Was she calling me a helicopter parent? My child was two years old. I couldn't exactly let him run wild with the others, unattended. Strangers often used the courtyard as a shortcut. He was vulnerable in so many ways.

*

I began to look out for Marley, or look for her. I'm not sure which. I brought River outside to play when he was content inside. I imagined scolding Hunter and Koda without cause just to make her appear, to see if she would. I asked the other parents about her, trying to appear naive: "What's that woman's name again?" It turned out everyone enjoyed the topic—*thinks she's better than us, anger management issues, orders takeout seven nights a week*—but no one really knew her. I did learn the boys usually spent summers with their dad, in Prince George, but for some reason weren't this year, much to everyone's dismay. She was a graphic designer, a runner, but that was it. What more did I want, or need, to know? There were other single moms in the co-op, but she seemed to have it figured out, how to parent and work and move through the world with a fierce, magnetic grace. I was struggling in my job as publicist for a small local publisher, which often required me to attend events in the evening, necessitating a babysitter. In bookstores, before pitiable audiences of friends, family, and the odd stray, I watched my authors monotone through their self-important work, reading longer than anyone in the room had an attention span for, all while the babysitting meter ticked. I just didn't care like I once had. Whereas I used to view the writing life as sacred, I now saw it as egocentric and my job upholding and promoting it complicit, void of any meaningful contribution to society. But how could I make a change when I had daycare and housing expenses forever bearing down on me? I couldn't afford not to care. One thing I could do, though, was contribute to my new community. It was an unofficial requirement of the co-op that a member from each household join one of the committees that met monthly to discuss and resolve issues related to their mandates—there were grounds, maintenance, parking, membership, and recycling committees. The latter of which, I learned, Marley was chair.

The recycling committee's next meeting was in a week's time, at the end of July. I anticipated it as though it were a date. The evenings were hot and I was tired from work and my commute, but I was a better mother with something to look forward to. I made watermelon slice and peanut butter toast picnics for dinner, which River and I ate in our underwear on our small sun-splashed deck. I knelt at the tub for longer than I would have liked while he wallowed in the tepid water and ate frozen blueberries. And I let him play outside a little in the evening, even though I didn't have the energy or desire to make small talk with my neighbours at the end of a workday.

"They're in Alberta by now, or Saskatchewan," a dad said to no one in particular, staring into his phone as I hurried along the main causeway, trailing River. I'd followed the updates that day too. The boys from Port Alberni were on the run, moving across provinces pursued by police. The media was calling it a manhunt. Journalists had descended on their hometown looking to interview anyone who'd ever brushed shoulders with the teens. Colleen was wrong: so far their mothers weren't being blamed, though their home lives were under scrutiny, particularly that of the boy who lived with his grandmother. There was a story there, a sinkhole in his past from which the darkness sprung. There was less discussion and speculation among the parents as new, grim details were revealed. Three people dead. Communities on edge. The long, glittering days of summer now cast a menacing light.

"Not in the face!" a mother shouted. "No shooting in the face! How many times do I have to tell you?"

I sat on a nearby retaining wall, watching the battle of water guns. River pedalled throughout the chaos in a stray plastic car. The bigger children ignored him, ran past and around him to refill their ammunition at the tap. Hunter and Koda weren't among them and despite the commotion there was a sense of ease to the play. Or maybe I imagined it. But no, the parents lingered with their evening drinks out of the line of fire and talked amiably about upcoming camping trips, triple-checking the weather forecast on their phones. There were shrieks and laughter and the odd injustice, but there was no ganging up on one another, no battle to achieve tears, as there would have been if the brothers were involved. One by one the children got cold and tired and were called in. I thought about the troubled fugitives bedding down for the night in mosquitoed wetlands. Were they sick with fear and remorse, or were they exhilarated, triumphant?

"Two minutes," I told River, preparing him to go inside. Just then Colleen's daughter, Violet, ran past and squirted River's car. I don't think a drop even touched him, but it was the act of being singled out and targeted that startled and set him off. Violet ran hooting from sight.

*

The conversation revolved around soft plastics—plastic bags to be precise. Apparently the city would no longer collect and recycle them. It caused flares of indignity among the five well-intentioned members who made up the committee. Marley, however, seemed tired as she took notes on the proceedings to share with the board. There were dark circles under her eyes, and her jaw muscles flexed noticeably when a sparrow-like woman named Anne spoke. Marley wore a black tank top and large gold hoop earrings, along with her trademark jean shorts. The door to the common room was propped open to encourage airflow, but only the whoops of children playing rushed in and out. I had hired a girl whom I'd observed to be one of the least disaffected among my teen neighbours to watch River while I attended the meeting. Her name was Sway and she rode horses on the weekend. Sway was outside with River. I'd instructed her to keep a close watch, to keep him a few steps removed from the play, safe from its volatile epicentre. She seemed to understand. I had not explicitly said, *keep him away from Hunter and Koda,* but implied it. "Some kids get carried away," I said, and nodded in the direction of the shirtless brothers whose torsos were scrawled with ballpoint pen depictions of flames.

Anne couldn't move past her dismay over the city's decision on soft plastics. "Why?" she wanted to know. But none of us could say.

"It just means you'll have to take your bags to a drop-off point yourself," Marley said. "It's not the worst thing."

"I'm retired," Anne said, "so I have time to do that. But how many people will?"

"Actually," I said, "I think most people nowadays pack reusable bags. There's definitely growing awareness about the evils of plastic."

"The evils of plastic?" Marley repeated. "Who *are* you?"

"Lauren," I said, though I'd introduced myself at the start of the meeting.

"No, I know. I just mean, are you some kind of eco-warrior?"

"Sorry?" I said. There was such derision in her voice. I looked around the table to gauge others' reactions, but no one appeared to notice. I grew hot and my face flushed extravagantly. I felt like an ant beneath one of the children's magnifying glasses: seen and deemed worthy of death.

"We'll need to include this in the newsletter," Marley said. "Maybe put a sign on the recycling room door, too."

The meeting shifted to the need to remind members to crush their containers to avoid bins overflowing before pickup day. Outside, the children's cries were growing increasingly feverish, crossing the line from play into overwrought. I hoped Sway had hauled River inside by now. I could've gotten out of my chair to look, no one would've cared, but I stayed seated. I didn't want to be singled out again by Marley. Anne continued to wring her hands over the plastic bags and decided she would write a letter to the city. This seemed to calm her. Marley's phone began to ring and she glanced at the screen.

"Meeting adjourned," she said, sweeping her notes from the table and heading for the door, phone to her ear. I heard her laugh and felt resentful. Why did I care? Why did I want to befriend the one self-exiled woman in a co-operative? Why not leave her to drift out there on the raft of aloneness she'd built? I can't say. Only that I felt compelled to lure her in to shore and burn that raft to ash.

*

It was Friday of the August long weekend and I'd taken the day off work. I must have mentioned it to Colleen because when I woke she'd already texted, suggesting we have coffee on the communal deck. Colleen was the best sort of neighbour: welcoming, unobtrusive, chatty. But I didn't want to be her friend, her confidante. I had no desire to map her quirks and failings the way I did Marley's. Colleen gave me everything up front, laid it all out there like garage sale treasures on quilts for every passerby to observe and comment on. I did not covet those kinds of treasures. I wanted a small glass swan slipped to me in the night, or beneath a table, and to know it was only mine to hold. Still, I texted Colleen back and told her I'd join her in twenty minutes, after River's breakfast.

"All we want is for our sons to become good men, am I right?" Colleen launched in as soon as I was across from her at the picnic table. "But how, exactly, do we do this when the patriarchy's been pinching our asses since we were nine-year-olds choosing penny candies at the corner store? That's just my experience. I don't know about you," she said, not waiting for a reply. "It should really be #mefuckingtoo because honestly, how is this a revelation to anyone? And, more importantly, considering how *we* came up, are we even equipped to guide our twenty-first-century boys?"

A wasp zipped around my mug and I swatted it away. "Good question," I said. I wasn't prepared for pre-coffee philosophizing.

"I like that you don't cut his hair," Colleen said, nodding toward where River was making his way in the direction of the sandbox we all knew was filled with cat feces.

"River," I said to his small, determined back, "not in there, please."

"Why do we cut boys' hair and let girls' grow long? It's so stupid, but it's a perfect example of one of those things we don't think about. Though clearly you do."

There was a wasp in my coffee now and I tried to tip it into a potted hosta without losing it all. "I'm not sure I do," I said, watching the wasp crawl about in the dirt. "I just think he has amazing hair."

"Well, whatever," Colleen said. "You're doing a great job."

"Thanks," I said. "We're all just muddling along, aren't we, hoping to get some of it right?"

"Some of us think we have it all figured out." Colleen rolled her eyes in the direction of Marley's place, where I could see the sliding glass door was open, a gauzy curtain catching the breeze. "She could learn a thing or two from you."

"I'm not so sure about that," I said.

Other doors began to open; children trickled out with unbrushed hair, eyes pinched against the sun. River was now digging with commitment in the sandbox and I didn't have the heart to stop him, cat feces or not, because I was drinking my coffee in peace.

"There must be a nest somewhere," Colleen said, flapping her hands and rising suddenly so that the picnic table rocked and more of my coffee spilled. "It happens every year."

*

I had plans to take River to the spray park on Granville Island, but the day kept getting away from me. After the sandbox he was tired, went down for a nap. While he slept, I answered a few emails, one from an author anxious for me to post a positive review of her work on social media before it became old news, another who'd found a misplaced comma in her biography on the publisher's website. Who's going to notice? I wanted to reply, but instead corrected it, let her know I'd done so, and thanked her for her keen eye. I filled a tray of juice popsicles and put them in the freezer, fished flies from the inflatable wading pool I'd set up on our deck and added some fresh water. But when River woke, he had a low fever. I tried to carry him to the pool, but he thrashed and moaned so that I abandoned the idea and gave him a dose of Tylenol instead. He fell asleep again and I saw our long-weekend plans—beach jaunts and ice cream stops—crumble into a rubble of indistinct hours spent nursing River's symptoms and streaming movies. I had no official summer vacation planned; I didn't have the money. And while I could've arranged to visit my father and his wife in the Okanagan, we'd have to bus both ways and be subjected to the fierce orderliness of their lakeview condo. The thought of keeping my sticky, cherry-juice-stained child off their white couches did not sound like a vacation.

Later that afternoon, River sat naked in my lap while I fed him green Jell-O. He took small, unenthusiastic bites and I wondered if I should take him to emergency at Children's Hospital. His body burned against mine and he shivered violently when I held a cold cloth to his forehead. He'd had colds in the past, many snotty-faced colds, but this was new for me. He couldn't even keep his eyes open for *Paw Patrol*. I heard parents outside, a discharge of laughter followed by a shout of reprimand. With River asleep again, I checked the news on my phone. An aluminum boat, presumed to have been used by the outlaw teens, had been found on the banks of the Nelson River, in Manitoba. Small communities in the area were setting curfews. The boggy forest along the river was too dense for a ground search, so helicopters beat the air overhead, trying to flush them out. I looked at River's small shape under the sheet. How did a boy go wrong? How to know when he's taken a fork in the road and call him back before it's too late? The sheet rose and fell with his breath. I put my face to his mouth to smell the hot, sugary life in him.

Colleen texted to invite me outside for a glass of wine. I told her about River and she said we could sit near my place, with the door open, so I could hear if he needed me. I said I had a headache and didn't think I could drink wine. She replied I could drink whatever I liked. I could think of no other excuse, so I took a glass of water outside to join her. The evening glowed with false promise that August would never end, that we would never again find ourselves in the grip of November rain. Colleen had told me it happened almost like clockwork in the co-op; come October, the doors closed and hibernation began. I wouldn't see most of my neighbours again until May. I welcomed the prospect of seclusion, quiet, but I also would have liked to have a friend nearby with whom I didn't need to make plans, who might just knock on my door and visit for an hour. I imagined Marley dropping by with sushi, eating with her amid the containers at my felt-pen-stained kitchen table while snow fell outside.

"Should I be worried?" I said.

"Kids get sick all the time," Colleen said. "He picked something up at daycare." She had two kids, a preteen boy and six-year-old Violet, one of the few girls roaming the co-op. When she spoke of them, or about children in general, it was with a weary knowledge that came from experience, and while she tended to set my mind at ease, she also shut down any discussion. There wasn't room for possibility with Colleen.

The water guns were out that evening and from where we sat I could see long arcs shoot skyward, into trees and over railings onto my neighbours' deck chairs. The children weren't background noise tonight, they were warriors on a mission.

Hunter and Koda were whipping up a frenzy, calling for teams, for battle.

"When they catch those boys, I hope they're locked up and psychoanalyzed," Colleen said. "I want to see brain scans and pictures of their bedrooms, the posters on their walls and the books on their shelves. The whole story's there, we're just not hearing it."

"It has to end soon," I said. "They're going to get caught."

"Of course they will. Teenagers are notoriously stupid."

Another cluster of parents were seated on a deck a little ways down from us, closer to the action. I wanted Colleen to join them, the livelier group. I wanted to go inside and imagine another life for myself and River, searching out vocational programs on college websites. Or I wanted to watch Netflix. I didn't want to think about those messed-up boys on the run. When they were found, a couple of days later, they would be dead, killed by their own or each other's hand. The videos they recorded before their deaths wouldn't be made public. And the public would gladly forget about them and the working-class mill town that made them. Their mothers would never be interviewed. Their mothers wouldn't surface, either, out of grief or horror or non-existence. What could they have said? What could they have done?

I gulped my water and said I needed to check on River. "I might be a while."

"I'll be here," Colleen said. "Violet's down there in the mayhem, so I'm not going anywhere."

Inside, River had kicked off his sheet and lay breathing steadily. His forehead was still hot to touch. I kissed his cheeks and his arm flung up involuntarily. He moaned, rolled onto his stomach. I scanned his back, legs, feet. Something caught my eye. On his soles: spots, pinpricks of red. I searched the rest of his body and found them on his palms too. I pulled out my phone and googled: *fever spots on hands and feet.* Apparently, River had a common virus among pre-school-age children: hand, foot and mouth. The spots would swell into tiny blisters and there were likely more percolating on the insides of his cheeks and on his tongue. I was relieved. Colleen was right: something he picked up at daycare. I pulled the fan from the closet and set it at the foot of the bed, wind rippling across the sheets. I was not an incompetent mother, only inexperienced. I needed people like Colleen in my life. She didn't have to be my best friend, just a friend. Did people even have best friends past a certain age? Generally, that was someone's partner, but River's father and I had messed that up, luckily before River was born.

When I returned outside, Colleen was gone. So was the other group of parents who'd gathered farther down the row. Had I been inside that long? Surely everyone's dinner hadn't arrived at the same moment. I heard traffic on the neighbouring street, an indicator of the absence of children's cries. A stream of water shot up into the giant maple that shaded the sandbox and gazebo. The water arced and broke apart in silvery chunks as it fell back to earth. Then another stream, another. No, they were two separate streams. Two water guns aiming at the same target. I moved closer to see what they were so bent on hitting.

"Knock it off, you guys," I heard someone say. A woman. "We'll need an ambulance if you keep this up." The streams of water continued, synchronous, deliberate, reaching for what I finally saw was a large grey cone fixed to a high branch. A wasps' nest. I moved to the stairs leading down into the courtyard. From there I saw Hunter and Koda, side by side, water bazookas in hand, determined to shoot it down. I understood the appeal, the desire to watch it fall and detonate on the pavement below, an explosion of wasps.

"People are allergic," Marley said to her boys' resolute backs. "You two, *enough*." The streams of water continued. The nest rocked a little. They were only managing to hit the bottom, the wasps' entrance, and I could see a small swarm gathering at the opening, trying to assess the problem.

"So, no video games for a week," Marley continued. "You two cool with that?" Target practice continued, unabated. It was as though they didn't hear. Parents steered their children away from the scene, toward safety and home. It was uncomfortable to behold Marley's ineffectual parenting, but I couldn't stop staring. Her gloss was rubbing off before me. I pitied her. I wanted to help.

"Hey, guys," I called out. "Listen to your mom." My words bounced off their gleaming summer bodies like a harmless spray of Nerf gun darts. Marley turned to me and I felt her focus intensely. Why the look of scorn? She was stubborn and ungrateful, an overextended mother with an inflated sense of self, raising two entitled boys. I almost turned and went inside right then. But I couldn't. What had begun as annoyance had undergone a chemical process in my veins; I was flooded with righteous contempt.

"Good riddance," I said, though Marley was too far to hear.

"Lauren." Someone said my name.

"Who does she think she is, anyway?" I said to no one in particular.

"Lauren." That voice again. Stern and authoritative. Colleen walked toward me, shepherding Violet along before her. Marley stood with her hands folded on top of her head. Tattoos of her boys' names ran along the underside of each arm, elbow to armpit, in ornate cursive ink. Did you love your children more if you needled their names into your skin, did it keep them closer, protect them?

"Let's check on River," Colleen said.

Hunter had moved to stand atop the electrical utility box with his water gun. This put him closer to his target and the stream of water made contact, causing the nest to swing on its branch. Koda refilled his weapon at the tap. Colleen gently took hold of my arm.

"Coming?" she said.

"No," I said, resisting her pull. I wanted to see what Marley would do next, how she would rein them in, if she even could.

Both boys were on top of the utility box now, hitting the nest simultaneously. It rocked above their heads like the lethal piñata it was. They were relentless in their attack; they worked in beautiful tandem.

"Guys," Marley sighed. She moved toward the box, reached up and placed a hand on Hunter's foot. "Listen to me. You need to stop." She stood almost directly beneath the nest, thirty feet up. Droplets from the boys' guns rained down on her.

"We've almost got it," Koda said. "You'd better move."

"This is the worst idea," Marley said. She looked over to where Colleen and I stood watching at a safe distance. "Move along," she said, and waved her hands to indicate we should go.

I shook my head no. We weren't going anywhere. The boys were right. The nest was going to come down. Were they more mischievous than other boys, or just curious? If they'd had another mother, would they be so disliked among my neighbours, by me?

They were just boys with water guns on a hot summer evening. They drilled into the nest where it connected to the branch.

"Any second now," Colleen said.

"Then what?" I asked.

Colleen shrugged.

The nest fell at an odd angle and a blur of wasps followed it down to land with a soft thud near Marley's feet, a throw cushion tossed from the couch. There was no explosion. It was constructed of paper, not mud, and built to flex with the wind. The boys whooped in celebration and Marley jumped back, away from the nest fizzing now that the internal hive had been disrupted.

"Shit," she said, grabbing her ankle. "Get inside," she told her boys. They leapt down from the electrical box, still eyeing the nest, wanting it to do more.

"Go," Marley ordered. This time they listened. The brothers jogged through the courtyard, spent water guns in hand. I knew that when a wasp stung its target, it also released a chemical message to its colony, ordering them to attack. Wasps flitted around Marley now, spun up and down her long limbs. She started to run for home, with her boys, then stopped and appeared to resist the impulse. She had to go another direction. "Fuckers," she spat, swatting wildly. She ran toward the underground parking garage, trailed by an erratic haze of insects. Out of sight, I heard her shriek—another sting, another several—and the sound echoed through the concrete bunker of parking stalls. Then a metallic crash followed by silence. Had she climbed inside a car? Had she tripped? People stored rusted, flat-tired bikes and other hopeless items where they shouldn't. I could've checked on her, I should have, but I was grateful to her for leading the swarm away from the courtyard, grateful she was gone from view.

"Mama?" I heard River say. Then louder, with a hint of panic, "Mama?"

Maybe later, once the wasps had fully vacated their ruined home, and if the raccoons didn't get to it first, I would tear off a piece to show him. I would point to the branch where it hung, the spot where it fell, and he would know one more thing to look out for in this world. The courtyard was empty, quiet. You could almost convince yourself no one was in trouble, there was no threat of danger.

"Hey, baby," I heard Colleen say. She'd gone to my house, where the front door stood open and River waited shivering on the threshold. "Your mama's right here." And I was, in an instant. I lifted him into my arms, buried my face in his hot neck, and made the sounds a mother makes to comfort her child, even though he wasn't crying, he was fine.

Liz Stewart

FUNNY STORY

Bullet vibrators are not meant for assholes, but I liked the feeling, I wanted it, and Shanna always gave me what I wanted. By myself, it always worked great. I still stand by the sensation, the gluttony of pleasure that encapsulated that whole era of my life, the unabashed lesbian sex I was finally having that first winter of living alone.

"I'm so sorry," Shanna called from the bed. "Would you like me to try?"

I was crouched on the edge of the toilet, fishing inside my asshole for body-safe silicone. I remember curling my toes around my dirty blue bath mat. I was so bad at cleaning that place. Mould grew up every cramped wall. In my memory, I had been sitting there for hours and she hadn't said a word, shocked or shamed into silence.

"No, Jesus. You should go home." I could not comprehend why she was still there. We hardly knew each other. The bathroom door was shut. I was practically begging for privacy.

"I think I need to take you to the hospital," she said. "It sounds like it's not coming out." That she could identify the state of my asshole by sound alone was enough to make me want to disappear. I looked around for a way to kill myself. Bedsprings creaked and I stuttered to my feet, making for the handle, ready to barricade myself in with the mildew if that's what it took.

Then the door opened and she was there, naked, ruddy, biting at her chapped lips. I covered my pubic hair with a free hand, as if she'd never seen it.

Her hair was the colour of a golden retriever and her face was the shape of a heart. She was short, thick-limbed, with distant, lime-sized tits. Apparently she was a wrestler, but I'd never heard of any rural Manitoba wrestling league, and I couldn't for the life of me picture her in a mouth guard.

"I hate hospitals," I told her, and brushed past her to put my clothes back on. The buzz in my ass was getting claustrophobic. Mid-stride, I vibrated, and froze in place to groan. The noises were in equal parts frustrated, pained, and rapturous. It sounded like it wasn't coming out.

What was I supposed to do? I couldn't call my parents. I'd die before I shoved my homosexual proclivities in their faces like that. I couldn't call my friends. They'd all moved to Winnipeg after high school. None of my ex-lovers would pick up the phone.

In the end, I went willingly.

Shanna got dressed and walked me to her parents' pickup, parked jauntily on the dead-grass driveway. It was nearing midnight. We both shivered while she turned the car on. April in the prairies, and the ground was wet with shrinking piles of old snow. I couldn't get comfortable in the red upholstered passenger seat.

"Jesus," I kept saying, "jesus, jesus, jesus."

Shanna peeled down Main Street and turned onto the highway. I didn't question it at the time. The hospital in town was small and there would be no doctor available this time of night. They probably would have sent us into the city anyway. Shanna was saving us time. So we started north, the long forty-five minutes to the city.

I was a live wire. Every second I was twitching, swearing, shrieking in anger-ache-ecstasy.

"Shh, shh, shh," Shanna said, not taking her eyes off the potholed highway. "This reminds me of the time my brother and I—"

"Fuck! Drive!" I was sweating. I was sick to my buzzing stomach.

"I am." Her voice was clipped and calm, a flatness I didn't recognize. What did I know about Shanna? I knew that she referred to her first time eating pussy as her "second baptism," and that when she did it, mid-March in the pitch dark of my basement, she pulled her face off my clit and begged me to tell her she was doing a good job. I knew she did whatever I asked with a timid openness that didn't exist in her clothed life. I liked her best when I slapped her in the face, rammed her into the headboard, and she cocked her head and bit at her lips like, *was that okay?*

We met on an app. Well, we met in high school, when she was in ninth grade and I was in twelfth, but it didn't count as meeting, I was trying so hard to disappear. Her profile was sunny and full of friends and drunken nights. One picture of her holding a largemouth bass on the edge of a dock, wearing a bucket hat, smiling. I was impressed by that. She was looking for "someone fun," same as me. Nothing too attached. It helped, I told myself, that she would be leaving soon. Actually. Concretely. She had an acceptance letter. She had her flights booked.

A highway empty as a hole, that's what I remember. And Shanna's lips bleeding, her tonguing at them, staring into the space between headlights. I arched my back and moaned.

"I am not comfortable with this situation. Pull over. I can call a cab."

"No, come on. Sit tight. I know it hurts, but it's going to be okay. We'll be there soon." A lie. We hadn't even passed Riverside.

"Boundaries, Shanna, boundaries. Let me out, this is too weird."

The truck swerved, straddled the yellow line, then righted itself.

"Something dead," Shanna said, her face twisted. Guts and a twisted head on the side of the road? Get over it, I thought. Think about me in this situation. My asshole burns.

"A deer," she said, and glanced at me. My face was not the comfort she was looking for. She turned on the radio.

The second time we hung out—always late, always at my place—she told me she hadn't caught the fish in the picture. Some ex-boyfriend had, and she put it in her profile as a joke, "to make me look more butch."

"Fuck!" I yowled, and spread apart my cheeks through my sweats to relieve some of the impossible pressure.

"Shh, shh, dear," she said, and put a hand on my knee. Whether she was being intentionally affectionate, or if she had been primed by the image of roadkill, I'll never know.

"I never see you like this," she mused tonelessly, staring ahead. "You know you're usually really hard to read? This is the longest I've gone without wondering how you're feeling."

I kicked the glovebox, wrangled the seat belt with my hands. We crossed the bridge with a rattle.

"How long has it been since you got me drunk and convinced me to go home with you?" she continued, and I moaned, "Two months? I don't think you've asked me a single question about myself. I can't tell if you like me. And I can't tell if you're using me, manipulating me. I have to assume you are. Trying to."

We crossed the #2 intersection, and the cab was momentarily lit. Shanna's neck, its blue veins, sprouted from the furry hood of her winter coat. She was biting a smile off her lips. I was still wet from the sex we didn't finish having, her spit still stuck to the inside of my thighs.

"You like me like this?" I asked.

"I think I do," she said. Her voice was soft, and I clawed the radio off to hear her say, "Like I finally have you. Attentive, for once. Present."

A lump rose in my throat. She hadn't driven me anywhere before. We never had a reason to go anywhere but bed together. My poor butthole rang like a phone, and her smile widened.

"Pull over," I begged my stranger, "please, pull over." I thought I might be able to push the bullet out. I thought she might fuck me and leave me on the side of the road. It would have been a relief.

I lunged for the wheel. We jerked across the road onto the gravel shoulder.

Then my palm was in her stubby fingers, bent unnaturally toward the wrist, which screamed in pain. Wrestler girl. For the first time, I thought she might be my type.

"Don't," she warned, and threw my hand away, pulling us back onto the highway. I rubbed my wrist, buzzed, and gasped, light-headed. Giddy.

"I want to know you," I told her. Declared it. "I want you to know me."

"I don't care anymore," she said.

I told her anyway. We approached the city lights and I told her about my childhood fear that a tiger would jump through my window and tear my chest out. I told her I wanted to start wearing boxers. I tried to convince her that I was not a broken person, but someone who was going through a metamorphosis and would emerge from that mouldy basement, some day in early summer, with a fully formed personality and a healthy attachment to others.

We pulled into the hospital. I kissed her knuckles and thanked her for the ride, and she thanked me.

"For the funny story," she said, and she left me there, at the front doors of emergency.

*

I only saw her once after that. Three years later. I had changed my name, started wearing boxers. I had moved to Vancouver for a girl, and it wasn't working out. I had found happiness like a cup of water, a continual thirst, absorbed and pissed away.

The wrestling opens were advertised on posters at the SFU library, where I was a regular loiterer. I checked their website to see that she was registered to fight.

I think I was in search of something familiar, sitting alone, wringing a program in my hands. And walking into the ring, she looked the same—her hair in two braids, her body rippling beneath a burgundy singlet. A whistle went and her hands shot out, grabbing the other girl's hair and, when they were slapped away, the back of her neck, and then her hands themselves, and they held each other, violently, until Shanna shook free and, leveraging the back of the other woman's leg, wrenched her onto her back. If it were me she would have stuck two fingers in my mouth. If it were me she would have spat. Bodies, thrust together and shoved away. A gasp and a cheer from the crowd, and I was with them, awed, lurching to my feet.

She didn't scan the crowd for me. I didn't try to catch her eye. Mid-match I realized I was being ridiculous and walked out. I caught a bus back to the new basement I was living in.

Caitlin Galway

////////////////

HEATSTROKE

The wallpaper was an inferno of curling red acanthus. If Fiona looked at it for too long, she felt it moving inside her, slipping between her organs. Other oddities: She noticed that gravity was strongest in small, atmospheric pockets right around her temples, and weighing against her shoulders. There were fruit flies on a water-warped corner of the ceiling, barely moving in counter-clockwise rotation.

Fiona sat by the motel window, looking out at a corner of downtown Vegas. Electric outlines glowed above darkened storefronts, green light harnessed and bent into the shapes of women's bodies. A pair of pink-neon lips twitched with the intensity of a heating coil. Fiona stepped off the bed, rings of cereal crunching beneath her bare feet.

None of this was right. She was not the way she was supposed to be. It was as if she had exploded and been too hastily reassembled, pieces misplaced or fitted upside down. All she knew was this: One week earlier, she headed out of Reno in her uncle's car, toward the Red Rock Canyon National Conservation Area. She hiked at least as far as the limestone ridge of the Moenkopi Loop—and then, a time-jump. She awoke on her side, in the sand, the sun exhaling its molten breath over her skin.

A map of Clark County and the Mojave Desert lay unfolded at all times on the motel floor. Fiona ran her finger along the lines, trying to channel her memory like a spirit through a Ouija board.

A route drawn in Sharpie led from Reno to Red Rock, among the easternmost parts of the Mojave, then to the salt flat called Groom Lake—AREA 51 scrawled in big daggered letters, more of a joke than a destination—then circled backward to an abandoned gold rush town in the Bullfrog Hills, occupied only by the ghosts of murdered prospectors and miners with phantom lungs like sacks of coal dust. It was meant to be Fiona's own bespoke road trip, marking the end of high school, the beginning of the newly unfurling world. As far as she could tell, she had only reached her first stop, Red Rock, when the journey ended.

Fiona understood that it was July 5, 1982. She remembered her mother and sister, their clapboard bungalow. Her friends Jody and Easton Maxwell, a pair of brothers who left Reno the previous summer, and now lived with their father on an old ranch in Moapa Valley. And the robot they constructed in middle school, out of scrap metal and a toy astronaut helmet. The siren they set into its chest—found in a ditch, cracked through the centre, like the once-wailing blue heart of a disintegrated spaceship.

She knew she should reach out to someone. Jody in particular would have understood, but each time she picked up the phone, an inexplicable hesitancy sacked her voice, and she hung up before the first ring.

Once she had found her uncle's car in the conservation parking lot, Fiona could have sworn she saw a second road float into view, like a soul ushered from a body. There were two roads now, overlapping. The correct one, and the one that she was on. But it was an error, a mutation of fate. She was stuck in the aftershock of some sudden divergence, a reality that never should have been.

July 2—The Dream of the Wrong Turn

Four hundred miles from the heart of Reno, the Creamsicle-orange Cutlass drives through the Sierra Nevada range. Soft white headlights pass us, their silence almost wild, like the eyeshine of a deer.

The driver taps the wheel to a euphoria of synth-pop on the radio. In the passenger seat, a child reaches out and tangles the wind between her fingers. I watch her from the back seat, far away in the side-view mirror—a deep, steadfast light blinking from the black night of her pupil.

So the dream played out. Wound back, played again, my mind swallowing itself until I woke, left to stare into the motel's comatose ceiling fan, the red wallpaper like a window into the bloody viscera of a whale. The dream had followed me from the desert and played continuously the past two nights. I sensed that its persistence was intentional. That it knew what had happened, wanted me to know.

Outside, people roamed Fremont Street under the winking observation of a carnival-lit cowgirl perched above the Glitter Gulch. I half watched them from the bed by the window, pulled back in time to a day I could not remember, the square cut clean from my memory's calendar. If I squinted, I could see the outer edges of the lost day, a shimmering dissolution like a mirage. But the hours between had collapsed, sealed themselves off, left nothing but a black hole.

*

Fiona bolted up on the mattress, breath squeezed from her body. She felt the coarse tongue of desert heat, tasted the grainy air between her teeth. The dream again, every night for that first week of July. It was 3 a.m. The clock, knocked onto the floor, branded the darkness with an insensate red glare.

In the dream, the child was always gone when the car stopped. Fiona would get out and follow the driver—known only as M., and identical to Fiona but for muted eyes unsullied by any puncture of pupil. Ahead lay the Mojave's burning sandstone, its sweeping rings of red and white, and distant mountains with gentle peaks and slopes, like a fading cardiogram.

M. would stand ankle-deep in a prickly haze of desert needle, taking quick-flashing photographs that shook the darkness like dry lightning. "The egg hatched," she would say, turning to Fiona. "And a hundred baby spiders came out, and they ate her."

Fiona curled up again in the motel's thin sheets. She clasped her head as if squeezing a splinter from her mind. Of all the films, why had M. chosen *Blade Runner?* The last line from Rachael before android hunter Deckard reveals to her that she is not human, and her understanding of herself splits: *Real. Unreal. Before this moment. From now on.* Fiona had seen the film in theatres twice that summer, her eyes wide and shining like coagulated wonder.

She fell back asleep and the dream resumed its loop, only now the green highway sign had changed. Before, its taunts were simple: *Wrong Turn Up Ahead*—a perky little arrow tilting left. Now there were a thousand arrows. It had replicated itself, split radially into an inescapable warning.

*

The owner of the motel never seemed to unplug herself from the network of hanging keys behind her, a broad wall of multi-dimensional connectivity, like an old telephone switchboard. Fiona scanned the keys, each one able to unlock a portal into someone's fitful world.

She had received an unexpected call from the lobby. Some business about a letter.

"Yeah, I'm pretty sure it's for you," the motel owner said, looking slightly confused as she handed over an envelope. "Fiona Moss?" When Fiona nodded, the motel owner clicked her nails on the counter. Her eyebrows pulled together. "Was it your sister or something?"

"What do you mean?" Fiona asked.

"Your sister, bringing the envelope."

"My sister? Not in Vegas, no, she's fourteen."

"She just looked ..." *Cleaner? Chattier? Less blood-flushed in the eyes?* "She just looked an awful lot like you."

Fiona felt an eerie omnipresence. Was the letter from M.? How could that be? She scanned the lobby's dimpled ceiling, the vacant cherry-vinyl chairs, the magazine rack neatly stocked.

"It's kind of like ... what was that episode ... ?" Fiona pressed the heels of her palms against her eyes. In the blotchy darkness, she saw herself huddled with her sister on the sofa, their faces a weird embryo-pale in the glow of *The Twilight Zone*. Watching as poor Millicent Barnes, *girl with her head on her shoulders,* is tormented by the sudden appearance of her doppelgänger in a bus depot.

"Honey, are you okay?" The motel owner touched Fiona's hand, startling her. "You seem a little young to be on your own out here. Are you meeting friends? Family?"

"No, I'm here for..." Fiona's thoughts knotted. What could she say? A small white statuette of the Virgin Mary stood on the counter by the window. Its reflection in the glass, cast in the ceiling's fluorescence, appeared superimposed onto the scene outside, an attentive presence watching over the cars in the parking lot. "I'm here because..."

Was it the light? Yes . . . a mothlike longing for the light had drawn her here. A lifelong reliance on the stars, or whatever light was most at hand for comfort, navigation. But how can one say *I came here to curl up in the city's manic radiance*? How does one explain that if they could not burrow into the space between the stars, hold themselves in place with the pins of Orion, then Vegas would have to do. An electric star cluster within driving distance.

July 1—The Day After the Wrong Turn

The morning cracked open, spilled onto me. I found myself staring at the prongs of cholla cacti, fuzzy and forked like freezer-burned coral reef. Strands of hair beat against my face. I swatted, saw browned blood on my knuckles. *What happened?* It took a long, sinking moment for me to ask: *What happened to* me?

Pain flooded my body as I tried to sit. I caught my breath, gazed into the clear, watery strata of blue sky streaming between the clouds. Every ounce of fluid had hemorrhaged out of me. I was still in the Mojave, with the giant sandstone formations, the occasional Joshua tree, branches contorted as if fossilized in a state of hysteria.

I could do this; I could make sense of things. Find the ridge. Follow it back to the visitor centre, the parking lot, my uncle's bright-orange car. I tried to trace my movements backward, salvage some sequence of events, but the harder I concentrated, the faster my footprints burned up like tissue paper.

*

Evening fell as Fiona sat outside by the edge of the motel pool, afraid to return to her room.

When Fiona had left the lobby and opened the envelope, she found a Polaroid of herself standing by her school's flagpole. Wearing her burnished-blue graduation gown, tipping her mortarboard like a Stetson. She had intended to give it to the Maxwell brothers but held on to it instead, struck by a sudden self-consciousness. Written on the back was some ridiculous joke about a Vulcan *passion fight* for her affections. Had it, in fact, been a joke, or her egging them on, trying to make Jody jealous, or Easton jealous, or both for some reason, or no reason at all?

Fiona's breath tightened, her throat a pinhole. Perhaps cross-contamination had occurred. She had failed to decipher the dream, and so the dream had come to find her. Fed up and determined, M. had attached herself like a burr to Fiona and travelled into the waking world. Fiona was not one to jump to impossible conclusions—but then, deserts and other untamed terrain had long been breeding grounds for unexplained phenomena. Geometrically pristine patterns in the wheat fields of

Wiltshire. Claims of portals appearing, quietly timed for twilight, in the Verde Valley of Arizona.

Fiona walked the length of the pool, intercepted by the shadows of zany-legged flamingo ornaments. Opening the envelope again, she eyed the photograph without touching it. As she searched it for meaning, studying the tie-dye sneakers and blooming cottonwoods, a clot of dark hair appeared in the pool. Fiona watched, alarmed, as it drifted toward her like the inky curlicues of a squid. She knelt and looked closer, a girl's figure taking shape in the pool's icy-green light.

Only now did it occur to Fiona, blood-rush filling her ears and body bracing to run, that she might have been wrong about the other girl. There was M., floating in the pool water, looking every bit as lost as Fiona. Staring up at her with a helpless look of embalmed serenity, like a specimen preserved in a jar. Eyes scrubbed of aspiration, of memory, no future or past. A self suspended in time.

Fiona crashed through the water, pearls of air spilling wildly. She swam to the other girl, took her hand, kicked to propel them both to the surface. But with contact, a sudden tessellation occurred. The two of them began to merge—a unifying feeling at first. Fiona could see M. as a little girl, crouched on her knees among the wispy wild rye, watching mustangs in the meadow below. There was a delicate, pinkish rain, each fast-falling drop catching the sunset. M. was trying to memorize every detail of the horses, the full breadth of their peacefulness. Incubate them in the warmth of her memory, so that they might be cherished, kept safe.

No. I know this memory. Did M. mean to consume her, like a fetus absorbing its twin? Fiona pulled away, afraid of draining from her own body. *It's mine. It's mine.*

*

Back in the motel room, the fruit flies had grown busy. Congregating in sticky takeout containers and pockmarking the walls. Fiona felt the doppelgänger fusing with her, inhabiting her. She tried to will her pores to filter out the other girl, let M. drip from her hair like the pool water. But her body only absorbed the invader more fully, locking her inside.

Fiona leaned over the sink and peered into the uneasy depths of her pupils, waiting for M. to Bloody Mary herself into the mirror. Fiona's mother used to call her own reflection her *better half*. Glimpsing it in the department store window, a puddle in the yard, the hallway mirror: "She never has to feel anything, does she," she would say, her eyelid like a slice of plum. Fiona remembered the punched-purple lids struggling to open, her mother's clear blue eye like the sky squinting.

She hurried to the phone on the nightstand and dialed the number to the Maxwell brothers' ranch. Nausea burned her throat as she forced herself to listen to each taut, frenzied ring.

The otherworldly, with all its strange possibility, had always been for her and the Maxwell brothers a conduit for shared curiosity. Jody had joined her sixth-grade class mid-year, but Fiona did not particularly notice him until the day he presented a shoebox diorama of post-apocalyptic San Francisco. He spoke softly under the class's laughter, in his green-corduroy overalls, holding a creased copy of *Do Androids Dream of Electric Sheep?* Fiona admired the glittered cotton balls stretched into golden radioactive mist, the plastic farm animals broken apart, hollow insides stuffed with wires.

Jody, soon accompanied by Easton, began to ride over from the suburbs to camp in Fiona's backyard. Easton would roll up singing off-key before dropping his bike onto its side with a hard clatter. Jody would carefully wedge his bike's kickstand into the mud, as Fiona waited inside the lopsided tent, wherein fervid debates arose over closed loops in space-time, the grandfather paradox, the diplomatic merits of Kirk versus Spock.

One morning in eleventh grade, Jody pulled Fiona aside by the foggy bleachers. He had been quiet throughout their usual walk to school. It was just the two of them by then, with Easton getting his licence and, along with it, a new-found embarrassment over public contact with his little brother. In the school hallways, he passed Jody without acknowledgement, and threw Fiona consolatory side-smiles that left her oddly thrilled.

"What's the matter with you?" she asked. Jody was agitated, readjusting his glasses and looking over his shoulder. He reeked of wet grass and unbrushed teeth as they sat on the dew-chilled steel of the bench.

"Something fucked-up happened," he told her. His lower lip was swollen. His sweater had a ruddy, poorly soaped stain down the front. "I can't remember it all," he said. "It's like the whole night's been scooped out of my head."

By his account: Easton's recent spurt in size and confidence shifted everything. Now, the absence of such a spurt in Jody formed a channel, hovering invisibly in the air, redirecting his stepfather's violence. Whatever happened that night, Jody never said, but it caused him to bolt out the front door, and race through the neatly hedged cul-de-sac—only to wake up lying in the middle of the neighbourhood baseball diamond, the night instantly gone, dawn clicked into place like a picture in a stereoscope.

"But that's not the fucked-up part," he said. "I saw myself, Fi. I could see myself standing there, watching from the infield. It was my face, my clothes—then it fizzled out, it was like radio static or something." A duplicate, staring at him with an almost feral tranquility, the soft black eyes of a raccoon. As Fiona placed her hand on Jody's shoulder, he shrank into himself. He rubbed his cheek and forehead compulsively, as if confirming the fixed existence of his face. "I look like me, right?" he asked, gripping her leg. "I'm still me?"

*

The phone shrieked to life. Fiona clutched it to her ear with both hands, nearly knocking the base off the nightstand. "Jody?"

"...Fiona?" It was his voice. The shy, ever-sleepy mumble.

"Did you get my message?" Fiona listened to his breath, caught and trying to loosen itself, before a fumbling click. "Jody? *Jody.*"

She lowered the phone, stared at it in her hands like she had cracked it in half. Her message on his answering machine had been clear enough for Jody and no one else: "The morning at the baseball diamond... it's happened to me too. Can we talk?"

Jody had never again spoken of what happened. That he had experienced some ripple in reality had never occurred to Fiona. And yet, reasonable people reported doppelgängers, catching sight of their own likeness on a bridge, a terrace, striding down the street in the opposite direction. Fragments of themselves roaming the world.

He had not seemed himself the last time she saw him, about six months ago, when he visited his mother in Reno over the Christmas holidays. He called Fiona in the middle of the night, pleading with her to drive over. Fiona had peeked out the window at her uncle's car, occasionally parked in her driveway since her father died. *Come on, Fi. Easton wouldn't come up with me, and everyone's out at some tacky office party. Will you come? Please?*

Without waiting for her to take off her coat, Jody led her, awkwardly by hand, through his living room. It struck her that she had never invited the boys into her own home. Maybe it was something in the way Easton tugged the string of her shorts, causing her body to seize up, or Jody's sulky conviction that his brother always got his way.

Jody, your mom … Fiona pulled back and gestured toward her soaked boot prints on the carpet, but Jody ignored them. His dark-syrup eyes peered into her, and though she could see him working through whatever he wanted to say, he never managed to say it.

Fiona clapped the motel phone onto its cradle. Why had Jody been so oddly tender that night? Watching *The Exorcist,* he had volunteered his shoulder for her to hide her face against, stroked her hair behind her ear when she thought she might throw up.

She grabbed the car keys from a heap of dirty clothes on the floor, shook off the flies. Had it even been Jody sitting with her in the dim intimacy of his house? Whose eyes, when he drew so close his breath warmed her collarbone, had she been looking into?

*

Light slipped over the hood of the car as Fiona drove down the Strip. Glancing in the rear-view mirror, she caught her eye, a bright gash of aquamarine—though the other eye was somehow bigger, somehow smaller, older, younger, like undulating oil in a lava lamp.

Fiona felt the city's wired, red-eyed restlessness running circuits through her, well after she had driven outside its borders, until somewhere along Route 95 her heart began to sink. The roadside thickened with brittle saltbush and cacti. A tremor electrocuted the small bones in her hands. They vibrated against the steering wheel.

She shook her head. "I don't want to," she said. "I've changed my mind." But as if on its own, the car slowed and parked by the unpaved road leading into Red Rock.

Fiona went still. Here was where the world had split in two. Become *before* and *after*. She looked out the windshield at the vast, open flatland. Listened to the low-roving wind, the screech of a bird in the reeling blue overhead. What good was it to remember? After her father died, she was asked to recount her memories, brutal and loving alike. Would a counsellor have her squish another squeeze toy and explain her every bruise, her mother's history of fractured bones? What purpose had it served to understand the violence? She wanted the violence gone. Dug out of her body like a bullet.

Dust skirted across the road. An inviting breeze rolled through the window and lapped against her cheek, but she could not get out of the car. The minute hand on the dashboard clicked with feeble determination, as time lay slumped and rotting around her. It would only continue mounting, this mass of wasted time, fortifying and isolating her. She hit the steering wheel. A hot, foul rush of memory began to rise, a magma chamber in her chest bursting.

June 30—The Wrong Turn

"Moss, wait up!" Easton readjusted his backpack, watching his step on the slick rock. I had darted up a crumbly incline near the base of the Calico Hills. I was showing off my stamina to Easton, and laughing at Jody who was flushed and panting behind us.

After nineteen years of living in the soft-palmed suburbs, helping out at his father's ranch had given Easton a quiet earnestness. He paused to study the asters and mauve-veined lilies, and photograph the mottled cliffsides. He had drifted back to us, too, since leaving Reno. Going to see *The Thing* in theatres with Jody, calling me late at night to discuss alien sabotage. He and Jody would be attending the University of Nevada in the fall, Easton having deferred for a year, while I would be moving to California to start at Berkeley. We had planned this trip together, a proper send-off, the sort of foray our childhood selves would have wanted.

We hiked through hills of rusty stone, where trees rose aslant, branches low to the earth, as though their bulk had been swallowed by quicksand. By early sunset, we began to wander off the trail, settling near a ground-level cavity among the giant sandstone forms.

Easton sidled up next to me, startling me as he touched my wrist. "What happened? Did you nick yourself?" There was a scrape on my forearm from the whip of a branch. "I have stuff in the pack, you should have said something." I shrugged, but he waited with his elbows out, hands tightening around the straps of his backpack. "Fiona. It'll get infected." I sighed, held out my palm, but rather than give me the antibiotic, he took my hand. "Be more careful, okay?"

Easton had a way of falling still, fully occupying a moment with his presence. He would seem to me then, as he did now, somehow altered. Eyes cool with jarring clarity. As he dotted the scrape with ointment, gingerly thumbing grease into my skin, I smiled at Jody, unsure what else to do. I could read his irritation; his mouth had thinned, tongue running along the inside of his lower lip as he watched Easton's hands, the little wound near my wrist.

Maybe nothing would have happened had I reached out for Jody. Had I not simply stood there, bewildered, as he stalked off into the tall, tunnelled complex of stone. Had I not watched him disappear so quickly that, after searching in flustered circles, calling for him, yelling at him, Easton and I could do nothing but return to the cavity and wait.

The sun hung low and full-blooded, gradually disappearing behind mounds of scarred rock.

"Don't worry, he'll find his way back. He has a map, some water." Easton's cigarette dangled from his fingers, emptying itself like an exhaust pipe. "It's been rough for him without you. He doesn't know how to make new friends."

"That's not a reason to just take off like that," I said, pacing and itching at my shirt, the swampy feeling of sweat under my clothes. "He has no idea what he's doing out there. He could get hurt, or lost." I was beginning to feel faint. I sat down next to Easton, leaning back against the rock wall now varnished in shadow. "I think I'm going to be sick."

Easton rose onto his knees and rested the back of his hand against my forehead. He took my jaw, gently tilted it back and forth. When I winced, he laughed. "Just checking your pupils, like Deckard."

The empathy test—how bounty hunters decipher who is human, and who amounts to nothing more than an assortment of parts, sentient shells planted with seeds of untrustworthy memory. "If I were an android," I said, "you'd never know."

I would never remember exactly how it started. Why he leaned forward and kissed me, what I did in response, if the twist in my face came before or after the stiffness in my spine. Nor the moment it all slid away from me, surprise at his eagerness swerving into swift, suffocating panic like a plastic bag over my head.

What would remain clear, palpable as the nightly chill of sweat on my scalp, was Easton's forehead hard against mine. His heated voice, *Don't be like that, don't make it weird.* My eyes opening to find Jody watching motionless, shock bleaching the sunburn from his face. The surreal terror of my inanimate body manipulated by another's hands, another's intentions, like a necrophiliac with a corpse. My helplessness, stunning. The weight of it, crushing me into the dark, breathless, bottomless cracks of the earth. And I felt some small part of me eject from the rest, free itself, as if I could preserve a single unbound piece, cast it like a bottled message into the light.

*

Fiona drove away from Red Rock without thinking, other than a nagging worry she had forgotten to return her Vegas motel key. The car now sat on the highway's muddy shoulder. Beyond it lay mangy flatland, a lone ranch, a laundry line bearing nothing but faded blue strips of sky.

There was a word Fiona would not use. A name she would not say out loud. She stared at the nearby ranch, but she did not entirely see it. Only its curtains, framing the kitchen window. The thin, weary cotton, a print of large green roses. A wholesome quality like the prairie-girl patterns of her childhood bedroom. In the window, a boy washed dishes over the sink.

Fiona touched the hospital wristband. *MOSS, FIONA. VALLEY HOSPITAL*—she stopped, looked away. Before arriving in Moapa, she drove from the conservation area to a hospital, where she was told an examination would be performed. Police would be called, yes, she would need to provide names. Photographs would be taken.

"Photographs?" she had asked the nurse. "Photographs of *what?*"

Before changing her mind and hurrying out, carrying all her weight in her knees, a doctor instructed her to lie back and concentrate on the poster stuck to the ceiling. Puppies wearing birthday hats.

It was easier for M., untouchable in the darkening windshield. Fiona had nearly given the hospital the name Millicent, but when her own name fell out, she was sorry for only offering M. an initial, an incomplete piece, like that was all either of them deserved.

The boy in the window dried the dishes, dabbed away the suds. Straightened the curtains. Such gentleness applied to cutlery and cloth. Fiona finally looked away from him and pulled back onto the road as quietly as she could. She drove into nightfall, past exits, down roads where salt grass and downy seep willow sprouted. She drove until she was bordered by valleys, where stars collected on still black ponds. The dream had not stopped, and she understood, with a knowledge stored marrow-deep, that even once it did, it would continue to swim up from the time-drowned murk of the past, while she prepared breakfast, or stood on the crowded bus in a nerve-spun cocoon. She knew, indefinably, that something—a way of being in her body, a certain freedom with which she might have moved through the world—would never be quite what it was supposed to be.

Fiona stopped the car and rolled down the window. She listened to her breath, how it mimicked the quiver of the grasshoppers in the valley. She conjured the scent of violets lifting from the resin-glazed evergreens as she and her father hiked along Lake Tahoe. His hand reaching back for hers, their hair flying in the winds of the foothills.

The moon drizzled its reflection across a pond. It hung full and pearl-powdered, so gauzed with light that one did not always see the heathered bruises, its surface cratered from the chaos of other bodies. The moon itself a piece broken from the earth, shoved into silent orbit.

Fiona looked through the windshield, into the sky, until the natural rhythm of her breath returned. Until there came a flickering recollection, an awareness of how she matched the moon, bright and pithy-eyed and solid. For a faint moment, she felt its enduring glow deep in her pupils, casting its beam down forgotten caverns and buried causeways, where she housed every ghost of herself—from that first small, balmy-faced progenitor, all the way to who she might become—illuminating the ever-rippling, collective memory of a life.

Saad Omar Khan

////////////////

THE PAPER BIRCH

Taha was nine years, seven months, and six days when he came to Canada; nine years, eight months, and eight days when his sister fell ill; and nine years, ten months, and one day when his prayers saved her life.

It was Faiza—not his parents—who told him they were moving. Ten years older, she swayed over him like a giant, telling him that Abbu had a new job in Toronto. He knew all about the city. Founded in 1793 as York. Population of 3,807,000 people. He memorized its facts, keeping them in the vault he kept inside his heart that only he could access. They would leave Hong Kong just as his international school ended in early June, and just before school in Canada finished. Abbu and Ammi wouldn't bother to enrol him in classes yet, Faiza said. His summer would come early and last long, and his sister's words came as a sign of good fortune to come.

He welcomed the change as long as Faiza was with him. She'd already been enrolled in university in Canada ("A place called York," he overheard her mother say to Atiqa *khala* in Karachi on the phone). As they were packing the week before they left for Canada, their large apartment in Tai Tam a rubble of taped boxes, he went to Faiza's room, asking her if she was going to leave him when she went to university.

"Of course not, *jaan,*" she said, dropping the sweater she was folding to embrace him. "Abbu said the university's near our new house. I'm not leaving you." She looked at Taha, her wide moon face shining down on her brother like a beacon. "Are you going to ever leave me?" she laughed.

He said no, never, never, never, repeating the word as if repetition itself would bond them forever.

*

Taha was a mystery to himself as much as he was to others. His frequent silences unnerved peers and teachers, his muteness broken only by awkward laughter when he heard what he thought was a joke. Teachers at his international school noted his troubling ability to withdraw from the world. When asked questions in class, he would answer cogently, if verbosely, his eyes otherwise wandering to the sky overlooking the South China Sea. He heard these comments when his mother was brought in for parent–teacher assessments, sterile meetings between adults in white rooms filled with money plants, speaking of him as if he were a ghost.

He knew his parents protected him. He knew Abbu was like the fathers in *Faerie Tale Theatre,* his absence from home a sign of devotion and conscientiousness. Ammi was never the evil stepmother, yet she still intimidated Taha with her stern, poised bearing. Like his teachers. Like everyone except Faiza. Always social, particularly with the wives of her husband's colleagues,

Ammi presented Faiza as her star, someone who could speak to the aunties with singular maturity. Taha was different. Introduced to his elders, he would only murmur his perfunctory *salaams* before rushing away to his room. The aunties would laugh, noting the personality differences between the siblings. "He'll grow out of his shyness, Amina," they would say, a note of confidence that she tried desperately to take to heart.

*

The bank allowed them to stay at a hotel their first week in Toronto before their house in North York was prepared. The grey ghastliness of downtown gave way to a green leafiness the first day they arrived in their new home. The streets were wide and quiet. Children rode their bicycles freely. Elderly couples waved hello to them from afar. Each house was made of near-identical red brick, every lawn wide and perfectly cultivated. This was a new world for Taha, a distant planet from the metal shards jutting into the sky in Central, or the lanky apartment buildings on Hong Kong's south side. It was one of Abbu's officers from the bank—a garrulous man named Daniel who constantly mispronounced everyone's name—who guided the family through the house as Taha clung to his sister's side, the home so big and cavernous it seemed as if it could swallow him whole.

Daniel took them to the deck to see the back lawn. Flat and green, lying peacefully under a partially clouded sky, it was arresting, so beautiful Taha was certain such images only existed on film. He was struck by a tree standing erect at the end of the lawn. "It's a paper birch. Taller than most birches," said Daniel proudly, as if he had cultivated the tree himself. Taha ignored the world—his parents, Daniel, even Faiza. Without speaking, he left his sister, stepped down from the deck, and approached the tree. Composed of three branches emerging from a single solid base, its bark was clear and white, its spade-like leaves casting a wide shadow on the ground. He touched its unblemished skin as he came underneath the canopy. Nature was an abstract concept to Taha, having never touched anything like this, not even the scaly-skinned palm trees in his grandparents' house in Karachi.

Ammi called him back to the deck. His reverie was broken, and he returned to the tour and the new home which would soon be theirs.

*

They settled into the house quickly, the summer days an excuse for Taha to explore the house, its grandness, the spaces where he could hide with books or watch television behind Ammi's back, who spent most of her days complaining to friends in Hong Kong or Pakistan of Canada's dullness, the loneliness of suburban life, the isolation her husband bequeathed her while he worked. Taha heard everything, understanding little, but feeling his mother's world was coming undone.

He tried to speak to Faiza about their mother. He knew something was wrong when she wouldn't answer his knocks, respond to her name, or even emerge from her room. He noticed Ammi becoming increasingly agitated with her silences, with Abbu spending more time at home. In the few moments when Taha could see his sister, he saw her metamorphosis. The gentleness that held him so close to her drained away. Her eyes, luminescent even in their darkness, drooped more every day, as if witnessing the world became exhausting. Sleep was never enough. On weekend afternoons, when he wanted nothing more than to read in her room, she would do nothing but face the wall, her chest heaving heavily. Taha would creep inside and touch her back to see if she was awake. Faiza would recoil, her back arching up as if his touch was too heavy to bear, her lips emanating a grunt or an annoyed *"mat karo."*

Taha's parents protected him from the anxiety that suffocated their home. His sadness coexisted with confusion. Canada seemed to bring a sense of disorder more than prosperity. In specks of conversations, he heard terms like *lymphoma* and *cancer* piercing through the walls. He was too young to know more—he heard Ammi and Abbu say that as well. Abbu kept a library in his study. Taha would sneak in occasionally to ransack his encyclopedias and read all he could of his sister's condition. He imagined it as a demon draining Faiza, poisoning her blood, the same blood that kept her warm all these years, the coldness Taha now felt the result of his sister fighting a malignant presence within her.

He wanted to tell his parents what he discovered. Faiza was the only one who paid attention to his bookishness. His enthusiasm for detailing every aspect of Hodgkin's lymphoma was met differently by his parents. Abbu would only nod his head as Taha used terms like *lymphocytes* and *lymph nodes* to describe the precise mechanisms with which the disease was ravaging his daughter, usually deflecting his son's words by saying, "Good, *beta,* your mother needs help." Ammi would hear snippets of Taha speaking as she would distract herself with cooking or cleaning, dismissing him by saying, "*Bas,* stop reading, it's rotting your brain."

*

Taha wasn't allowed at the hospital when Faiza started chemotherapy. He didn't question why.

Faiza was a ghost the first time she returned home. He saw her from the windows of his room, the family's black Volvo sliding into their driveway, Abbu exiting the car and taking Faiza by the arm to bring her inside. Taha bounded from his room, flying to see his sister at the front door. He situated himself at the stand in the foyer where their family portrait and a copy of *Ayat al-Kursi* was placed.

The door opened. Taha saw Faiza come in, their father lifting her from the side, a jacket armouring her from the summer breeze. He bolted from his crouching position, terrified of what he saw, the image of his sister drained of vitality unnerving him, burning his soul as if the world had betrayed him.

*

Tears rained at night. Taha heard them through the walls. Even before they came to Canada, he had known his mother to bear a deep sadness that shaded her life. His father's tears chilled him more, stopping his heart when he heard their heavy gruffness speaking of despair and anger. Taha's only peace was the birch. When alone, he huddled next to its side, the branches sheltering him from his home's discord. Light shone through the leaves, illuminating the tree from within. As time went on, he identified with it: solitary, ignored, rooted in its place like a sylvan sentinel monitoring the activities of the humans who took its presence for granted.

He looked longingly at the birch from the kitchen table when Abbu and Ammi sat him down, explaining what Faiza's life would be in the next few weeks. Seven cycles of chemotherapy, they said. She'd experienced the first two. He'd have to be accustomed to her absence. "She's going to be weak for a long time. You have to give her space," said Abbu with authority, as if giving advice to one of his clients.

They didn't soften their words. He saw beyond their faces, beyond the ache pulsating behind their eyes that spoke of lost sleep and invented hopes. All he heard were unconvincing bromides from his mother. "Everything will be good, *beta*. She'll heal well, *inshallah*." Taha lost himself in her voice, his eyes straying beyond his parents, immersed in the sight of the birch, as if the gentleness coating those words emanated from the tree alone.

*

Abbu locked himself in his study. Ammi retreated into prayer, supplications of self-pity rather than appeals of the faithful, loud enough for Taha to hear, making him wonder if God needed a threshold of pain for people to experience before he would intervene. Perhaps it was a matter of volume, a set number of tears falling on Ammi's prayer mat that was needed, each droplet nourishing a seed that would grow toward heaven.

Taha saw little of Faiza. He feared her degeneration. He experienced his sister's immurement in her room by ear, the sounds of nauseous retching reverberating in the corridors.

One night, he saw Ammi in the television den watching a Pakistani satellite channel. Her eyes were vapid. Taha recognized the sight: pilgrims in Mecca wearing white robes worshipping at the Haram al-Sharif, pictures of the Kaaba, the black cube in the centre of the Haram, visible on the screen.

Ammi beckoned, patting the empty space of the grey couch next to her. He hesitated coming near, as if the sadness he saw was infectious. She continued to beckon, whispering *"ajao"* in thin whispers. Taha drifted forward, taking a seat beside her. His mother's attempts to mimic a smile were tepid as she drew him close. Almost out of duty, he placed his head in her lap, his mind contemplating how he could assuage his mother's loneliness.

They stared at the television as Ammi stroked Taha's hair. He was afraid to speak. Ammi filled the silence by describing the experience of pilgrimage: the circumambulation around the Kaaba, the stoning of Satan at the three pillars of Mina, the seven-lap circuit walking between Safa and Marwa, visiting the Holy Prophet's mosque in Medina, and finally the shaving and trimming of hair for male and female *hajjis* at the end of the holy journey.

Taha was mesmerized, not by his mother's words, but by the visions in front of him. Each *hajji* gleamed in their ihram under the lights as they bowed themselves toward the Kaaba, its blackness contrasting with their white robes. Over the Urdu narration, the scenes changed back to pilgrims circling the Kaaba, looking like a darkened iris in the sea of a divine eye.

Ammi noticed Taha's absorption. "The centre of the universe," she said with awe. "They walk around the Kaaba seven times, you know. The same number of times they walk between Safa and Marwa."

"Why?"

"Seven is a holy number."

The holiness was apparent. The imagery of thousands of pilgrims circling the cube shifted in pace, speeding up in time-lapsed shots of a cyclone of humanity whirling around the black cube, looking still and immutable, inoculated against the wear of time.

"Why do they go there?" asked Taha.

"That's where our prayers go."

"Can God hear them from home?"

"Of course. But you can always get closer to God."

"What do they pray about?"

"Everything. Their families, their homes."

"Have you been there?"

Ammi paused. "Yes. With Abbu. Before Faiza was born."

"Can you go again? Maybe if you and Abbu go, you can pray for Faiza."

Ammi's silence grew. Her lips curved downward. Fear gripped him, the fear of upsetting the balance between her stoicism and her heart's disintegration, the fear of realizing that he did not know his mother, and could barely understand the recesses of her soul.

Ammi let go of Taha, staring at him for a wordless second before ordering him to bed.

*

The images of the Kaaba lingered with Taha throughout that night, like a memory of a previous life recently discovered.

He woke up early. He left his bed, compelled, as if by an unknown message, to go down to the kitchen, to see the birch on the lawn. Light had barely kissed the day. The birch was sturdy in the semi-darkness, a time between day and night that Taha had never witnessed.

A veil dropped. A spark glowed within him, that God existed in all things, the God his mother prayed to imbuing creation with his spirit. The birch must have been one of them. He knew—he felt—its uniqueness. Would only *hajjis* in Mecca feel close to the heart of this world? Could he not also feel that centre here? Would his prayers be heard with more clarity, accelerated upward to heaven?

He timed everything with precision. He would make his own pilgrimage to the birch every day Faiza had chemotherapy. Seven cycles, his parents said. Five more cycles to go.

*

Dawn prayers were close to four in the morning. He could sneak out through the back door to behold the birch by half past four when Abbu was asleep and Ammi had gone back to bed after praying. The time was perfect, the blazing hour when the sun seared the sky, the yellowing hues of morning fully ripened.

The whiteness of the bark was incandescent in the morning light. He knew no particular prayer to say. He had to make up his own pilgrimage. His mother taught him a few prayers when he was younger. He recalled one—the Tasbih of Fatimah, its simplicity sticking to his mind with ease. He wore a white *shalwar kameez* without socks, the same *shalwar* he wore the past Eid. Closing his eyes, he recited the litany—*subhanallah, alhamdulillah, Allahu Akbar*—dozens of times each. He pronounced each phrase carefully as he was taught, with the knowledge that God understood all, but could abide few mistakes. In measured paces, he circled the tree, leaves on low-hanging branches hitting his face like a loving reminder of the birch's presence.

Taha stopped moving after the seventh circle. Opening his eyes, he put his hands together to say a *du'a,* asking for God's protection over Faiza, asking for her to be healed and made right. The branches flickered in the wind, the ground beneath him soft and nourishing. Lightness overwhelmed him, as if an inner weight on his heart had been lifted, feeling, for the first time since Faiza became ill, that he felt anything close to the warmth she gave him.

*

He felt pity for his family. The mysteries of the birch would be unknown to them, its healing power trapped within his heart.

A few days later, he visited Faiza's room, seeing her with her head bound in bed, her face turning to him as he peered from the door frame with trepidation. In her weakness, her smile reached out to Taha like a beacon, trying to assure him all was well. He expected her to be better, as if the blessedness he felt from the birch could transfer quickly to his sister. Instead, her face was still withered, as if being slowly erased from the world.

The chemotherapy cycles continued, as did the cycles of trepidation in the household as Faiza spent more time in the hospital. Taha continued with his pilgrimage, convinced that its continuance was the only solution. Seven cycles. Seven pilgrimages to the birch. He had to complete the ritual.

Summer suffered its dying days sooner than Taha expected. The mornings became colder, yet he persevered, hiding his rites from his parents. At the end of the sixth cycle, the week before his new school would begin, he saw from beneath the birch's canopy a figure on the deck. It was his mother, wearing a green *shalwar kameez* underneath a worn cardigan. She stood, arms crossed, staring at Taha and the tree wide-eyed, as if staring at a spectacle she would not have imagined possible. Taha stared back, stunned, realizing his mother had been watching him. *She knows,* he thought. Ammi understood what he was doing. She came down the three steps from the deck to the birch, arms at her side, walking in quick steps where Taha stood. The birch dwarfed her, and yet it was her immensity that overwhelmed him as she looked into his eyes, rage resonating from her body.

She slapped him. It was a quick, unplanned strike, the tips of her fingers barely making contact with his cheek. Taha's eyes welled with confused tears. Before Ammi could raise her arms to correct her assault and hit him again, she hesitated. She lowered herself and threw her arms around his neck. She put her head back to look at him, her anger softening as she stretched out her arm and took Taha by the hand, hurrying him inside, away from the morning cold, away from the birch.

*

They went to the kitchen. Ammi made him sit at the table. She sat across from him, barely moving aside from an intermittent trembling of her lips. Taha knew she had something to say, no furious word, but a question. She broke the silence by asking him what he was trying to do.

He didn't know how to answer her. "I need to make one more," he whispered.

"One more what?"

"The circles."

She crooked her head. "I don't understand you."

Taha began to cry. Ammi went over to his side to hold him. He could feel her own tears dropping to his face. "I wish I knew you better," she said. "I wish I could take us away—"

Ammi stopped herself. Taha could only grasp slivers of meaning from her words. His head deep into his mother's chest, he separated himself from his own sadness, wondering if his mother longed for a pilgrimage of her own, to a place where her daughter could always be well, where Abbu was always home, where God could remain rooted in a single place to answer her questions.

"Promise me you won't go to that tree again," she said.

He nodded and said he wouldn't.

*

School started. Taha's homeroom teacher, Mrs Crawford, seemed kind. The students largely left him to wander the perimeter of the verdant playground during recess and lunch alone. He came home dejected, Faiza still at the hospital, Ammi being the only one to greet him.

She seemed different. There was a change in the way she looked at him, her eyes softer, almost out of fear. Her embraces were tighter, a cocoon insulating him from his daily loneliness. "I know you need her," she whispered to him one day after school. "We all do."

Taha avoided the birch. He barely looked at it, acquiescing to his mother's instruction. He still longed for the presence it gave him, that link to God that could heighten his prayers, like the *du'a*s he made before sleeping for his sister to return. These supplications came through two weeks after the start of school when Ammi and Abbu delivered the news at the kitchen table: Faiza would return a few weeks after her last chemotherapy cycle. "She's coming back, *beta,* you should be happy," his father said. Taha said nothing, his mouth slightly ajar. He felt excited, if bewildered, anticipating her return, yet feeling it was anticlimatic, wondering if his acts of worship had the power he thought they had.

Ammi came to his room later that night. She sat next to him as he lay in bed. "I know you've been doing a lot for your sister," she said, brushing his cheek. "I want to get you a gift, but I don't know what to give you."

He kept silent. He knew she was talking to herself more than she was talking to him.

She kissed his right cheek. "I think I know what to give you."

She left the room, leaving Taha alone pondering the mysterious decision his mother had made in her mind.

*

Faiza came back on a Friday. He was still at school. When he came back, his heart thrumming with love and the fear his sister would be unrecognizable, it was Ammi who told him to wait in his room before she was ready. After an hour, Ammi brought him to her. His sister sat in a metal folding chair atop a towel. Ammi held scissors in her hand. Faiza's head was unwrapped, threads of wizened hair draping over her shoulder. Her face was thinner, but her smile remained the same, worn by exhaustion but still intact.

"Are you ready?" Amina asked Faiza.

"Yes," she said. They both looked at Taha standing with hesitation in the doorway.

"What do the pilgrims do before leaving *hajj*?" his mother asked him. He said nothing, only nodding in understanding. With her scissors, she lopped off every stray strand of hair from her daughter's head, further denuding it with a pair of electric clippers from Faiza's dresser table.

Amina cleaned the room. She and Taha helped Faiza back to bed. Under the blankets, he came to her side, silently nuzzling next to Faiza like a stray animal huddling for heat. "*Jaan,* she still needs to sleep," Ammi said softly. "Let's go down. There'll be time later."

She led him downstairs to the kitchen. Slices of green apples were placed on a white plate for him. He picked one up, asking himself if this was the gift his mother promised him, the gift of finality, telling him his mission was accomplished, his prayers completing their own circuits somewhere between the soil and paradise.

He looked across the lawn. The birch was in its place, tinges of colour speckling its summer green, the leaves preparing to fall, its splendour ready to be shed from its body.

Cody Caetano

MIIGWETCH REX

I lived and died with the lake that Mino Bee told the world he came from. I never understood what made the shirk go full tadpole, as if he ever hung his jacket there or knew somebody with a hook. Hard to know why he did that when not him nor his dad nor his dad's daddio ever dipped a rickety pigeon toe into Crop Lake. And what locals from the bird's throat quit trying to figure out long ago is who Mino was, or whether the ancestral hereditary title in his artist statements and ever-changing bios and interview quotes belonged to this dried-up gulp or the next, and if it even matters since it now all lays below kilos of mummied trash that I piled on each week until I died and joined the grandfathers myself.

When the coats first showed up at the lake, they brought with them garbage. Not just wickedness or gaslit, dour teachings about our wickedness, or the shame that afflicts those who mess around with guilt trips and scripture, but stinking garbage. The concept of it. Sometimes after I cleaned up the kitchen table, my pops would tell me to sit back down and listen up. And then he'd tell me stories of when the ancestors first saw the coats and tunics piling scrap deemed valueless at the bottom of a dug hole, along with any cloth-wrapped tchotchkes or Euro trash they brought with them and tossed after one measly use. What the coats did after Hudson's pulled up with fleets of mayflowers is dig even bigger holes, what we now call landfills, and in them would go stringy intestines and unwanted meat pieces, their constipations, discarded bits, ripped woollens, blackwood, partridge bones, ashes and any other immediate sweepings at the elbows of hunting trails and near the sites they buried their young and then ours. Generations afore passed down stories of those great steaming heaps. Of course, there was more than one heap, roughly a heap per fleet. Those stories were not about the garbage so much as how dumb it was for them to shit where they fish. No wonder they got sick and then we did too. Sometimes they'd just pile their rubbish at the edge of the lake if they felt lazy, and when the ancestors demonstrated circular knowledge and how to repurpose the items in question, whatever coat who led the troop would command the next to polish more shine onto the donned copper because it wasn't bright enough, clearly.

As an artist, Mino Bee built his "practice" on the country's waste. He called his six-decade career "Mino Bee's Ways of Throwing." The country loved the whole series, not a poorly received work in the catalogue, especially when considering how feedback loops and unsustainable power systems could entropy cities and towns overnight, undo the experiment, and that aki quit putting up with the comforts and abuses of humans altogether. Made the people feel good about themselves while they could, at least enough to keep filling those big, ugly coloured bins.

No matter how unpredictable the predictable, Mino kept popping off. Keep in mind that Little Miss Dominion's prime minister at the time hit a sixth consecutive term, and about a month into it, he struck countersigned addenda for each treaty and pledged support from every assembly of heretical worm-tongues in political office and on tribal council. The addenda offered a fated clause that made the ministry liable to enact all ninety-four calls to action for the Truth and Reconciliation Commission over the following three decades, a desperately massive component of their tented campaign platform. It won over most constituents and helped secure the NDN vote. Little Miss promised many empties, namely that we'd get our children back, our regional dialects taught in the cloud at both the elementary and secondary level. They promised to ship hydrolyte after E. coli mutated and ruined the great and regular lakes (Crop included) and what little fresh water that aki had left got mad pricey, replace the dainty national anthem with a banger remix by the Halluci Nation and we'd even get cell service from Dominion Mobile on the rez. All these well-meaning gestures under one stinking condition: a generational bond to Little Miss D's "Sposal" program.

Underneath the public eye, Little Miss Dominion's "Sposal" program was just some tech mogul's scheme for more digital coins. But at our level, the program involved fielding and then dumping shipped garbage from urban centres into new landfills on each and every rez under treaty. We picked up everywhere settlers lived, from surveilled metropolises for heat migrants and gated cloud towns for the lucky few thousands that lived there. The minister's cabinet framed it publicly as a sort of reverse paternalism, like nates would become the rightful stewards of the land once again, and permitted us the byline for any new prospects considering natural goods and resource development on the mainland, which was fine for them since big oil fracked the good and badlands altogether and moved on to the untapped Arctic. They delivered to every community a management (rather than treatment) system unique to their territory and ordained each with enough jurisdiction for any waste-making policies that involved it. But with that sovereignty and agency came the stinking reality that hundreds of trucks loaded with the rest of the country's garbage would roll up and dump, come hump day. And leave it to Mino Bee to apply for and secure decades of council grants, a few settler badges, plus all the coverage and industry connection "Ways of Throwing" would ever need to keep going based on our struggle. And those ways of his rested on a central figure named Miigwetch Rex.

Miigwetch Rex is a Bojack-slacked Jurassic big head. Little Miss Dominion's national mascot. Anthropomorphic tyrannosaurus, he rocks a beaded hoodie, Timberland moccasins, medicine wheel pins, a vintage STRONG/RESILIENT/INDIGENOUS dad hat lazily painted tangerine, and a pair of camo slacks. The lore behind Miigwetch is that he's one of the waste depot drivers. But there's only one piece from "Ways of Throwing" that finds him behind the wheel, hand straddling the gear, the stick made long enough to accommodate those HR-ready forelimbs. Never mind that paleontologists never dug up any dinosaurs around Crop Lake. But it doesn't matter anyways, since most pieces find Miigwetch off-duty and away from the bird's throat, enjoying impossible vacations: surfing the northern lights, snorkelling in the acidic Georgian Bay, plunked beside a campfire at the top of Mount Assiniboine, tripping on LSD at a holographic Arkells concert. He's always framed in realist composites, removed from this world like a Monkman piece, or maybe one of those Ralph Lauren sweater teddies. Most people liked it. Unless they drove a truck.

But again: nobody knew who Mino was. Perhaps it had to do with him going full Banksy from the start, had no photos in the cloud-verse, no public appearances or YouTube interviews, and any recordings of him speaking that surfaced were vocoded and droned like Jigsaw or Anonymous. All the country had was a clipped avatar of Miigwetch looking back at the voyeur, blinking and occasionally yawning. Underneath, Mino put "Crop Lake First Nation" as his pinned location. Not even his talent agent or publicist knew what he looked like, admittedly, and there were threads online and theories made to find out who was behind it and why. Although I don't know who, I do know why: Mino brought Rex into this world to animate the country's fantasies of escapism, which he did. Even landed Rex in his own Pixar flick and Tim Hortons advertisements. Canada Trust campaigns for days. And as Rex took form and shape, he produced more by simply existing, and began to replace Mino's appearances, speaking on his behalf and acting as a proxy for any situations that required his presence. But what bothered Crop Lake the most about Mino was that he never drove the trucks. Anyone who did could just tell from the one piece: the gratitude above Rex's chin, the strokes that composed his whistling. Just Mino's hard-working fraudulence doing its thing. Yet despite the poor imitations, he got to speak on behalf of the Crop. It was unclear which one of us he was or which house he came from, and anonymity like that was impossible at Crop Lake. And so began this dangerous and uncertain period where we stopped trusting each other, quit believing if we really were who we said we were, especially whether we were Mino. Really, anyone with a computer and access to the Adobe Suite could be Mino. I'd work and drive across the wastelands furious until I'd get back to the bird's throat, and then when I'd get home I'd lie awake in bed, thinking about how mad that dino made me, until I fell asleep.

After Rex showed up, I kept dreaming the same dream. Once REM set in, the sleep pictures would cloak a thin membrane around my first sensory memory, beginning with long strips of light that flicker and fade along a shaking wall of blackness.

In the dream, I'm barely two and throwing fist after useless fist against Pop's bedroom door, which is where he used to put me when I acted up. And while I crave release from the separation anxiety, what I really want is to get away from the glowing television in the corner that plays a well-loved VHS tape of 1993's *Wallace and Gromit: The Wrong Trousers*. Pops often relied on those British Claymations about a hapless inventor and his loyal dog to phase out an overused Kenny Rogers cassette that worked magic tricks during my colicky days. The TV is rolling a shot of Gromit the beagle, who looks mournful in his doghouse out back. Gromit began sleeping out there to accommodate the scheming penguin, Feathers McGraw, who prefers Gromit's bedroom over the spare. Grief nibbles Gromit when he sees Wallace enjoying dinner with this fraudster, and it is too much for one pup. So Gromit packs a framed photo of Wallace and him, one analogue clock, and a doggy bone into a polka-dotted bindle and ties a knot, dons his yellow raincoat, and walks off cloaked into the stormy street, looking for another place to sleep. Gromit wakes up the next morning in a tin garbage bin, and then the TV cuts to white noise. The shadows cast from the deception followed by the tape's salt-and-pepper fuzz had me ping-ponging around the room in tears. But to balm my nocturnal meltdown and attend to my unanswered calls for freedom comes Rex, who in a great swoop picks me up by his teeny arms for a dangle-legged hug, hush-hush, anything he can do to shut me up, only to shove my head into his mouth. And then I would beat my work alarm by a few seconds.

The end of my life began like any other morning. Wake up while it was still dark out, shower, and slip on my neon hazard coat, and drive in the truck on up the road to the collection depot, where I usually bumped into my circle of co-wasters to have a coffee and bust guts about the dogshit it all was and probably still is. A crowd of wasters had their backs to the door of the depot foyer after I checked in, and when I made my way to the front of the meeting room, I could see why.

Facing my fellow wasters stood Miigwetch Rex, dad hat and all. He was blinking and occasionally yawning, and his arms hung slack in front of him. But instead of the usual fit, he had a hazard coat overtop, and there was a seamed hole for his tail to poke through, and goggles nice and snug over his carnivorous peepers. I walked as calmly as possible toward the impossible to get a better look.

"Miigwetch Rex," I said. "What the hell?"

"Boozhoo," the dinosaur said. "Miigwetch Rex ndishinikath. Crop Lake ndoonji."

I looked at the other drivers working that day, who just looked back as puzzled as me.

"What the hell is this?" I asked. More importantly, I was thinking, *how the hell is this.* It's not every day a dinosaur shows up in the flesh, but then again this wasn't like every day.

"The creator has sent me to help," Rex said, without prompt, and sincere as a dinosaur could be. We made eye contact, and when we did, I got a fierce brainpic of Gromit in the trash bin, except I was Gromit and Gromit was me, crying at the TV for what he was about to see, had just seen.

I turned to the manager, who stood cross-armed and next to Rex.

"Think we're stupid?" I asked them. "CBC sucking Mino off again?"

"Pipe down, Dane. Rex is on a research trip. Show some respect to our guest. Matter fact, he's gonna shadow you today."

"No way I'm hopping in a truck with that thing."

But then he explained there was no way forward without it. So in the truck we went.

Rex and I made it on the highway shortly after daybreak. We drove to a prairie metropolis a half-hour north to grab a load before going back to the bird's throat. I told Rex that he had to get ready for the garbage.

"I am always ready for everything," Rex said.

"Really? Everything? Okay, how about a question, then? You're always ready for those."

"Only the guilty are not ready for questions."

Sure, I thought. And then, "Why a dinosaur?"

"Indigenous peoples have long since been treated like dinosaurs," Rex said while staring out at unceded land. "There's not a lot that can be done about the image lodged in the colonized mind, one that is in many of our minds too. No matter how many attempts are made to show that our people can play video games and innovate and lift weights and change light bulbs, we're still dinosaurs to everybody else and ourselves at times too. And when it comes to representation, the creator has no limits as to what counts and what doesn't count. It's all game. There are no limits for us anymore. Besides, it's not like you're even real, Dane."

"You sure about that?" I tightened my hand around the wheel and pulled into the drop-off to join the truck queue. "You—or sorry, the creator—think just because you're a dinosaur and wearing some hat that you have the right to assert values and beliefs? That's why you're my shadow today, yeah? Cuz Mino already has all the textures down pat. Pretty sure you're just like any other rat. Another ultramodern fraudster banking our lived hardship. Bet Mino's a group of people. And if I'm not real, then why can I chew cheek and pass gas and collect garbage?"

"The creator is not a person," Miigwetch said. "He's beyond this realm. But you are very much from within this realm, and only serve those who think they're better dinosaurs than everyone else. As though you know what's up because you're the real deal, right?"

"I'll tell you what's up," I replied.

"Okay, Dane. What's up?"

We continued like this for most of the pickup. When we left the drop-off, I noticed the long, cascading morass of plastic and debris introducing new horizons had grown even bigger since the previous week. The freaky thing about the trajectory of garbage is how much of it there is. How consistently it arrives week after week after week. No matter how many bans or sanctions or fines or limits for the makers, there is little to do to halt it all or dig a way out of the trash. As we drove back to the lake, I knew what I would do next.

"Another question for you."

"Any question, Dane Green."

"Who is Mino Bee? Why can't he show his face? Thinks he's Pynchon?"

"That was three questions. And we've already covered it. I can only speak for myself. Besides, the creator works in mysterious ways. I am privy to those ways, just like you. I pray every day and smudge when I need cleansing and participate in the ways of throwing, just like you do."

"You don't know what I do, Rex. What I'm about to do."

At that moment, I cranked the wheel and slammed my foot into the high pedal, and off we went barrelling into Crop Lake, slow motion and all.

I drove into the lake that day because dinosaurs don't know how to swim and sure enough, neither could Miigwetch Rex. But when the truck hit the surface and then sunk below, I began to realize how tough it actually is to get out of a sinking vehicle. Gravity and pressure work in tandem to keep the sinker sinking. Sure enough, Rex just sat there. He didn't unbuckle himself or squeeze out the window or struggle without oxygen, just opened his mouth and let the Crop fill his insides with E. coli. I did everything he didn't do. I fought against the struggle, but the efficiency of the lake made us sink to the bottom in no time flat, and I drowned in his plot.

The worst part about the end were the memorials held in Rex's honour afterwards. National coverage of the incident took over the news cycle for a week, and the tragedy turned into one of those cycle-suckers that dominated all things Native and makes everyone forget about the issues that really affect communities. The minister turned it into a national day of remembrance, and the critics described the death of Miigwetch Rex as Mino's strongest toss yet.

Glenna Turnbull

BECAUSE WE BUY OAT MILK

Each morning starts with a cup of coffee, because who can function without that first hit of caffeine—but not too much caffeine so just a half-caf latte for me that I make at home because it's cheaper and doesn't create more waste with those takeout single-use cups, and not with cow's milk because cow's milk was meant for baby cows, that's what Eric says, and never almond milk, because, well, Eric is convinced the almond milk industry is run by the mafia and uses too much water—water that Eric would rather secretly snake out when nobody is looking, late at night in well-hidden hoses that slither into the cedar hedges they tell you never to plant in the Okanagan because of the drought and the fires that rage here—fire season, heat domes, we are doomed, but especially doomed if we put cow's milk in our coffee so we only buy oat milk because *mares eat oats and goats eat oats and little lambs eat ivy* and the ivy grows up on the side of the house, its tendrils gripping on for dear life but Eric says it will crumble the bricks if we leave it but we can't kill it because its leaves are filters for all the carbon monoxide we are producing, the greenhouse gases which have very little to do with the greenhouse Eric built in the backyard which then became my job to tend, to make sure the bugs don't get in and if they do then I have to kill them because it's okay to kill the bad bugs just not the good bugs and then everything gets watered with more of the water we're not supposed to be using but it's okay, because if we grow stuff in our yard then we aren't contributing to the greenhouse gas problem by having to drive to the store. Except to buy oat milk. We don't grow oats.

Eric leaves for work like he does every weekday at ten to seven in the morning in his orange Ford pickup truck and I don't point out the amount of carbon monoxide he puts into the air as he lets it sit idling in the driveway for five minutes to warm the engine up or that the truck burns oil or that rust really isn't orange at all but more of a brown colour, brown like the leaves that the house-eating ivy turned after the heat dome we had last summer, or maybe it was the wildfire smoke, so thick we couldn't see the houses half a block away, that made its colour change, and I had to keep the kids indoors, letting them play on the computer or build things with Legos as they watched television so they wouldn't be breathing that brown into their lungs—lungs already strained from wearing masks in school all year long—well, that Ethan and Emma had to wear but not Ellie because I kept Ellie home with me as Eric said she didn't really need to go to kindergarten, that I could teach her way more at home and he didn't want her first experience of school to be scary, with everyone hidden so only their eyes showed what they were thinking, which I actually kind of liked in a way because it is harder for most people to lie with their eyes than it is with the rest of their face. I try to always believe what I'm saying is really true and make sure my eyes remain fixed straight ahead as I talk but not too fixed because if I stare back too hard, then Eric will know if I'm lying, right?

Ellie started grade one this fall and with the cost of food and the interest rates climbing faster and higher than the house-swallowing ivy, Eric says I need to go back to work full-time because really, how long does it actually take to do bookkeeping for my few remaining clients since Covid coughed up the rest of their businesses like a giant hairball and what else do I do all day but run errands and make meals and go grocery shopping for oat milk and squish the bad bugs in the greenhouse? He thinks I do nothing because he came home from work early one day last spring sick with Covid and discovered I had the TV turned on while making supper so he is convinced I sit around the house all day watching soap operas but really it's only *General Hospital* and I've been watching that since I was a child when I'd sit underneath my mother's ironing board and she'd forget I was there and I learned about way more things than I would have if I'd been in kindergarten, things like affairs and passion and love and betrayal and how to lie without looking like you're lying when you say things like, yes, I still love you, or I couldn't be happier, or of course he's your son! It's also where I first learned about abortions.

Making lunches, no peanut butter for Ellie as someone in her class has a nut allergy, so I put in cucumbers and carrots from our greenhouse and yogurt from the same store we buy the oat milk from and not the soy yogurt that is so gross nobody will eat it, but the one with the catchy jingle in the commercials that play during *General Hospital.* Eric says it's okay if there are still a few cows on the planet trapped working in the dairy industry, enough to make the cow's-milk yogurt he likes which comes in the little plastic containers that kids eat with little plastic spoons that all get thrown in the garbage when they're half-done because, really, who has time at their school to clean out all those little plastic containers and wash all those little plastic spoons and then haul them all to the recycling bin along with all the plastic bags everyone's sandwiches came wrapped in, but it's okay because we don't have plastic straws anymore and Ellie, Ethan, and Emma can grow up teaching their children to only drink oat milk as they wander through the barren spaces where old-growth forest once stood on Vancouver Island, or the burnt black toothpick-like Okanagan woods that were once green, a different tone of green from the greenhouse-plant green or the ivy green or the greenhouse-gases green, a colour they might only read about in books if there are still books—oh please let there still be books!

Drive the kids to school because we're too late to walk, pumping more exhaust into the air, then it's time to walk Einstein—Einstein, who doesn't live up to the potential of his name, because Eric said if we got a dog it simply had to be a doodle because, well, everyone else has doodles now as they don't shed which makes them so much cleaner but you have no idea what happens when a doodle like Einstein sticks his head into the water dish and the hairs surrounding his muzzle soak up the liquid faster than a cannula pump, his fur like an old-fashioned wringer mop that hasn't been wrung out so he leaves a trail of water across the kitchen floor like a greenhouse slug that has to be squashed, then I need to get out our Bee mop with its artificial sponge head to clean up but Eric says all this helps to keep our kitchen floor clean—Mr Clean, Lysol, Vim, all the cleaners lined up all neatly hunkered in their bunker in a trench under the sink, a little army in their plastic bottles full of chemicals and perfumes that mingle with the Downy Unstoppables poured into the laundry so our clothes stink like an old woman's purse for weeks instead of only days because Eric likes to smell perfumy-clean, especially after standing out back behind the greenhouse smoking the cigarettes he thinks I don't know about but I do because really, how can you sleep with someone and not smell the nicotine oozing out of every pore in his body when he sweats on top of you even when you say it isn't a safe time and he needs to stop and that you really mean it, then you lay under the blankets and find you can't sleep because your mind won't stop thinking about the Brazilian rainforest or Fairy Creek or your extended family in Ukraine being blown up in their sleep or oil companies announcing record billion-dollar profits at the same time we're told we aren't reducing our carbon emissions enough to keep global warming under 1.5 degrees or the unwanted life that might be brewing in your belly and it's sweltering in here because Eric has turned the mattress pad up to high and he is radiating nicotine-infused heat like the atomic waste they keep burying around the world created by all the clean energy nuclear power plants that aren't really clean or leafy green at all, forging their power out on those long straight lines that span across the sky like lines on a musical staff or lines on a street, lines that get crossed, lines across a Covid test. Or a pregnancy test.

I caught Eric siphoning gas out of the old lawn mower because it's now over two dollars a litre, and he got mad when I said it should cost even more so more people will park their cars and ride their bikes to work but not the electric bikes because Eric said they use child labour to make the batteries and here in North America our children can't even pick up their toys, and if I step on one more piece of Lego I might just throw them all in the garbage or at least the recycling bin because they're made of plastic but the recycling company says you can't recycle plastic toys so what do you do with the unwanted Legos or the children who won't pick them up and what do Americans do now that *Roe v. Wade* is gone and they can't afford a fourth child?

Separate the whites from the colours but then add them in anyway because you know Eric gets upset if you waste energy running the washing machine when it's not a full load and then climb back up the basement stairs, careful to watch for Einstein's water marks and navigate the small pieces of Lego that wait like bees to sting your feet except the bees are disappearing, and what will pollinate the fruit trees so heavily sprayed with pesticide for codling moths and aphids and leaf curlers, hair curlers, curling irons, ironing board, soap operas, lying, lying with my eyes to Eric when he asked this morning if my period came yet.

O Canada, our home and native land, Native land, Native, First Nation, residential schools and treaties and promises, here, have a blanket that wasn't properly separated in the laundry to cut down on the washing bill, wrap your baby up tight and rock it to sleep, deep sleep, to sleep my baby, to sleep forever, my Canada, O Canada where I thankfully still have control over my body so when my doctor confirmed it was no bigger than a garden slug or small piece of Lego, I could choose.

At the Kelowna General Hospital, which is very different from *General Hospital,* I walk past the protesters who circle around and around outside its doors like privileged children who don't have to pick up their toys, around and around like a merry-go-round, *round and round the mulberry bush*, each carrying signs that tell me I'm about to become a murderer and will burn in hell, *pop goes the weasel*, that Roe was a hoe and Wade, being a man, knew oh so much better, then I check into the same front desk that I checked into while in labour with each of my three kids before the elevator whisked us up to the third-floor delivery rooms but I don't head to the delivery room today—instead, I go down a different hallway to the special area set aside for all of us careless flippant about-to-be murderesses who just went and got ourselves pregnant again because it's always our fault it happens (didn't you say no?), and I put on the robe that ties in the back (but did you really mean it?), and I want to leave my socks on because it's cold in the room, but the nurse says they have to come off because somehow having warm feet might interfere with the ability of the cannula pump to suck this fetus out of me, this little Lego piece that doesn't fit into our family plan, family planning we learned in high school—how to put condoms on bananas and how to say no, say it like you mean it, say it with your eyes, just say no, to just say no, to say, to just say. No!

I lie there patient as a cactus waiting for my turn to come around and I stare straight into her eyes as I tell the nurse yes, I have a lift home, because it's not a complete lie—I don't tell her I'm the driver and that I need this to be done in time to meet Ellie, Ethan, and Emma at the school gates with Einstein on his leash and a smile on my face as if everything is fine fine fine even if my eyes are bloodshot and I reek of sadness.

Back at home, I send Ethan out to the greenhouse to pick cucumbers and tomatoes and turn on *General Hospital* so my brain can switch off, my cramping body slumped across the couch and I listen as Ellie and Emma giggle upstairs sneaking pieces of their Halloween candy, and even though I keep thinking about the poison and chemicals they're pouring into their little bodies, the artificially flavoured sugar that's coloured with products I can't even pronounce, I can't seem to rally enough to stop them and it's not until Einstein starts whining at the back door that I finally give in and begin to peel myself up off the sofa, the bulky blood-soaked pad between my legs feeling thick as a hotdog bun.

I swing my legs over the edge of the cushions and my foot comes hammering down onto a tiny piece of Lego no bigger than a small garden slug, and the full pain of the day takes over, thick as a blanket of forest fire smoke, swaddling me in brown, crumbling like a brick house, taking me down down down.

Kawai Shen

THE HANGED MAN

Queenie liked playing dumb with Ryan. Not when it came to intellectual matters, for it was obvious to them both that she bettered him in this domain. No, Queenie liked to pretend she had no idea Ryan was attracted to her. It amused her to deflect his tentative, elliptical advances, to neither encourage nor reject him, but instead to spin him around until he was facing an entirely different direction.

Her first impression of Ryan was that he was, incontrovertibly, a white male. Disenchanted and atomized by modernity, liberated from the fetters of religion and social tradition by reason alone, he was someone destined to claim his rightful place at some unspecified pinnacle of achievement. With his modest upbringing, gangly build, and lack of intellectual prowess, Queenie understood that this left Ryan with slim pickings when it came to blazing his übermenschian path to glory. His fate had cast him so far from the domains of finance and industry, medicine and law, creative or philosophical genius, athletic prowess or good looks, that he had to content himself with less attractive domains to colonize, like the quest for spiritual enlightenment. Within moments of meeting him, Queenie had already pegged Ryan as the kind of man who had spent his teens in a suburban bedroom plastered with band posters, consuming second-rate philosophy and copious amounts of acid in order to expand his consciousness. He might have picked up a trendy vipassana or yoga habit along the way.

Her second impression was the recognition that, in spite of herself, she had fallen in love.

Of course, Queenie had no interest in having a relationship with the man; the very prospect was humiliating. There was no comparison between Ryan and her common-law partner Eunice, a feminist activist and clinical psychologist who ran studies on eating disorders at the Centre for Addiction and Mental Health. Eunice sat on the board of directors for an Asian-Canadian arts collective and co-chaired their annual fundraising gala. Eunice came out to her family when she was sixteen and was living on her own by eighteen. Eunice wore vintage YSL and drew her eyeliner so sharp, a mere glance could slice your self-esteem to ribbons. Eunice was an equal; Ryan collected tarot decks. But Queenie was self-aware enough to recognize her humiliation as part of the attraction.

The unlikely couple met in a café equidistant between his work and her home. Queenie liked to arrive after lunch and stake out her favourite spot in the corner by the power outlet. Ryan would usually shuffle in sometime in the late afternoon. She found him suspicious-looking because he always had his hands in his pockets. She would later learn that he kept gem-stones on his person for grounding.

It took several weeks for Ryan to work up the nerve to speak to her. They were both seated by a shared coffee table where Queenie was ostensibly working on an assignment. In reality, she had already spent an hour scrolling through social media for "inspiration." Frustrated, she took a quick break to purchase a second latte. Ryan seized the opportunity as Queenie resettled herself in her leather armchair, pretending to be distracted with her drink.

"Would you be interested in a Tarot reading? For free?"

"You mean right now?"

"Sure, why not? I'm Ryan, by the way."

Before she could respond, Ryan retrieved a drawstring tarot bag of Chinese brocade silk with an occult sigil embroidered into the fabric. Queenie noticed that while Ryan was not a handsome man, he had beautiful hands.

"I'm Queenie."

Queenie received the tarot deck into her hands as if it were an illicit drug.

"You can shuffle the deck until you feel ready. But if you have a question or issue in mind that you're seeking counsel for, it's better."

"Do I have to align my chakras first?"

Ryan paused and appraised her expression. His gaze was not objectifying and she found that unnerving. "No, but there has to be some respect for the process, or else it won't work." *How convenient,* Queenie mused, *of course it only works when one buys into the bullshit.*

"I was just teasing. I'm curious and I have a question."

As Queenie shuffled the cards, she thought about her assignment, then the phone bill she forgot to pay on time—which would piss off Eunice—then dinner with Eunice's parents that she was already dreading, even though it was weeks away.

"When do I stop?"

"Whenever you feel ready."

Queenie handed the deck back to Ryan, who spread it out face down on the table and pulled out three cards: the Hanged Man, the Four of Cups, the Nine of Discs. Ryan paused, staring at the cards over hands tented theatrically before speaking with an unyielding voice: "You're dead in the water. Suspended. Stuck." He tapped the first card, which depicted a man suspended by one foot, his abstract face lacking any features or expression. "But it's comfortable, pleasant even." As Ryan said this, he tapped the Four of Cups and pushed it toward her. Pale waters spilled from a dusky lotus suspended from a grey sky, cascading into four weary chalices. Ryan tapped the last card, which appeared upside down. Nine coins arranged in a geomantic form emitted a muted light. "What was once satisfying now leaves you cold. You may not be as independent as you think." *Was that a neg?* Ryan began to replace the cards in the deck.

"My question was about completing an assignment that's due this week."

"Okay."

"But I still don't know what to do. That was rather oracular."

"The Tarot doesn't answer what you think you want to know, but a more profound truth. It reveals what your unconscious, what your deeper Self, wants you to know." Queenie suppressed an eye roll. *What's the point of thinking of a question if The Tarot is just going to bypass that anyway?* She managed a noncommittal "Thanks. It's something to think about."

Ryan now couldn't look her in the eye. With the cards packed away, he seemed shy again. He traced the threads of the sigil of the tarot bag with his finger in a manner Queenie found disarming. She stilled his hand. "My turn," she said. "You shuffle; I'll read."

"Wow, you read Tarot too?"

Queenie laughed. "No, but would you like me to anyway?"

"Sure! Yes, I mean … you already look … not sneaky, but kind of …"

"Mischievous?"

"Yes, you look very mischievous right now."

"Maybe I'll be a mischievous reader."

Ryan shuffled and handed the deck to Queenie, who spread the cards out on the table with a magician's flourish. "Pick one." Ryan pulled out a card and she flipped it over as if they'd already established a routine. On the card, a goat with spiralling horns stood before a stylized phallus and rested upon abstract testicles within which small human figures twisted. "Ah, the Devil. Well then," Queenie began. She tapped the card like Ryan had. "The Tarot is telling me you will be possessed by creative forces leading you to produce penetrating works of seminal genius." She smiled at her own cleverness; Ryan returned her smile. It would occur to her later that he wouldn't have caught her play on the word *seminal*.

"You *are* a mischievous reader."

Queenie pantomimed a pensive expression. "Morning wood. That's what your unconscious wants you to know."

"That's good to know."

"That your junk's in working order?"

"And that you're a natural. On a path to becoming a master reader."

Queenie shuffled the cards and returned them to Ryan. "In that case, maybe next time I'll charge you."

Now, sexually charged banter with a strange man was by no means a transgression. But even then, the transgressive trajectory of the relationship could be easily plotted by anyone. The predictability, the banality of it—that was what excited Queenie. After all, The Tarot was right. Her life did feel mired in stagnancy. She was often cynical and bored. She was tired of self-sufficiency and containment. She knew she had been raised with a generic image of perfection, yet was discovering that even your garden-variety perfection was asymptotic; the closer you curved toward it, the clearer it would become to you how you would always remain flawed. Queenie was also beginning to understand that the more one approached perfection, the more the law of diminishing returns came into force. She failed to see the point in putting in any more effort.

Eunice, on the other hand, seemed content to deny this logic. Blithely ignoring any evidence to the contrary, Eunice pressed onward, as if everything she encountered was a malfunctioning machine to be dismantled by force, hosed down with a water-cannon stream of common sense, then snapped back together again. In this manner, she steamrolled her way through the world, riding a relentless momentum of her own making. It was almost as if she didn't even notice the tightened budgets, EDI policies, and optimized resources she left in her wake until someone thrust yet another award in her face. *Nike,* Queenie would sometimes call her, the Greek goddess of victory.

Quite understandably, then, Eunice was late for dinner again. Queenie had missed the butcher's shop before it closed, so she made tuna casserole from pantry staples and left it in the oven to keep warm. As she waited, she set up her laptop at the kitchen table, working on mock-up logos for her latest client: clean, curvaceous gold vectors for a spacey white woman who was starting up a retail store in Parkdale selling heavily marked-up

CBD oils and tinctures to nervous rich ladies and their equally nervous lapdogs. Eunice arrived after eight, tossed her jacket and tote bag onto the couch, and made a beeline for her desktop. "Hey, aren't you hungry?" Queenie asked. Eunice logged into her computer and began typing.

"Euny?"

"I just need to print this file," Eunice replied in a tone that translated into an order to remain silent.

As Queenie spooned the casserole onto their dinner plates, Eunice roused herself from her laptop and came to the dining table.

"I thought you said you were making steaks for dinner."

"Zanakins closed early," Queenie lied. "They had some kind of leak."

"That's annoying."

"It's whatever. How was your big meeting?"

Eunice shook her head. "Sorry about earlier. I have had *a day*. The artists are organizing a protest against one of the AACT directors. He's an old white cis man who's been defending this white Sheridan grad who's been making the rounds on social media with these"—Eunice sighed deeply before finishing—"weird portraits of Chinese people in cyberpunk Mao uniforms. God, you have to see them."

Eunice displayed her phone and swiped. Queenie grimaced.

"That's, like, Yellow Peril territory, like all Chinese people are swarming CCP spies."

Eunice threw a hand up in the air. "Yes, it's racist. But are these artists going to find us another major gift donor to replace our director? I don't think so. I—" Eunice's phone chirped, but she pressed onward: "I mean, why should all the at-risk Asian youth enrolled as a part of our upcoming exhibit get punished because some ignorant white men decided to double down on their ignorance, as if this doesn't happen all the time already? That grad's work has nothing to do with my organization." Eunice reached for her phone. "Sorry, I know, no phones at dinner. Just let me put it on silent."

Queenie suppressed the urge to argue her point. She wasn't volunteering on the board of the Asian Arts Collective of Toronto, after all. She could also see that Eunice was suppressing the urge to respond to her text. "Anyway," Eunice said, "I know all this is not very interesting for you. Tell me about *your* day."

Queenie shrugged, but even before her shoulders had settled, something wicked sparked.

"Well, this really awkward white guy at Slanted Portal hit on me and, like, pestered me for almost half an hour. I was obviously trying to work—"

"Ugh. I'm so sorry."

"—and like, you wouldn't believe his pickup line. He kind of, like, leans over with a pack of tarot cards and asks if I want a reading. And I'm like, uh-huh yeah, I'm *working*—"

"You're too polite."

"—and like, he starts going on about my *aura*—"

Eunice shook her head. "Oh god. Let me guess: tribal arm band, blond dreads." The couple laughed.

"Euny, that's so nineties. Tribal finger tattoos, mala beads."

Eunice narrowed her eyes, reminding Queenie why she'd first been attracted to her. Eunice's wrath was always so beautiful.

"You know what booster shot you need, babe? Yellow fever vaccine."

Later that evening, as Queenie and Eunice sat side by side in bed wearing Korean sheet masks, Queenie received a series of texts.

About The Hanged Man, Aleister Crowley
wrote, every man and every woman is a star.

I don't know why but thought this might
mean something to you.

Queenie put down her phone. She forced herself to peel off her mask and massage the serum into her skin before responding.

                                        Who is Aleister Crowley?

A famous english occultist. He made the tarot
deck I used with you.

The british press called him the wickedest
man in the world

                                        Sounds like a bad boy.

He was!

                                        And what does Mr Crowley have to
                                        say about The Devil?

Knowing crowley, likely something about
one's junk being in working order :P

"Who's texting you?"
"CBD Lady." Queenie turned off her phone and placed it face down on her bedside table. She began kissing Eunice's neck and

shoulder and sliding her hand under her lover's silk slip, tracing her fingertips up an inner thigh.

"What are you, ahh, fuck..."

Eunice closed her eyes. As Queenie stroked Eunice's clitoris, she observed Eunice's mouth widening with a moan, the jellylike bio-cellulose mask contorting with the shifting contours of her face. Queenie became fascinated by her lover's sightless, masked expression, how the material clung to Eunice's face so seamlessly, it was as if her skin was secreting its own glutinous white film. Queenie could never get her sheet masks to fit so smoothly.

With her non-dominant hand, Queenie stroked herself in time with Eunice. As Eunice finally climaxed, the sheet mask, still glossy with collagen serum, seemed to all but meld into her skin. It gave Queenie the disconcerting feeling that she didn't recognize Eunice at all. She began to touch herself more urgently. It had been a long time since she had been this aroused. Her orgasm took her by surprise. It seemed to crest out of nowhere, waters pitched from the lip of a weary chalice finally toppling over.

The next day, Queenie arrived at Slanted Portal just past noon, even though she knew Ryan never showed up until the afternoon. After Eunice left for work, Queenie spent twenty minutes trialling outfits before settling on a jersey slip with a revealing cowl neck, followed by another thirty minutes painting her face—primer on the lids, lipstick applied with a brush, a liberal dusting of translucent finishing powder—only to realize that she was advertising all the effort she was making. She changed into a pair of skinny jeans and a plain T-shirt that hugged her breasts just so, then melted down her work on her face and started over. *I'm a thousand times prettier than him anyway.* Despite this, she had overestimated the time she needed, and, unable to concentrate at home in her no-makeup makeup, smelling of Eunice's Noir Épices perfume, she packed up her knapsack and left.

When Queenie reached the café, she was surprised to find Ryan had already arrived. At the sight of him, an unfamiliar warmth rippled through her core. Queenie ordered her regular matcha latte and settled into the chair beside him. "You're early," she said.

"Had to save you a seat. Plus my shift doesn't start for a couple hours?"

"So tell me about your bad boy."

Ryan looked at her with a blank expression. *God, he's slow.*

"Crowley," Queenie prompted, "the wickedest man in the world." Ryan's expression lifted in the way that only an introvert's can when weary of small talk and suddenly presented with an obscure conversational topic of intense interest. He proceeded to deliver a disjointed, ten-minute lecture on Crowley's life, laced with apocryphal anecdotes of the going-ons of the Toronto lodge of the OTO, Crowley's secret occult society. Ryan mentioned that his roommate had been initiated into the group six months ago. *Of course he has.*

"So you have a roommate?"

"Yes, but he's not around much."

"I take it, then, you have the place to yourself a lot?" Queenie asked with a coy smile. "That's good to hear."

Ryan nodded.

"Must be nice." Her smile grew. "I have a lot of roommate horror stories."

Queenie knew that this dynamic of manipulation, which was to continue for the following month, was a diversion. But Queenie needed a diversion. She couldn't afford to get away like Eunice, who had planned a week-long yoga retreat in Guatemala. "It's not a beginner trip," Eunice had said. "You've never been to a developing nation before." And Queenie knew without further elaboration that had she been able to afford the retreat, she was not invited, that this was Eunice's time, time that was not to be spent worrying about Queenie messing up her meticulously plotted itinerary.

The farthest Queenie had ever travelled was when her family drove to Florida for her cousin's wedding when she was fourteen. Ryan, on the other hand, promised to take her to another dimension.

"You should come check out the store I work at," he said. "The Eighth Dimension."

"I'm not sure I got past the fourth dimension of time."

Ryan took this as an opportunity to launch into another unsolicited lecture. "Well, the eighth dimension is, like, it goes beyond reality. In the Jewish faith, everything comes in sevens, right? Seven days of creation, seven days of shiva, seven blessings for marriage, seven, seven, seven. So seven is like the totality, it contains everything, life, death, all of it.

"But the eighth dimension is *beyond* that. It transcends what can be defined. It has no limits, it can't be contained, it—"

"So the owner is Jewish," Queenie interrupted.

Ryan paused, his mind skidding to an unexpected halt. "Huh? No. I mean, I don't think so." He paused. "I mean, Kate's like a Kabbalah master."

Queenie struggled for something to say that would be the least likely to trigger another logorrheic response.

"Oh, I see."

"Have you ever heard of the Kabbalah?" The only thing Queenie knew about the Kabbalah was that Madonna had been into it during her yogini-*Ray-of-Light* phase and that the controversial rabbi she followed had died in disrepute.

"Hasn't your shift started?" Queenie gestured to the clock on the café wall. She knew he was already eight minutes late and it would take him maybe another six to walk there. Ryan nodded, but didn't seem hurried.

"I mean it: you should come see me where I work."

"Seriously?"

"Why not? I'll give you the grand tour."

Queenie and Ryan had a few more coffee "dates" before she visited Eighth Dimension. Even though it was in the neighbourhood, she'd never set foot in the store. It was not at all what she had expected. It was the scent of petrichor that struck Queenie first, like thrusting her bare hands into cool, wet earth and bringing her soiled fingertips to her face. The retail environment, if it could be called that, was equally evocative. Instead of a dusty, incense-burning hovel, Eighth Dimension was like a woodland grove for raving. The psytrance music pulsating in the background was more conducive to dancing intoxicated than browsing wares. The staff had covered every conceivable surface with convincing tangles of artificial ivy and the floor featured dried grasses and craggy stones. The greenery was studded with crystal points, feathers, and glinting pieces of broken mirror. Wind chimes, animal bones, beaded medallions, and abstract wooden carvings were suspended from the ceiling with fraying hemp ropes slung about the room like jungle vines. Tinkly fairy lights crept over the walls, winking to reveal new crevices and corners. Every inch of the premises offered symbols of some kind, painted or carved into surfaces: runes, geomantic figures, Hebrew letters, astrological glyphs, I Ching hexagrams, Sanskrit, all carefully rendered.

Queenie's eyes swept over the inventory. Pricey wellness products in minimalist packaging were interspersed among beeswax candles, essential oils, and crystals labelled with earnest messages in aesthetically challenged "tribal" fonts making every kind of claim from dispelling curses to improving your ability to communicate with angels. Near the back, there was a dried goods section featuring such mundane items as raisins and pantry spices alongside herbs she had never heard of, like damiana and motherwort.

The back of the store also featured its centrepiece: a giant stone-cast water fountain carved in the shape of a lotus flower where the staff had hung garlands of fresh flowers and on which they had placed gemstones. Queenie resisted the urge to touch it; she had the premonition that just placing her palms in the water would have a calming effect.

"It's beautiful, isn't it?" Ryan said. "We all call it the Mandala."

"Why would you hide this in the back?"

"Oh, we're not trying to hide it. This was the best placement for it according to feng shui. You can tell it's a good placement, too. See these flowers? They're from my garden. I bring them here and they'll keep looking fresh for almost two weeks."

"You made these intricate garlands? By yourself?"

"Yeah, my ex was from Thailand and she taught me how. Anyway, I should probably start my shift, but stick around and feel free to ask me about anything here."

Queenie lingered in the back, unwilling to pretend to browse anything other than the civilian goods. There was also something thrilling about being able to observe Ryan standing servile behind the cash counter. At first, Queenie felt like gloating. Yet instead of speeding up to accommodate a growing lineup of shoppers, Ryan became engrossed in a genial conversation with another man buying an oracle deck. An oracle deck with Native Spirit Animals. By Ryan's animated expression, Queenie judged that the topic at hand was probably Jungian archetypes again. With this, her thrill was swiftly displaced by the co-morbid feelings of pity and disgust. Only a small-town white boy could be this satisfied with his total lack of material ambition. It took a specific kind of privilege to remain so heedless of the world's merry-go-round of physical threats—illegal eviction, unemployment, sexual assault, what have you—threats that could, on Queenie's blacker days, grip her like a centrifuge, an invisible force pinning her to the wall as her rationality dropped out from beneath her. Rhetorical questions laced with contempt marched into her mind: *What is it like to not give a shit over financial security because you're too busy pursuing a life of Authenticity and Self-Actualization? What is it like to go through the world with absolutely no instinct for self-preservation?*

Queenie understood Ryan's white maleness as not just a privilege, but as a consignment to a special kind of ignorance, one that doomed him to narcissism: wherever he looked, the world reflected the rightness of his image back to him. The man lacked all ability to imagine prostrating himself to forces outside his control that didn't invoke some notion of psycho-spiritual personal growth. With this realization, Queenie decided she would cease batting him around and just fuck him.

That was how Queenie found herself in a basement apartment on Lansdowne with a ceiling too low to be up to code and reeking of pot and frankincense. Initially, she had invited Ryan to her apartment; Eunice had finally departed for her yoga retreat. But the improbable prospect of Eunice returning unannounced and catching the two of them together gripped Queenie's nerves like pincers, and after two restless nights she called Ryan to reschedule last minute. In a stroke of propitious timing, Ryan's roommate Kwento had left to visit his parents in Ottawa.

As Queenie followed Ryan down the sloping stairs of the basement unit, she immediately noted that its walls were covered in posters of deities of various religions: Baphomet, Kali, Eshu, Isis. Behold, the settler who killed his own god now buys everyone else's instead.

Still, the unit was tidy and clean. The men had affixed patterned Nigerian textiles to the ceiling above the living room area and this gave the dwelling a cheerful look. Throughout the space, Ryan was successfully nursing multiple pothos cuttings.

Queenie sat at the kitchen table as Ryan cooked dinner using a hot plate. "I make a mean pad Thai," he'd promised. As he prepared their first meal together, Queenie eyed the small bookshelf that doubled as a kitchen island. She was taken aback by the total absence of the English literary canon. Ryan collected books she could not even imagine a market for: *The Hero with a Thousand Faces; Exploring Jupiter: The Astrological Key to Progress, Prosperity and Potential; The Mothman Prophecies*. There was also an entire row of different tarot decks.

"You can borrow anything that interests you," Ryan said. Queenie picked up a dog-eared copy of Crowley's *The Book of Thoth*. She recognized the illustration style of the tarot deck Ryan had used for her reading. "I thought you'd pick that one," Ryan said. "It's really philosophical."

She flipped through the pages and stopped at the passage for the Hanged Man. The quote Ryan had texted her caught her eye, for he had underlined it in purple ink: *Every man and every woman is a star.* Queenie read onward:

> *"Pity not the fallen! I never knew them. I am not for them. I console not: I hate the consoled and the consoler." Redemption is a bad word; it implies debt. For every star possesses boundless wealth; the only proper way to deal with the ignorant is to bring them to the knowledge of their starry heritage. To do this, it is necessary to behave as must be done in order to get on good terms with animals and children: to treat them with absolute respect; even, in a certain sense, with worship.*

Queenie didn't understand how these words were supposed to relate to the image of the man with the geometric face, hanging from one foot with a snake coiled around it. Instead, the passage made her think of permissive white parents, the middle-class liberal kind who preferred to verbally rationalize every child care decision.

Shortly after Queenie moved in with Eunice, she once overheard their next-door neighbour struggling in the hallway, trying to cajole her three-year-old son into wearing a pair of mittens. She felt ashamed on behalf of the woman, a grown adult, late for her appointment, reduced to pleading with an infant. From behind his copy of *The Book of Thoth,* she observed Ryan contentedly slicing scallions with a blunt peeling knife and imagined his own mother pleading with him to perform the most basic of tasks, listing all the reasons he should consider obeying, like she was a defence lawyer, and her son, her jury. She imagined his nameless

Thai Ex-Girlfriend indulging him in his mediocrity, teaching him how to thread floral garlands and where to buy the best tamarind paste. Maybe she even taught him how to correctly pronounce the names of the Buddhist gods that decorated his apartment. Probably not.

As they ate dinner, Ryan asked Queenie what she dreamed about. Queenie paused. It had been so long since she had thought about what she wanted.

"Well," she said, riffing on the spot, "I was thinking of maybe enrolling in a program to study fashion design. I've been really inspired by the Antwerp Six lately. Everyone's into Margiela, but like, some early Ann Demeulemeester is amazing, stuff like the fluidity and breezy silhouettes of her Spring 1997 collection." It was true that she often thought about that show.

"Oh, that's cool. But I meant when you're sleeping."

Queenie felt embarrassed, like she'd been tricked. "I don't dream."

"You dream," Ryan said. "Everyone dreams, but it takes practice to recall them."

Queenie bristled but let it pass. "What do you dream about?"

When Ryan didn't answer, she asked, "Did you dream about me?" She had only been teasing, but Ryan looked down at the dinner table. After a long pause he said, "I know you have a girlfriend. I mean, as a partner." Queenie paled. *Was this motherfucker actually psychic!* When she didn't respond, Ryan continued: "I've seen you both at the Slanted Portal. You'd come in together, holding hands. Once, you kissed her at the door."

Queenie scolded herself for even entertaining the possibility of psychic powers. As if that rebalanced her, she quipped, "But you approached me and flirted with me anyway." For the first time, Ryan looked irritated. "She doesn't own you. She doesn't even see you."

"Careful."

"What are you doing here, then, if that isn't true?"

Queenie pulled away. "I should get going."

"Wait, I'm sorry. Don't go. I was out of line."

"Why did you invite me here?"

"Why did you come? You came because you felt something." *Boredom. Self-deceit. Neurosis. Internalized racism.*

"You came," Ryan continued, "because you wanted to feel more of that something."

It had been so long since Queenie had been intimate with another body that every touch registered in relation to Eunice, as if her measurements were an imperial scale for all things. Ryan's torso was broader, his muscles firmer, his skin rougher, his biceps thicker, his kisses longer. With each caress, Eunice's presence seemed to erode. That burgeoning feeling Queenie couldn't recognize or name, that feeling she was making space for, not only excluded Eunice, it excluded herself. So when Ryan drew her ankle up to lick the arch of her foot, she did not recoil; she moaned. And when he asked her to spit on him, an act she had never done to anyone, she complied and, inspired, slapped him. And when she had risen in the morning to get dressed and return home as she knew she should, and Ryan had said "stay," she stayed. She stayed so long, she would have been late to pick up Eunice from the airport had the flight not been delayed.

Eunice returned from Guatemala with guilty handfuls of jade and chocolate. With Eunice, it was always the best for Queenie: the most exquisitely designed, heavy jade pendant necklace; the most aromatic, fruity chocolate bars made with rare criollo beans.

Queenie knew Eunice had likely spent obscene amounts of time choosing these just-right gifts for her. And that spending time in this manner was preferable, and possibly more pleasurable, than time that would have been wasted on Queenie if she had come on the retreat as well, forcing Eunice to correct all her bumbling, privileged tourist mistakes.

Queenie dutifully wore her new necklace to visit Eunice's parents for dinner. Eunice's mother, Evelyn Wong, had mercifully picked up a sushi tray and seaweed salad from the grocery store. Like many Hong Kong women of her generation and class, Evelyn was a travesty in the kitchen; her idea of home cooking was what a maid served you.

At the Wongs' family dinners, there was a tacit understanding that the opening conversational topic would always be career success. "I have been working with a new client," Queenie said, the image of a child tap dancing coming to mind as she quickened the patter of her pitch. "She's a female entrepreneur, and I really enjoy working with trail-blazing women like her. I've been thinking of ways I can differentiate myself as I'm starting out, and I'm finding that when you're really upfront about who you are and your values, you attract clients you work well with and where there's a mutual understanding."

Evelyn coolly raised one pencil-thin, pencilled-in brow. "So how does this client share your values, Queenie?"

The only mutual point of interest between Queenie and CBD Lady was that Queenie was willing to accept this client's vague instructions, lapses in communication, and repeated demands for time-consuming tweaks and alterations, often based on criteria that Queenie would only learn about after the fact.

Sensing Queenie faltering, Eunice replied before Queenie

could fumble the response: "She's an ambitious entrepreneur. She just opened an upscale health and wellness storefront in Parkdale that was featured in *Toronto Life*."

"Hm, health and wellness," Evelyn echoed. "Brisk business selling 'self-care' to women these days, isn't it? In fact, I recently saw another upscale health and wellness boutique open in Yorkville last week." Another eyebrow raise. "The inventory was primarily organic skin care products. They were selling jade facial rollers for fifty dollars."

Queenie tread carefully. "Those are very popular these days, it seems."

Evelyn dipped the edge of a California roll into her mini-saucer of soy sauce. "It seems to me that white women love to pay through the nose for 'traditional Asian beauty secrets' from other white women, don't they?"

Normally, dinners with the Wongs made Queenie hyper-vigilant, sensitive to the most minute changes in Wong Tai-Tai's voice and facial expressions. But tonight, her mind's eye was focused entirely on three images: the Seven of Cups, the Seven of Swords, and the Hanged Man. Before she had left Ryan's apartment, that noon after they had first had sex, Queenie had given herself another reading with the Thoth deck as Ryan showered. The first card bore the title Debauch; the second, Futility. These two cards made sense, but she didn't understand the last one. Weren't hanged men those tried and convicted? Why was it, then, when she'd looked up Hanged Man cards in different tarot decks on her phone, these figures always had a peaceful expression? In every deck, it was the same: a man suspended from the top of the card by one foot, his beatific visage crowned by a halo of light. The Hanged Man, his helplessness, his sanctimonious gaze—they irritated Queenie. It disarmed her, made her feel ridiculous, how this enigmatic, two-dimensional image kindled a desire to humiliate the man, but also to seek refuge in him.

Queenie could not deny that the night she had spent curling into Ryan's embrace was the first in a long time she had slept soundly; she had even woken up with him still holding her from behind. The two were silent in the first moments of that morning, as if both struck dumb by their shared transgression. Finally, after some time, Ryan confessed: "I have dreamt about you." Queenie took his hand and threaded her fingers between his.

"It was before we'd ever spoken. I was watching my body from above. I was naked, maybe dead? I was laid out on a slab of something cold, like stone. A black bird, an ibis, you know the kind with a really long beak? It flew toward me and landed on my stomach. It pierced my chest with its beak, like it started my heart again, so that I was bleeding? And as the ibis fed on me, it became human … it became you. And I knew I was alive again." Queenie turned to face Ryan, brushing his hair from his eyes.

"Strange dream. What does it mean?"

Ryan looked away, shy once more, as if he hadn't spent the last night with his face between Queenie's thighs or seen her face contorted by her climax. "It means you're my anima," he replied. Uncharacteristically, he did not explain what that was.

Queenie had two more trysts with Ryan before convincing Eunice to come with her to Eighth Dimension. She didn't know why she'd suggested it. All she knew was that her heart was beating faster before she'd even crossed the threshold of the store's door-way. Eunice entered first and was greeted by the sound of Hindi women chanting mixed with a pulsing trance beat. "Queenie," she said, frowning. "You'll see, it's so cheap," Queenie said, ushering her deeper into the store.

With Eunice present, Queenie saw Eighth Dimension anew, appraised through Eunice's eyes. The retail space, once entrancing, looked like a high school theatre set. Statues of decapitated Buddha heads were shelved on the left; bundles of sage for smudging were stacked beside Indian incense on the right. For the first time, Queenie noticed the display carousel of correspondence cards featured thin white women dressed as shamans gazing at their viewer with come-hither eyes, or straddling dragons between their pale thighs. "I *know*," Queenie muttered in a conspiratorial tone, steering Eunice toward the bulk spices.

Upon seeing the prices of the pantry goods, a brief yelp of pleasure escaped Eunice's lips. "Babe, these are almost like Costco prices!" She immediately began filling her basket. Queenie kept her back turned to the counter, unsure of whether she wanted Ryan to be there or not. He was there. As the women approached the counter to pay, Ryan's face froze in disbelief.

"Queenie."

His voice was raw. "Hey," Queenie replied and smiled despite the fact her heart felt like it was pumping peroxide. The man had no talent for deception. His total lack of guile made Queenie near apoplectic. Eunice looked at the adulterers. *She knows. She knows!* "Do you two know each other?" Eunice asked.

"Sure," Queenie replied, her face betraying nothing. When Eunice didn't react, Queenie couldn't help herself and added, "Ryan's checked me out a few times now." Queenie pantomimed casually brushing her long hair back behind her shoulder. As she did so, her vision was darkening at the edges, the rush of blood in her ears drowning out all sound, the corners of her lips suppressing a mad grin that would have drawn her lips back behind her teeth like the muzzle of a threatened dog.

Queenie had expected to be afraid, but this couldn't be fear. Fear made you contract and run away; these sensations were propelling her onward with a demonic force. She found her mouth and tongue producing the following sounds: "He's the one who helped me find that Cajun spice you like." Eunice turned to address Ryan. "If you keep your prices this low," she said cheerfully, "I promise you'll be seeing us a lot more." Ryan blanched. He managed to sputter out a thank you before rapidly scanning the items in Eunice's basket. His slender fingers trembled so badly, he dropped a baggie of cinnamon.

After they were out of earshot, Eunice raised a brow. "What was up with that guy?"

"They're all like that here," Queenie replied. "They're high in the *eighth dimension,* Euny. That Ryan guy does a lot of drugs. He was probably coming down from some ayahuasca trip or something. Hallucinating about shamans and spirit animals. You know that whole burner scene." Queenie was deliberately trying to slow the pace of her speech, but her perception of time seemed so warped, she wondered if she was babbling. Eunice seemed not to notice; she rolled her eyes in solidarity. It was as if Queenie could feel her kidneys halting any further production of adrenalin. Eunice's phone buzzed. Queenie took the opportunity to look back at Ryan. His head was bowed, his eyes closed. His hands were shoved into his pockets.

When Ryan did not return to Slanted Portal for two weeks, Queenie returned to Eighth Dimension shortly before closing. The lights out front had already been turned off. She found Ryan restocking jars of reishi mushrooms by the mandala.

"Hey you." Her voice was unexpectedly tender.

"We're closed," he said, avoiding eye contact.

"You left the door open. I locked it behind me."

"Thank you." He still wouldn't look at her. "Why are you here?"

"I wanted to see you."

"Well, you've seen me. Kate's already left for the day so you should probably leave."

"Come on. She had no idea."

"Why would Kate—"

"I meant my girlfriend."

Ryan finally glanced at her, briefly. "That's not the point." He shoved more reishi onto the shelves. "What you did was really fucked up. I don't think we should keep seeing each other."

Queenie mentally flinched but quickly recovered: "Is that what The Tarot said?"

Ryan paused. "Actually, yes."

"And which card was that, Ryan? Was it the 'Queenie is an exotic prize here to guide you on your journey toward enlightenment and now that you can't play the white saviour you don't need her anymore' card? Is that the card you pulled?"

Ryan turned toward her, his face contorted. He was so predictable.

"It's not like that at all. That's not why I need you!"

"You don't need me. You *want* me. And that's not the same thing. Not even close."

Ryan began shaking his head. *What was it now?*

"Queenie, why are you always so sad?"

Queenie blinked, twice. She felt it again, the sense of standing at the precipice of something immense, a rising sensation of something she could not identify, something that wasn't factoring her in.

"You think I'm sad," Queenie repeated.

"Yes," Ryan continued, "you're bored with your clients. You're distant with your girlfriend. You feel like you're way too smart and beautiful for this, but that's not it. You're not holding yourself accountable and it's making you miserable. You're cheating your true Self."

Queenie's lips curved into a painful smile. "My 'True Self'? You think I'm sad because I have … *first-world problems?*"

Ryan's guileless expression goaded Queenie on. "I'm not sad," she retorted. "Sad is fleeing your home because colonizers have plunged your country into intractable political violence. Sad is being separated from your family, holding down temporary jobs in a country whose language you don't speak and paying taxes for critical services you are denied. Sad is living under a government that committed genocide against your people and being policed into recognizing their continued authority over your land. What could someone like you possibly know about sadness?"

Yet Ryan was undeterred. "Queenie, everyone suffers. And you're not different just because you're not … I don't know, stuck in some refugee camp, okay?"

She wanted to slap him again. She wanted to shove his woo-woo platitudes down his throat until he choked on them. And he knew it. Ryan's eyes were softening the way they always did, as if he was willing her being to penetrate and wound him. It took his nascent white guilt toward somewhere far more inchoate. It occurred to Queenie at that moment that Ryan looked like an Aryan Jesus Christ, a starving Norseman with dreamy blue eyes and flaxen hair, his silhouette cast with a backlit glow of divine forgiveness. The man was born to be sacrificed, Queenie thought. His pliancy, his yielding nature, all but begged to be lashed to the cross.

Queenie grabbed two fistfuls of shirt and shoved Ryan against the shelves. Before he could protest, she covered his mouth with her hand.

"There's no one else here in the store. Do you understand? Nobody's watching over us, and nobody cares." Queenie pulled her hand from Ryan's mouth and found he was already hard. She dragged him down to the shop floor and mounted him without resistance.

When Queenie arrived home, Eunice was still working late on her laptop. To avoid facing her partner, Queenie took a quick shower, claimed she had a headache, and went to bed early, feigning sleep when Eunice slipped under the covers. In the silence of the bedroom, her eyes closed, Queenie could not stop her mind from replaying the sounds Ryan and she had made as they moaned together, how their cries and frantic slaps of flesh merged with the steady sound of running water, trickling over the stone lip of the sightless mandala.

Something cold is dripping on Queenie. She looks up and sees The Mandala. It is alive and electric and breathing. To look at it is making her dizzy. Its manifold petals are continuously peeling back from its centre, row upon row of plant matter replacing the next, as they unfold like shark teeth. Instead of water, the liquid that flows from within the lotus is silty with filth, leaking contaminants that stain itself. Viscous droplets carrying sludge thread downward like saliva, or semen, before landing on Queenie's skin.

Panicked, Queenie looks down and sees her foot trapped and bound with rope to the floor. The knots are simple and loosely tied, yet each time she almost releases one, her fingers fumble and the knots seem to tighten. Her torso grows heavy and bloated when she realizes her foot is not on the floor; she is, in fact, suspended upside down, hanging over The Mandala. This realization terrifies her. Her blood is rushing to her head, her temples pounding. The pain is growing more intense. Queenie tries once again to reach the knots, but now her limbs feel leaden, as if moving through mud. She understands that if she cannot right herself, she will never die.

When Queenie wakes up, it is still dark and she is trembling. Eunice, always a deep sleeper, lies snoring and undisturbed beside her. Queenie turns away from Eunice and massages her temples. She does not remember her dream.

Christine Birbalsingh

COUPLES' THERAPY

I tell our therapist that I tend to shout. This is not how you should start your relationship with your therapist. Just to be clear: I didn't shout this at her. I was simply trying to be honest because I thought that's what you do in therapy. So I agreed when Ryan, not shouting—because Ryan is very calm, some might say unemotional, some meaning me—told her I shout. As it turns out, though, if you're honest about something your therapist doesn't approve of, you don't get points for being honest.

This is our first couples' therapy session after nine years of marriage. We have one seven-year-old with special needs, although we're still trying to figure out what those needs are. At the moment we just know he can't do a lot of things other seven-year-olds can do. I don't want to add the breakdown of our family to the list of what he has to deal with. Between SLP, OT, and PT appointments, not to mention school homework, there's only one afternoon a week we can play Clue Junior, his favourite game.

You know that scale of forty-three of life's most stressful events? They've done one for kids now. Death of a parent is number one, which makes sense, but makes me question the adult scale, which doesn't list death of a child. In fact, the adult scale doesn't list anything about children, other than pregnancy and a child leaving home, as if everything in between isn't at all stressful.

But aside from the death of a parent—we're both still alive—an unplanned pregnancy—impossible for Noah at this moment in time—and getting married—again, impossible—parents' divorce is the next most stressful event of all possible life events. Divorce or separation, in fact, are number two and three on the adult scale, in between death of a spouse and imprisonment, which, I would argue, might all be the same thing, metaphorically speaking.

So this is why Ryan and I are in couples' therapy. I'm lucky Ryan's agreed. It's rare, I think, for a Gen X white man who was taught boys don't cry. Millennials, undoubtedly, and whatever other generations come after them, are far more progressive. I'm clearly a Gen Xer too: I punctuate my texts, for instance. But when I was growing up and was taught girls don't shout, I didn't listen.

I had to pick and choose which rules to follow. If I followed all of them, as a Black girl I would never have gotten into the Science Club in elementary school, for instance, or become friends with Nancy Parker down the street whose father banned me from their house. We broke his rule and played together in the park instead. Ryan has the privilege of being a rule follower. He won't cross the street on a red light even if it's a Sunday morning in the middle of a snowstorm and there isn't a car in sight.

But I think he wants to fix things as much as I do. Divorce is common, I know, but it's like a natural disaster or being hit by lightning. You never think it's going to happen to you.

*

"Let's rewind," Tammy says. She's sitting behind her desk on a cheap black office chair with wheels. She closes the file in which she placed various confidentiality forms we just went through. She then labels it "The Carlsons," even though I told her I don't use Ryan's last name.

We're sitting on a rather worn utilitarian couch in a rather worn utilitarian room in a rather worn utilitarian house. Tammy's house. This is her home office. There are baseboard heaters emitting an almost imperceptible humming. But at least it's warm. We came in through the slush and snow of a back entrance, where we removed our boots and coats in a tiny vestibule and were ushered into this windowless basement room with beige walls, beige shag carpeting, and faded prints on the wall. If Tammy wasn't in her sixties and somewhat immobile, I might be scared.

"Why do you shout?" she asks me.

"Because I'm annoyed," I say. "Or excited, or happy, or angry."

Tammy peers at me. She has straw-like blond hair that looks as though it wants to reach her shoulders but just can't quite make it there. She wears wide, translucent-framed glasses. Her body is quite hefty. It takes her great effort to move around. It's not just because of the heft, I don't think. Maybe she's had some sort of joint surgery. I feel a bit sorry for her. I wonder if I should offer her the beige cushion behind my back. It's not as if it's comfortable.

"I mean, was there a particular incident?" Tammy asks. "It's easier to work with an incident rather than deal with hypotheticals."

I look at Ryan. We're sitting rather far apart from each other. I suppose that's indicative of how we've been feeling in our marriage.

"It's just in general," Ryan says. "I feel like I'm being attacked all the time."

"Attacked?" I exclaim, my eyes likely bulging. "How can you possibly feel attacked?"

I realize that Ryan looks like he's feeling attacked right now, so I unbulge my eyes, which is kind of hard to do because my eyes are large to begin with, the dark of my irises rather intense, or so I've been told. I look at Tammy as unbulgingly as I can. I may be squinting, actually.

"I'm expressive," I explain. "I raise my voice because I feel strongly. I show my emotions. I wouldn't even call it shouting." I pause because I can see Tammy isn't convinced. "I just speak loudly. It doesn't mean I'm attacking him."

"You understand he's telling you he feels attacked, though, right?" Tammy asks.

I notice she has a really big head. It's so big, I can see her pores. Or maybe that's a function of the room being so small. Either way, I don't imagine her pores are clean. She wears a ton of makeup. Or maybe I only think that because I don't wear any. And that's not because I don't need makeup, although does anyone really? But rather it's because I can't be bothered. Plus, finding the right shade of "nude tan" or "caramel" or "deep sand" is an exercise in ultimate exasperation, where I end up cursing the racist patriarchy. Either way, the point is I'm regretting having chosen Tammy.

Ryan and I had both researched therapists. He had chosen an older white man with decades of experience helping couples, but who also—Ryan missed this bit—talked a lot about God on his website. God, we both agreed, had no place in couples' therapy for two people whose son regularly goes about telling people God doesn't exist. We have to pretend he picked that tidbit up at school.

I chose Tammy because not only did she have many four- and five-star online reviews—which I admit did feel a little odd at the time, choosing a therapist like you choose a mechanic—but because she was older. I figured she would have already gone through menopause. And since I'm in the throes of perimenopause, I figured Tammy would empathize with the hot flashes, lack of sleep, and everything else. We'd have a secretive wink-wink-nudge-nudge feminist bond that would no doubt benefit, well, me.

"Right, Naomi?" Tammy nudges me, but not the kind of nudge I had envisioned. "Just because you tell him you don't mean to attack him doesn't mean, in the moment, that he can talk himself out of feeling attacked."

Isn't that exactly what it means? I don't say this. "I can't change the way I express myself," I say. "My family is from the Caribbean. This is how we speak. We don't hide our feelings. It's how I am. It's who I am. It's like you're asking me to be someone else." I pause, contemplating whether or not I should say what I want to say next because I don't want to hurt Ryan's feelings. I say it anyway: "I'm not going to become quiet and unemotional, like … Ryan."

She laughs.

That's an odd reaction, I think.

"Ryan and I are just quiet, repressive WASPs," she says, and she laughs again.

I haven't heard that term in decades. I look at Ryan. He's nodding. Oh, my god. I realize the feminist bond I thought I would have with her is nothing compared with the WASP bond she has with Ryan.

We all say nothing for a minute or so. Tammy finally says, rather authoritatively, "You did move here."

Wait. What?

"To Canada," she clarifies.

I'm stunned. I don't say anything. I don't even tell her that's not true, that I was born in Toronto. Instead, just in case I missed something, I check the calendar on the wall behind Tammy—she's obviously not a millennial either. It actually is 2022.

"When you move somewhere," she says, "you want to do what people there do. You know? Like when in Rome?"

Are you fucking kidding me? I don't say that.

Chelsea Peters

MUDLARK

The girl in front of him was skinny, the large, round bump of the belly beneath her hoodie evident even from behind. He'd been waiting behind her for at least ten minutes, and had drawn up a whole story for how she'd gotten herself into this situation: young, pregnant, and alone at the blood clinic. Absent parents, a rotten boyfriend — he was sad for her. For all their troubles, at least his girls had both escaped their teens without getting themselves knocked up.

As they finally approached the doorway into the actual waiting room, where they'd get to sit on chairs instead of standing in the hall like chumps, the girl stepped briefly out of the line to look intently at the grandfather clock that stood incongruously against the peeling white walls of the clinic hallway; probably donated by some magnanimous patron, who'd imagined it ending up somewhere grander than it had.

The girl had a long black braid and large ears. He tried to picture his girls' ears, how they wore their hair these days, but couldn't. When the girl was done looking at the clock—an action that endeared her to him—she returned to staring at her phone and twirling the braid around and around her wrist. She seemed bored, had none of the serenity about her that Sally had always had when she was expecting. He'd always loved her the most when she was pregnant, and when she was newly un-pregnant; her body all soft in an attractive, forgivable way; the new baby all pink and peach-fuzz-skinned against her milk-filled chest.

He'd left Sal alone at home, stroking her hot water bottle in its velvety red cozy like it was a baby's back. She'd been shopping for pajamas, the cursor hovering over satin sets in luridly bright jewel tones, a red heart blooming in the corners of the images she clicked on. He thought of the heaps of ballooning, silky material she already had to envelop her from 7 p.m. to 6 a.m. each day, and wondered what she needed with them any more.

She'd been so vain before the babies that he was always surprised, and a little disappointed, that she no longer seemed to care much about how she appeared when it was just the two of them. She'd never fully lost the weight from either of her pregnancies; never even seemed to notice when he occasionally gave her pouchy stomach and puckered thighs sidelong looks as they got ready together in the bathroom, hoping she'd see as he flicked his eyes back to whatever he was doing, a measured shadow of mild disappointment crossing his face.

The curvy nurse finally took his blood, declared him free to go. It was a routine checkup—"Good to keep an eye on things at your age," as the nurse said; his doctor would call him in a couple of days if anything was off this time. He passed the pregnant girl, still waiting in her chair, on his way out, and tried to smile at her, but she remained gazing resolutely at her phone. As he shoved open the door to the outside he remembered that girls didn't really like men to smile at them anymore—Sal had told him this recently, during a particularly fraught shopping trip—but surely he was getting old enough now for it to be permissible.

He was fifty years old today, born less than five kilometres from the clinic he now exited. The ground would have been frozen that day, fifty years ago; the river swollen and covered by three or more feet of solid ice. It had been one of the worst winters—shortly to be followed by the worst flooding—that the city had ever seen, the winter in which he was born. This year, by contrast, they'd had hardly any snow, and just a handful of days that hit a seasonable minus thirty. He could go to the riverbank and squish his boots in the mud as if it were springtime, and after his appointment he did just that, indulging himself because he'd overpaid the meter, and the river was just a handful of blocks from the clinic.

Once he got down to the bank, he scoped the ground casually for glints of silver or gold, or the bright of white ceramic against the grey of the claylike mud. He didn't usually come down randomly like this; this was a bonus visit, an indulgence he allowed himself because of the day. He didn't have any of his mudlarking equipment, and didn't expect to find anything much in the hour or so he had before Sal was expecting him home, but he selected a long and sturdy stick from the bank, trained his eyes on the muck, and began to poke at it nonetheless.

The air felt positively warm. The river moved at the steady speed it usually reserved for the summer. There were even a handful of jokers boating along the murky water, paddling or motoring their way down. A pair in a red canoe passed him now, waving when they spotted him on the bank. He didn't wave back, but the next moment he felt a sudden, surprising surge of nostalgia for his days spent by this very river in his childhood, with his dad and brothers and his little fishing rod. The world had been simpler, friendlier, then—and so had he, he supposed. Now he was standing around, fat and alone, irritated by people who were kind enough to wave at him. What would Lacy and Cora be nostalgic for when they were his age? Whatever pop stars had populated the top of the charts when they were teens? The thought made him desperately sad.

As he climbed back up the bank, having found nothing but bits of garbage in the muddy clay, he thought of the girl and the clock again. He wondered what had stirred in her to make her step out of line to gaze so intently at it; what it was about the clock that had drawn her attention away from the pull of her phone for such a relatively long amount of time.

*

He went home. Sal greeted him with a quick peck before pointing at a plate awaiting him on the kitchen table. She'd fixed him a lunch of mushroom ravioli with bits of something green on top.

"How was it? Was the wait long?" she asked as she put the last of the dishes she was washing in the rack. Then, before waiting for a response, "I called the girls. They'll be here at four for dinner, as requested. Or so they say." She gave him a wan smile and another kiss on the cheek, before returning to the couch with her hot water bottle and her laptop in hand.

He always marvelled at the fact that she'd completely hidden her periods from him until they'd been married almost ten years, especially now that she didn't hide them at all, and he could see how bad they were. She was slightly hunched over as she shuffled to the couch and flopped herself down with a deep sigh. She was forty-seven, though—nearly forty-eight; surely they'd dry up soon.

A few months earlier she'd started making what he supposed were healthy, longevity-minded decisions, partaking in activities like doing yoga in the park with a dozen other women and a handful of saggy-assed jokers at dawn. She kept a tub of Vaseline beside the bed and slathered her hands in it before going to sleep. She wore sunscreen every single day, even in the winter, and even when she was spending the whole day inside. As he chewed his ravioli, he remembered when they'd both been cavalier about their health; eating crap and barely sleeping. Now one of their favourite pastimes was to spend the morning arguing over which of them had had the worst sleep.

He got a shock from the next bite he took. He'd forgotten what he was eating—his nose had told him cake, when in fact it was this mushroomy pasta. The night before, in bed watching the soft-core porn now available on Netflix in the form of raunchy historical dramas, he'd turned down the brightness when he meant to turn down the sound, concerned that the actors' increasingly heavy moans would wake Sal as she snored next to him. It had taken him a moment of staring blankly at the dimmed, naked figures on the screen to realize what had happened. Little slips like these were starting to seem more familiar than being in control. He washed his final bite down with a gulp of beer and stood, pushing his plate into the middle of the table and leaving it there without a second thought.

*

After lunch Sal took two big Tylenols and they went out to buy his birthday gift, which would be a new metal detector for his mudlarking. Sal dressed for the springlike February weather they were enjoying, while he donned his parka, heavy boots, hat, neck warmer, and garbage mitts, as if it were the temperature it ought to be this time of year.

When they were out in the world, Sal made a show of making friends with everyone she considered subordinate to them in some way. He supposed it was sweet, or would have been, if he thought it were rooted in genuine kindness. At Canadian Tire she chatted with the kid who showed them to the section they were seeking for a full five minutes after he'd brought them to the row of metal detectors in aisle ten. He knew so many people like this. They made these efforts at kindness so they could tell themselves that's who they really were. If only they could get every busboy and gas station attendant to speak at their funerals, he thought, as he waited for Sal to wrap things up with the kid so they could get his gift and get out of there.

A couple of years after Lacy was born, a friend of Sal's had disappeared. It turned out an ex-boyfriend had killed her, but at first the police mounted a big search, thinking she might just be tucked away somewhere, hidden or hiding. Sal had given an interview for the news in which she'd cried into the camera, little Lacy in her arms, and asked her friend to get in touch to let everyone know she was okay. When the spot aired, she'd recorded the appearance on VHS, carefully labelling the tape "Mona's Disappearance—CTV Interview" and slipping it in next to the Disney movies lining the shelf beneath the TV. It was one of the moments that had clarified her to him, back when they'd only been married for a couple of years, and still didn't really know each other—not properly, at least. For some reason this memory had stuck with him more than most of the others;

continued to define her to him, even now. He wondered, now, as he stood in the aisle while Sal looked at the row of metal detectors, if this was completely fair, but the thought left his mind as quickly as it had entered it.

"Here we go." Sal held up the box with the metal detector he'd told her he wanted. "This the one, baby?"

"That's the one."

The same kid who'd helped them find it checked them out. He thanked the kid quickly and turned to leave, then stood for another five minutes with both hands atop the upright box, looking at the ground as Sal confirmed the details of the kid's plans for school, before she gave a final dazzling smile and led the way back out of the store.

*

That afternoon he shopped for pajamas for Sal while she took a nap, sneaking onto her computer to purchase the ones she'd let him see her singling out with those little hearts that morning before he left for the clinic.

Sal's birthday was just a week after his, something that had absolutely delighted her when they first met. He was late, as always, in ordering her gift, and would have to pay extra for express shipping, but it was fine: this was all part of their system. Once he'd already left things too long, she would make a show of browsing online for the items she wanted, and then he'd "surprise" her with them a week later, earning himself a wet kiss when she opened the gift and, later that night, the chance of some rare, tepid sex.

The women modelling the pajamas in the photos were all standing or lounging in the same bedroom set, a fake window behind them lit with fake sunlight. The pajamas were all jewel-coloured and printed—bright and gaudy. All this colour. When did people start wanting so much colour?

One woman recurred in a few different photos, wearing an array of outfits. Most of the photos didn't show the models' mouths, just their bodies from the neck down, but this woman's mouth was visible in all of them, and in each photo she was smiling—not like a model, not like his daughters smiled, pushing their lips out farther from where they naturally sat in their faces. Smiling like she was happy, like she meant it.

In another photo, a woman's bare stomach was visible above some frilly pajama bottoms that looked more like underwear. This stomach had a slightly pudgy softness to it, and a poorly air-brushed scar just below the belly button. Though her face wasn't visible, he imagined that this was the woman with the smile.

He glanced at the door to the bedroom. Sal usually napped for half an hour—he had a few more minutes. Saving the pajamas he'd narrowed it down to with one hand, he unbuckled his pants and untucked himself from his underwear with the other.

*

Lacy arrived for dinner first, half an hour early. She kissed him eagerly on the cheek after hanging her jean jacket carefully on one of the hooks by the door.

"Happy birthday, Daddy!" She beamed at him, handing him a card. She was a sweet girl, Lacy. A good girl. She bounced into the kitchen to help her mother with the salad, and the two of them proceeded to gossip happily over the crunch of the iceberg leaves being ripped to shreds.

Cora was late, arriving just in time for them all to sit down.

"Hey, Dad." She gave him a somewhat tight grin and let her jacket fall to the ground beside her chair. Sal glared at her as she scooched her own chair up to the table, though this scowl melted to a smile fairly quickly once she started in on the rosé.

He was quiet throughout the meal, mostly focused on his food, and occasionally on the little gestures or turns of phrase that revealed the ways his daughters had changed slightly, even since he'd last seen them just a week or two before.

He could see how they'd each shaped themselves to other people, instead of finding identities of their own. Cora wrote ironic poems in the style of a young female poet whose book she'd bought him for Christmas, but not as well. And Lacy seemed to have lost her own personality somewhere in her early teens; he could remember when she was a nerdy, sensitive little kid. Emotionally open and unwittingly charismatic. At some point she'd shifted, after a period of deep melancholy when she entered high school that he could still remember, into this people-pleasing cartoon character, all sunshine and pleasantries, who wanted to be everyone's favourite person so badly that she'd given herself a stomach ulcer at the age of twenty. He'd never understood what had happened with her, but he'd also never really wanted to know.

Lacy. He'd worried about that name, the potential playground associations, but Sal had insisted. It was the only name she liked out of the hundreds they'd peeled through, lying cuddled together in bed so many years ago; the only name that didn't seem to remind her of someone or some TV show character she hated. Or had it been him who'd been so picky? He couldn't remember.

Cora mostly spoke over the rest of them, though Sal held her own pretty well. His thoughts slowly receded into considerations of the items he'd found on his last proper mudlarking visit to the riverbank, a couple of weeks before. The old glass pill bottle had been a real find. He suspected it was 1920 or so, but he'd know for sure once he'd posted its photo to the online mudlarkers forum and his fellow larkers had weighed in.

"Dad."

"Mm? What?" Cora was staring at him—more like glaring, really; a look so like the one Sal had given her earlier when she'd arrived late.

"I asked if you've looked for those photos of Gran like I asked you to."

"Oh. No, I haven't."

"Could you? I'd really like to see them ..."

"Sure, sure." Cora kept talking, but he stopped listening. Didn't ask why she wanted to see these photos; couldn't see why she would: his mother hadn't been much to look at, and she and he hadn't been particularly close.

After Cora ran out of news she wanted to share, Lacy kept trying to salvage the conversation, which had lulled into near silence by the time he blew out his birthday candles. His older daughter kept returning to the same safe topics of food and television and celebrity gossip, and he worked hard to scrounge up a smile and a semi-interested response whenever she tried to draw him in.

She was a sweet girl, Lacy. They were all sweet, really—his girls, his women—in their own ways. They were here, weren't they? They were here, and they were showing him love, even if it wasn't the exact kind he wanted, and surely that was better than nothing.

*

After dinner Sal took the girls to her sewing room, which had once been Cora's bedroom, to fit them for the dresses they were reluctantly letting her make for them, like she'd often done when they were little.

He was enjoying his moments of quiet peace, pouring himself another Scotch, when he remembered with a jolt that he'd never finished buying Sal her pajamas that afternoon; he'd simply finished himself off, shut the computer, and moved on. He stopped mid-pour, paused, then took his tumbler with him to retrieve Sal's computer.

Sal had clearly used the computer since he had: the window with the pajamas no longer greeted him when he flipped the screen up to face him. He sighed and started clumsily dragging his finger around on the trackpad, trying to orient himself, clicking through the dozens of tabs that were open in the browser.

He wasn't sure what happened—he supposed he'd closed one of the million tabs by mistake—but he was suddenly staring in surprise at Sal's email inbox.

He'd never been one for snooping—he didn't care that much about other people's lives, not even Sal's—but his eye caught one sender's name over and over again amidst the dozens of emails about online sales and other spammy things.

He heard the girls giggling from Sal's sewing room, then Sal's deeper laugh joining in. He hesitated, then opened one of the emails at random, which brought up an entire thread of exchanges between Sal and this J. person. He sipped his Scotch as he began to read.

*

The river was receding slightly, depositing bits of colour in the form of leaves and garbage throughout the grey mud. He was later than he'd wanted to be, even though he'd asked for dinner to be at four thirty so that he could make it here with his new metal detector before he completely lost the light. He'd asked the girls if any of them wanted to join him, but even today they'd just laughed and sent him off on his own.

He went to his favourite spot, close to an old dock that still got occasional use from the water bus in the summer, and at which a large and grand old sternwheeler was moored—permanently, it seemed; he'd never seen it in use in his many years of larking along this stretch of the bank.

Two years earlier he'd found his favourite-ever artifact in this very spot: an old jackknife with a genuine silver handle. The mudlarkers on the forum had helped him date it to the early 1880s. You were supposed to turn things like that in to a museum; he'd told the other larkers he'd done this, though the truth was he'd kept it for himself.

He strolled up and down the bank for over an hour, waving the new detector over the mud, finding nothing. He was returning to the place where he'd started, by the dock, ready to give up and climb the bank back to his truck, when he heard car doors closing and voices carrying over to him from the road at the top of the bank—probably some kids, coming to drink on the dock. He turned and strolled back in the opposite direction from the dock; he was in no mood for teenagers right now.

Once he'd gained some good distance from the dock, he stood looking out, in the opposite direction from the voices, at the darkening water. After a few minutes, he heard footsteps in the distance, joining the sounds of the voices; rumbling hollowly over the wood of the dock. He turned to look back in that direction, surprised to hear the hard, crisp sound of heels instead of the plodding of sneakers upon the wooden planks some thirty yards away. Even more surprising: at the end of the dock the old sternwheeler was all lit up; through the boat's big windows he could see the small figures of a few servers dressed in tails wandering around, setting up a bar.

A soiree was making its way down from the shore to the old boat. He stood in his dark spot on the bank, invisible to the revellers, watching as a train of thirty or so of them tottered across the gangplank and onto the boat deck, many of the women dressed head to toe in thick furs. He stood, hands in his pockets and his elbow resting on the metal detector, a little awed by what he was seeing; that boat hadn't sailed for years. It had a funny name—the *Paddle Girl* or the *Paddle Queen*, or something like that.

He stood watching until they took off, some fifteen minutes later. The boat inched smoothly down the river, toward his spot farther down the bank. Jazzy music from the 1920s started playing soon after they departed, reaching him sounding vivid but somewhat hollow, like all noise does after travelling over water; that curious, flat echo that sounds really like a lack of echo.

As the boat sailed slowly past him and prepared to round a bend in the river that would take it from his sight, he could just make out two women emerging from the bright depths of the boat, approaching the railings at the stern. They were too far away, too bundled in their fancy furs, for him to make out their faces or ages, but he could tell from their hairstyles that they were women. Their body language told him they were close—that they loved, or maybe were in love with, each other. Cora seemed to have plenty of lesbian friends—maybe these were two of them.

His thoughts drifted to his women, back at home—were they standing with their arms around each other in the kitchen? Probably not. He could picture Sal, slumped on the couch, knocked out by the wine and Tylenol, while Lacy finished the dishes in the kitchen behind her. Cora would be either on her phone or gone already. Or were they maybe, just maybe, all together still, laughing, like they had been when they were in the sewing room without him?

No one really tells you that people can pass in and out of your life. That they can change, and that you're supposed to change along with them, or at least acknowledge that they've grown; that if you want them to stay with you, you have to latch on and refuse to let go. You have to make an effort, or they'll round a corner and never look at you again. It was just another one of those things people seemed to be expected to pick up along the way—probably from their parents—and which he was beginning to realize he hadn't. What did it say about you, if you hated all the people around you—your loved ones, your family—for what you knew were small, petty reasons, then hated them even more for not loving you in the exact way you wanted them to?

Un-evolved. That's probably what this said about him—that he was un-evolved, like a caveman or an idiot. That was the word that had appeared most often in Sal's emails to J.—whoever the fuck that was—which were much longer than J.'s responses to her; she seemed to email him at least once a day, sometimes more, complaining about her sad life with her un-evolved husband.

He'd found nothing at all on the bank, not even a comb or an old toothbrush. He realized he wasn't likely to, now that the dark had fully descended. He looked back up at the boat, the only bright thing he could see, as it neared the corner in the river.

Suddenly, he felt compelled to wave to the women standing at the boat's stern, before they disappeared around the bend. He raised one arm, in what felt like a cool, casual gesture, but soon raised the other as well. He waved them both slowly at first, and then almost frantically, like he was marooned, and hoping they'd save him.

After a minute or two he put his arms down, embarrassed by how short of breath this minor exertion had left him. All that happened was that a beautiful laugh rang out as the boat disappeared around the bend. It reached him in the same flat echo as the ripple of the water, the warble of the music; the tremble of all those happy, laughing voices.

Beth Goobie

//////////////

DARK RAINBOW

Philly slipped out of the dorm's north entrance, into the face slap of a brisk November wind. Cloud wisps scudded across a crescent moon; at 1 a.m., the college campus was quiet, with just the underfoot crackle of leaves. Twenty feet from the girls' dorm lurked the Administration building, a long, hulking shadow with a single overnight light on above the front entrance. Clutching her jacket close, Philly headed up the building's west flank toward a little-used side entrance that was protected from the casual glance by a small copse of aspen. Hunched in a bomber jacket, Quinn stood waiting, breath ghosting his lips. They kissed, another cirrus cloud ghosting the moon, and she unlocked the door.

They removed their shoes by the light of the Exit sign and carried them up a short hall, which served several faculty offices. Turning left, they started along the building's main corridor. The bible college was small, its 1982 student body under two hundred. Set in a residential area close to the city's downtown, it was founded in the 1930s, the groundbreaking funded through donations raised by congregations across the country. Admin and the girls' dorm were two of the initial buildings constructed, and they had the feel of the people who had paid and prayed them into being—solid and utilitarian, a collage of sober browns and beiges. Philly loved the high-ceilinged, creaky grumpiness of the girls' dorm, the plain, no-nonsense thrift of Admin. *If Admin were a food, it'd be a perogy,* was one of her favourite jokes. To which Quinn would reply, *Potato and onion, with liver for dessert.*

The main hall's south side contained the office, which faced the student mailroom and bookstore. Several classrooms were located farther down the hall. A few steps along the corridor's north side, Philly stopped at an unmarked door and consulted her key ring. The summer after her first year, the college's custodian had retired and she had been hired to fill the gap until his replacement arrived that September. It had been a simple matter to have keys copied without the office secretary noticing. In a bible college, people had faith; they trusted what they needed to believe.

Now in her senior year, Philly wasn't sure whom she trusted or what she had faith in, but she knew she still wanted to believe. Believers walked through alternative landscapes, tuned to vibes only they could perceive. Philly remembered living inside those vibes; she remembered how they made her heart swell with pipe-organ glory and haloed her with divine sweetness when she knelt to pray beside her childhood bed. Somewhere along the line, though, that sweetness had faded. Philly had continued getting down on her knees, but the vibes had deserted her, along with those alternative landscapes where everyone and everything encountered was a personal message sent by a loving God to bring her closer into relationship with Him. Philly couldn't pinpoint the moment she had stopped believing; rather, belief seemed to have taken itself out of her life as if she were no longer worthy. Loneliness was being left behind, not knowing why.

The keys to the kingdom—that was what she called them. If the ring of keys in her hand couldn't open lost places of the heart, she still possessed these moments of opening still-dark rooms in the dead of night—rooms that sometimes felt as if they were waiting within herself.

Philly slid the key into the lock, gave it a careful turn, and listened as the click travelled the silent corridor. Then she slid the ring of keys into her jeans pocket, double-checking to ensure they lodged snugly in place. Ahead, a staircase rose into a deeper darkness. Philly started up, her socked feet noiseless as Quinn eased the door shut behind them. From several steps down, he felt for her, his hands settling onto her hips, his forehead resting against the small of her back as they climbed. Above, darkness roosted in greater and lesser definitions, and then Philly's head was rising out of the stairwell into the college's former chapel, consigned for over a decade as storage space.

The new chapel had been constructed in the late sixties, an off-white concrete void with narrow window-slits and rising tiers of upholstered flip-up seats; it doubled as a classroom. Here in the old chapel, a hardwood floor muttered as the eye lifted to an overhead dome of stained glass, easily ten feet across and mysterious with royal blue, forest green, a scarlet that stopped one's breathing. The dome's geometric design glowed with an eerie beauty that carried Philly deep into herself. Brought into stillness under its post-midnight bloom, she settled into an inner beyond. These days, it was the closest she came to a relationship with God.

Padding up behind, Quinn wrapped his arms around her. Together, they watched the dome's come-and-go glow under the overcast moon. "A profundity of colour," Quinn murmured.

"It lives at the top of my brain," said Philly. "All day long, I feel it glowing there."

She would not have said the same that morning, at least not initially. The college was accredited with the local university, and Philly took courses at both institutions. Just after eleven, she had been on her bike, cycling to meet a university class-mate who worked as a legal aide at an office on Portage Avenue. Several blocks after the turn off Main Street, she had pulled out from the curb to pass a bus that had stopped to take on passen-gers. Seconds later, the bus had started moving, just as another bus had come up on Philly's left. Caught between the two, Philly had put on a burst of speed in an attempt to pull ahead of the bus in the outer lane. Just as she had reached its mid-point, the now nearly parallel buses had begun to close the gap between them. The space on either side of Philly's handlebars had shrunk from six, to five, to three inches, and she had grasped that neither driver knew she was there. Putting on the brakes, she had allowed the buses to pull ahead, her shoulders cringing in the expectation of furious honking from the drivers who were watching the tail end of her bike emerge from the buses' rear ends. But no one had honked; instead, room had been gently created for her to wobble her bike, chastened but safe, to the curb.

Looking back on it, Philly realized that she hadn't panicked at any moment during the entire event—not even with the apprehension that neither bus driver seemed to be aware of her presence. In retrospect, it felt as if she had been travelling up

Portage Avenue under the night glow of the stained glass dome, its slow, deep certainty. She wanted to believe this.

"Colour—is it noun or verb?" she asked, turning to Quinn and leaning her head against his throat. It was a game they played, though they usually targeted people. For instance, Cynthia Newson, hailing from Dartmouth, Nova Scotia—music major, dedicated shoulder pad wearer, and "God is good" cheerleader. Was she an adjective or an adverb—adjective, as in merely auxiliary to essence, or adverb, as in part of its muscle and drive? "I get confused," Cynthia had confided to Philly in her first year. "Is Banff in Manitoba or Saskatchewan?" Quinn, after little pondering, had relegated Cynthia to adjective status. Last fall, Philly would have been quick to agree, but this year she was … restless in her thinking. And restless now in Quinn's arms as he stood, breathing his way through her question, letting his time-lapse thoughts develop.

"Colours are angels," said Quinn. "Thoughts before words, imagining new realities for God."

"So we're all God's imagination?" asked Philly.

"In the beginning," said Quinn. "Then we take over and imagine ourselves."

He withdrew his arms and sat down cross-legged in an open area directly beneath the dome, then pulled out some weed and started rolling a joint. Philly sat opposite, watching blurred angels of green and blue caress the heavy eyelids, the long flared nose, the full lips. Her body felt taut and lean, a strip of black velvet cut from the night sky. She knew it drew Quinn, was drawing him now like a thought before words. When Quinn wanted her, it was with an all-out absorption that raised the hair on her arms, even from a glance sent across a crowded classroom. Until his glance shifted, settling onto someone else. Quinn was a force of nature, and like the weather he was always changing.

He lit up, inhaled, and passed her the joint. Sucking in deep, Philly handed it back. With a quick pivot on her butt, she stretched out supine and let her gaze wander the dark play of colour above. "Colour—noun or verb?" she pressed.

"Angels are verbs," Quinn grunted, as he sighed his body into position beside her. He nudged her leg with his own; lifting her right, she let him slide his left underneath. For the past three years, they had started off the fall semester like this, both of them homing in on each other as if tuned to subatomic vibes. When Quinn's eye had wandered the first year in mid-November, Philly had been subsumed by an emotional sinkhole that had hung on into January. In spite of this, the following autumn the subatomic vibes had kicked in again, and she simply hadn't seen it coming—the eye that had started to meander, earlier this time, in October. This fall, however, when they had started up again, Philly hadn't allowed herself assumptions. The future, and all that it portended, was a noun, and she was a verb—an active verb.

"Your turn," she said, floating a hand through the air and watching it shift from scarlet to green. "Story me."

Quinn sucked in again, then offered her another drag. Philly shook her head—she liked a mild buzz, one that left her mind connected to her body. Quinn butted out carefully and slid the joint into his shirt pocket.

"Brashwackle Creek," he intoned. "Harvest Festival, all the locals gathered in the village square. Full moon rising, barrels of beer on tap. Uncle Billy, as usual, has drunk himself stupid. Now, Uncle Billy is an exceptionally long pisser. When he heads into the can, guys follow him in and take out their watches to time him."

"You told this story two weeks ago," Philly interrupted. "Only it was Uncle Fred at the OK Corral Bar."

"I did?" mumbled Quinn. "Well, Phillipa Upchurch, you tell one, then. You're better at this than me."

"It's your turn," Philly demurred. This was another game they played—making up stories for each other. *It's all imagined* was their mantra. Besides, a mind in story mode made for better sex, the storyteller's voice on slow reverb through the listener's body, plot lines getting ready to head off anywhere …

Quinn considered, his gaze conversing with the overhead seduction of colour. "Okay," he said. "I've been thinking about this one for a while. It's not ready yet, but here goes. There's this girl who can hear music coming from other people's bodies. Sometimes just one note, sometimes an interval or chord. Every now and then, a real hymn sing. That's how she knows if she likes you—by the song your body hums as it goes about its day. No one else can hear what she hears, and none of this music is coming from anyone's mouth. No, it's humming right out of their skin."

He paused, running his fingertips over his chest. Philly watched his profile. This was the way she loved him best—pensive, slow-paced. Quinn went where angels feared to tread, but at a turtle's crawl.

"She can hear singing from trees," he continued. "Flowers and grass. Stones, too—at a lower pitch than, say, daisies and lilacs. And at night, she can hear the galactic trilling of stars.

"The question is," Quinn added, his voice deepening, "did this drive her insane? Everything singing its own opera—is it like the choirs of heaven, or like standing in the basement hallway in the music building when all the practice rooms are going?"

Both barely competent singers, Philly and Quinn could manage basic harmony on "Just As I Am," but they hardly qualified as one of the music majors who floated around campus, trailing perfectly pitched notes in their wake. Even to herself, Philly had trouble admitting the resentment she felt when one of these divas let loose with an exuberant trill just for the delight of it.

"Cacophony," she agreed.

"On a bad day, yeah," Quinn hedged. "So this girl is now twenty-two, and in her grad year at college. And she falls for two different guys. Each guy puts out a different note, and she finds them both easy to harmonize with. She can't decide between them, and to make things worse, God's gone quiet on her. This girl used to hear Him everywhere and now He's just silence." Quinn rolled onto his side and propped his head on a hand. "What's that sound like, Philly? The silence of God?"

His face was shadowed; Philly watched an orb of royal blue shift across his hair.

"Heartbeat," she said, savouring the answer as it sank through her body. She breathed deep, listening to the pulse in her throat, then picked up the storyline. "So this girl who's twenty-two and can't hear God anymore," she began, "she also takes an English class at the U. And she makes a friend there, a woman in her late thirties who works as a legal assistant. They agree to go out for lunch, and to meet at her law office first."

"Names?" asked Quinn.

"Darlene," said Philly. "And . . . Philly."

"Anyone I know?" asked Quinn.

"We'll see," said Philly. Lifting the hem of his shirt, she slid her hand onto his belly, felt the tense and release of his sigh. "Actually, Philly and Darlene have gone out for lunch several times, and each time Darlene asks Philly to meet her at the office first. While she's there, Darlene's boss always comes out and talks to her."

Quinn's breathing stopped; Philly absorbed his stillness through her palm. "Darlene's boss is always very nice to Philly, he seems... just very friendly," she continued. "The law office is obviously high rent, near the Bay on Portage—third floor, gorgeous wood panelling, stairs maybe of marble."

"Not marble," Quinn objected.

"He's obviously loaded," said Philly, her voice slowing as she recalled the first time she climbed those stairs: *Marble! Who put marble on the floor to walk on?* "Anyway, he's just nice to Philly," she went on, "and that's all she thinks of it. Even when Darlene tells her, 'My boss really likes you,' Philly just nods and thinks, *That's nice.* Except today at lunch Darlene says it again, and when Philly just nods at her as usual, Darlene looks her right in the eye and adds, '*Really* likes you, hon.'"

Again, Quinn stopped breathing, but this time Philly's focus was on the dome. The colours had started rippling free of their geometric boundaries—angels escaping definition, angels becoming verbs. Across Philly's body, the dome's reflected pattern glimmered with angels on the loose. She giggled.

"Philly finally gets it," she said. "She stares at her friend, she's so *completely* stunned. 'But he must be in his fifties!' she says. 'Isn't he married?' Darlene arches a cool, secular eyebrow. 'What's that got to do with it?' she says. Philly feels dirty, besmirched with filthy cobwebs. 'Is this part of your job?' she asks. 'Do you get a raise if I ... go out with him?'

"Darlene loses her smile *slightly,* but not her secular cool. 'It could work out very well for *you,*' she says. 'My boss is generous, he likes to give gifts. All you have to give him is your silence.'"

Philly took a long, slow breath, then recalled, "Philly decides to give Darlene some silence and walks out. Her body feels cold and clammy, with red-hot wires that jump-start her every move. She bikes home, her brain so buzzed she doesn't hear traffic, just one loud church bell bonging back and forth in her head."

"He's a shit!" Quinn blustered. "So is that legal assistant-pimp he's got scouting for him."

"Ha!" Philly crowed, stark with relief at his response. "Darlene a pimp! Well, no one's talking about paying me money. And I am twenty-one. It's probably quite legal. But I still feel kinda creeped out. Girls who do that—I guess I thought it was obvious I wasn't that type. Sure, there are guys who stare and stuff, but to seriously think…" She paused. "To *imagine* I would do that…"

"You wouldn't," Quinn assured her. "You are who *you* imagine you are."

"Maybe," said Philly, thoughts hesitating, half-formed, on her lips. "All of a sudden, it feels like I'm living in a world Darlene's boss dreamed up. Since September, I've met her at that office three times, and then we've gone for lunch. The last two times, was it because he wanted to see me again? And the first time—was it because she thought he might be interested? He's had some kind of power over me for months and I didn't even know."

Quinn let out a whoosh of air and pulled her in against himself. His throat pulsed, warm against her forehead. "You won't," he said, stroking her back. "He's just some guy out there. Just cuz he thinks something about you doesn't make it you."

Beads of sweat had formed on Philly's upper lip; she licked at it. "It's like he has a key," she murmured, "and he's opened a door I didn't know I had in myself. I can't stop thinking about it."

Quinn's hand stopped stroking. Eyes closed, he breathed and waited.

"Last Saturday night," said Philly, "you were out on a date with Roxanne. She came back to the dorm glowing. You could almost see the words *Mrs Quinn Golway* glowing on her forehead."

Quinn groaned and rolled onto his back. "We're doing a presentation for Gospels class," he mumbled. "Roxy's an adjective. She decorates a sentence, sure, but you're all verb—"

"Ah," said Philly, cutting off the lie in his voice. "Care to parse *your* grammatical state these days, m'dear?"

Quinn rubbed his face with both hands. "A dangling participle," he grunted. "A murder of crows, a mess of intentions, sneaky and self-serving. I'm a shit, I'll admit it. What gets me is that we're still friends. After all these years, you still hang out with me."

Philly eased the knife-edge of disappointment from her heart. "Is that what we're doing?" she asked. "Hanging out?"

They lay in a bruised silence, Philly's sense of herself deepening and expanding. Rolling onto her side, she lay facing Quinn. "D'you think we're *bad*?" she asked, her voice hoarse with intensity. "Do we *want* to be bad?"

Quinn's eyes remained closed under their heavy lids. He sighed, releasing something. "Because we want to see what's on the other side of good?" he asked. "Some days, I could fuck *any-thing*—doughnuts, a pride of lions, a tube of toothpaste."

Philly snorted and he cut her a sheepish glance. "A very *large* tube," he amended. "Anything with a hole in it, basically. Just let me go out in a flash of pure pleasure, I don't care if I ever see any of this"—he waved vaguely at the surrounding darkness—"again.

Why did God give us this ability to feel pleasure if He didn't want us to fuck our brains out? Okay, I know I've been a slime. I've hurt you, more than once, and I'm sorry about that, I really am. But are you sorry we've fucked? Would you rather we never did?"

"No." Philly's comprehension was instant and complete. "I'm glad, Quinn. I *am*."

Quinn's sigh exploded. "I'd make a shitty husband," he confessed. "I get so *itchy* sometimes. The way everyone walks around here—as if they know all the answers, they're the light of the world, God's waiting on them to answer all *His* questions!"

Philly rested an arm across his chest; picking up her hand, he played with it. "I don't think I want to be Mrs Married either," she said. "Not now, maybe not ever."

A blur of green on Quinn's face intensified. "So," he murmured, "you don't want to marry me, then? I sort of thought…"

Philly swallowed hard, convulsively. "I'm going to do it," she said abruptly.

Quinn closed his eyes, his face shuttering. "He sounds like a creep," he muttered. "In his fifties, coming on to a twenty-one-year-old. D'you even know if he'd use a safe? D'you think he'll actually care about you? Will he tell you that you're all verb, your breasts are like antelopes—"

Philly choked off a giggle. "That was sexy three thousand years ago," she muttered.

Into the pause that followed her comment, there came the slow, tentative shifting of hinges at the foot of the stairwell. The uneasy sound ricocheted through Philly. Quinn went still, his head turning toward the stairs as a flashlight beam stabbed the darkness of the old chapel. Heavy footsteps started up the steps. *A man,* thought Philly, her heart a gong, reverberating. *A big one.*

The flashlight reached the top of the stairs and turned on them, blinding, apocalyptic. Philly lifted a hand to shield her gaze, the motion like pushing back the weight of God. Behind the flashlight's glare, someone stood stretching out the moment—invisible, all-powerful. Philly's blood pounded with shame.

Fuck that, she thought. Pulling herself into a seated position, she let her hair fall across her face. "Okay, so you've got a flashlight and we don't," she said gruffly.

"Yeah," agreed a male voice. "And I've got you two, pinned at the end of my beam, just where I want you." The flashlight shifted from their faces to the floor as the speaker crossed to a nearby steamer trunk and sat down. Briefly, he shone the beam upwards from his waist, revealing the ghoulishly shadowed face of Leroy Shockle, the college's general manager.

"Mr Shockle," said Philly, as Quinn sat up beside her.

"Phillipa Upchurch," he replied. "Quinn Golway. Senior students, the both of you, expected to be role models for the student body. Tsk tsk tsk." Sniffing pointedly, he shook his head. "Not the scent of cigarettes I'm getting here. What d'you say—do I put in a phone call to the police and ask them to make a little after-midnight visit, maybe press charges for trespassing and possession?"

The question was a clammy tongue, filling Philly's mouth with dread. Quinn cleared his throat.

"We—we'd appreciate it if you didn't, sir," he said.

Shockle played the flashlight across their faces. Even with her veil of hair, Philly had to turn her head away. "How'd you get in?" Shockle snapped.

Again, softly, Quinn cleared his throat. "The side door," he said. "Earlier in the day, we jammed some cardboard between the lock and the frame so we could open it tonight."

The flashlight ravaged their faces again. "Do this often?" Shockle demanded. "Come here for a little hanky-panky when everyone's asleep?"

Head down, Philly watched the blurred light through the fall of her hair. The two men continued to negotiate, Shockle smug and insinuating, Quinn appeasing with hesitant replies. Neither looked to her for a response, and within the respite provided by their dismissal, Philly's thoughts crawled toward coherence.

"So you think I should keep your little secret?" Shockle jeered. "Do you a favour by keeping my mouth shut about your little affair?"

"We won't do it again," said Quinn.

"Ah," said Shockle, "but the piper has to be paid, eh? What's in it for me? Upstanding man in the community, general manager of this honourable and decent institution—I could lose my job if someone found out I let this slide."

"We wouldn't tell," stammered Quinn.

"No," Shockle purred. The smile in his voice oozed up Philly's spine. "You won't tell and I won't tell. The question is what we won't be telling about."

The flashlight beam shifted, pinioning Philly. A pause followed, loud with the unspoken.

Leroy Shockle was a big man on campus. Tall, broad-shouldered, he had a guard-dog gaze—Philly had always thought of him as Cerberus, three-headed guardian of the underworld. College staff and students alike responded to him with obsequious respect; Shockle held the threads of an invisible network that pervaded all their lives. That kind of power could make one careless, obvious. In the dense, calculating silence, Philly didn't need the flashlight's glare to illuminate the intentions of Darlene's lawyer-boss surfacing into the man opposite. *She* was the price about to be paid, at least as far as Shockle was concerned. He was a man who brought light into darkness, killing uncertainty, the in-between, the dark rainbow. Everything he saw, he remade in his own image. Philly would not have hazarded a guess as to whether Leroy Shockle believed in Jesus, but she understood with an awful certainty that he believed in himself. He was a man to whom you could say, *I am new, I am beautiful, I am strange, and I am worthy,* and his taxidermist heart would kill and stuff you as a salute to what he ruled.

Yet she possessed the same keys to the kingdom that he carried in his pocket, a fact of which Shockle was unaware. Furthermore, thought Philly, the realization tingling through her, she and Quinn weren't the only ones prowling Admin at 3 a.m. while the world slept.

"And why are *you* here, Mr Shockle?" she asked, her voice harsh in the breathing quiet. Flipping back her hair, she tried to make out his expression. "You don't live on campus. I've been to your house for prayer meetings—you're twenty minutes east by car. What could possibly bring you here in the dead of night, with a flashlight no less—so you wouldn't have to turn on lights, so you wouldn't be noticed?"

The flashlight beam wavered, dropping its attack from her face to her chest. Philly leaned all her luck into the moment and pushed hard. "You're not about to tell anyone about us," she said slowly, "because that'd mean we'd be telling about *you.*"

Quinn let out a whoosh of air. The flashlight beam subsided to the floor. "Ain't nothing to tell," Shockle drawled, but a titch had crept into his voice and he coughed. "Nothing about me, and maybe nothing about either of you. Just don't let me catch you in here again. Now get out."

"Yes sir," said Quinn. Philly stood and followed him to the stairs, her limbs clenched as if walking in the crosshairs of a gun. They descended the stairwell's darkness, Quinn fumbled for the doorknob, and then they were in the shadowy hall and heading for the side entrance. Stepping through the doorway felt like emerging from a netherworld. Philly eased shut the door, then collapsed against the wall next to Quinn, who stood with his eyes closed, breath after breath juddering through him.

"Oh man," he moaned. "I didn't know which way that was gonna go."

"Sure wouldn't want him teaching Christian Ethics," Philly muttered. "What d'you think brought *him* here in the middle of the night?"

"I don't know and I don't care," Quinn groaned. "I'm going to sleep this one off."

He started off along the building's west wall and Philly let him go. Alone, she stood, pondering what had happened—Shockle's predatory glee, how quickly it had crumbled when challenged. Imagination could create reality, she mused, as long as you kept an eye out for a world that looked too much like your own reflection. Somewhere in the city night, a high-priced lawyer was awaiting her approval, and she possessed a ring of keys that could open the door to Leroy Shockle's campus office. A week, two weeks, a month—she would bide her time, but his kingdom was going to unlock at her touch.

Kate Cayley

A DAY

My mother was worried about our raincoats. My sister's was red-and-white stripes with a yellow lining, mine pink with purple scallops along the hem. We would stick out, she said. The rest of the outfit was easy: jeans, plain T-shirts, our long hair fastened with brown barrettes. She'd picked out our clothes weeks in advance, along with her own. White blouse, grey skirt, nondescript but well-fitting. She couldn't resist wanting to impress, her necklace carrying the smallest hint of something chosen. The necklace (a flat blue oval of glass sunk into tarnished silver, held on a wide chain) evoked a woman standing at a counter, pointing. Pausing over this one, that one. She wanted to show my aunt that she had an enviable life.

She didn't go too far; she took off her rings. When she seized our hands to leave the apartment, I felt the naked indents at the base of her fingers, the more faint indent from her wedding ring, though I couldn't tell if I felt that only because I knew where the ring had been.

But now it was about to rain, and we had to take the raincoats in a bag, just in case.

The clouds were bilious, yellow-grey. My mother checked her hair in a storefront window before we descended to the U-Bahn, took out a compact and reapplied her lipstick, which was burgundy. She fretted at her face, turning her head, examining the corners of her mouth, then snapped the compact shut with what seemed to me (I was eight) an enviable decisiveness, as if being an adult meant showing impatience without consequences. As if she was the last word.

*

Coming out on the East side and climbing the stairs to have our passports checked at the turnstile before we could go out into the street, I thought that the city looked cleaner and duller, like a plate that has been scrubbed with something rough. I wanted everything to feel perilously new. But really the station looked like any other station, like the unused stations we were used to passing through, routing through the East side on the way to somewhere else West. I would press my forehead to the dirty glass, looking at the empty platforms. I liked how the desolation made me feel an important sadness.

I counted the stairs aloud. My mother pressed my arm and Greta made a face, but neither of them said anything. For days before we left, my mother had drilled us in not calling attention to ourselves. If either of us were asked a question, not only by the guards, by anyone other than our cousins and our aunt, we would look at her before answering.

The guard didn't ask any questions. He checked over our papers absently, glancing up once at my mother's face, which she composed in a half smile, conveying that she hid nothing. He did not recognize her name (I had been terrified he would, convinced she was better known than she was). When he handed back the papers and waved us through the checkpoint, her hands were shaking. She took us down a side street and stopped, looking around.

"Are we lost?" I asked.

"No."

A woman passed by, carrying a brown vinyl shopping bag, her hair in little grey curls like a poodle. When she turned the corner, my mother let out a long breath, lit a cigarette.

"They'll be here soon," she said, and smoked in silence, Greta staring balefully up at the sky. It wasn't raining yet.

I looked at my mother. She seemed chastened, even with the cigarette, striking poses half-heartedly, putting her free hand in her pocket then drawing it out, angling one foot behind the other like a ballerina then shaking the foot as though she had pins and needles. She ground out the cigarette before it was finished, was about to throw it, thought better of it, and put it into a little bag in her purse, her lips pressed together. I couldn't tell what displeased her, and thought it might be me. If I wasn't what displeased her, I could easily become so. She worried me even more when she took out a tissue and wiped off her lipstick, leaving a tiny crease of colour in the left-hand corner of her mouth. She looked bereft, her lips raw.

At home, she was expansive, shouting to friends she saw across the street, shouting to her editor into the phone, late for appointments, careless with the details of our lives. My sister usually made sure the bills were paid. Whether or not my teachers liked our mother depended on whether or not they liked, or knew, her books, I found. I hadn't decided which was more embarrassing: their respect, or their blank stare when she referred to her work. Either might put her in a bad mood, depending.

"Elena! Elena!"

A woman scurried toward us. The children with her slowed to a walk, moving nearer to each other, the boy older than my sister, skinny and gangling with a pronounced Adam's apple, the girl a little younger. The woman reached my mother, kissed her cheeks, my mother gripped her sister's shoulders with tears in her eyes, but it still seemed like a pose, an idea of herself she hoped would fit.

My aunt Rosa was disappointing. We had photographs of her all over the apartment, from babyhood on (my mother, five years older, balancing her on her lap), holding dolls or plates of cake, then, later, in front of a curtain in a studio, then getting married. I imagined her as the antithesis of my mother, someone who would serve a meal on time, who would keep track of when I should go to the dentist.

In person she was tremulous and untidy, her hair frizzy and escaping from a plastic clip, the tip of her nose pink, her eyes small and tired, set close together. It didn't occur to me until much later that she'd travelled all the way from the town where she lived, taking a bus and then a train, sitting up while her children slept, their heads pinning her to the seat, her permission papers in her purse, her eyes shutting and then jerking open as the train lurched forward or she imagined that her suitcase was lost.

*

Greta was already shaking hands with our cousins, first Rainer, then Marina. Both made a slight diffident movement, like a gesture toward an embrace. Greta kept her hand out. Our mother and our aunt burst out laughing and Greta blushed, furious. I waited; she'd only recently, at thirteen, outgrown tantrums when she felt a loss of dignity. The women laughed harder, their laughter making them easy with each other, suddenly younger, strangers to their children. My mother stopped first, Rosa still giggling in little spurts like steam from a kettle.

"And this is your baby."

She kissed my hair, pulled me into her waist, my cheek mashed into the bulge of her belly over her skirt. Looking up, I could see sweat under the arms of her blouse.

As we walked to the restaurant, I could see why my mother worried about our raincoats, fussed over our clothes. She, even with all her effort, looked out of place, and not only because of the necklace. I didn't think we had much money, and we didn't, but she looked like money, like the possibility of sophisticated and assured vanity.

*

I stared at the Wall as we walked by it. It was looped with razor wire, the concrete unblemished, as if no one had ever touched it since it was made. Men in uniform held their guns loosely, standing at intervals and looking ahead. Our apartment was near it, on the other side, and I'd practise running at it, leaping, kicking off as hard as I could, only thinking of how hard I could propel myself backward, not of what it was. Covered in blaring graffiti, it seemed almost cheerful, as much part of my everyday as my school or the grocery store.

*

My mother had left in 1968, twelve years before I was born. She still had the suitcase she'd brought. She had told no one except her sister. Rosa stayed behind with their parents, married her boyfriend, had two children, worked as a secretary, bore the added restrictions and limitations that my mother's leaving created for her and for her husband, which would extend to their children's futures. She had looked after their parents, neither of whom had lived to be very old.

I had never met my grandparents, and we had fewer photographs of them. A phone call, when my grandfather died, my mother running out into the street, and the three of us (my father still lived with us then) watching her from the window as she set off, her coat flapping behind her. I was afraid she would walk to the Wall and demand to be let through, but my father laughed at me (he wasn't cruel, but he wasn't imaginative either, couldn't remember childhood, that precariousness, that dread) and she came back at dinnertime, her dress wet from lying on the grass in the park.

*

We used to play with the suitcase, which was blue, with a darker blue lining, hardly big enough to be called a suitcase. We would drag it out from under the couch, fill it up with toys, and say we were leaving. This game was played with the lights off and the curtains closed; we darted from shadow to shadow, squabbled over who got to carry the suitcase, over who got to be the one to finally go, shutting the living room door with a sigh, leaving the other standing in the space between the couch and the wall. Greta usually got to be the one who left, since she was older.

*

This day had been planned for a year. At the end of the afternoon, we would say goodbye on a side street, go back, and wait. Rosa had been given permission to travel, to visit a great-aunt who lived in a West Berlin suburb and whom we never saw, and the office that had processed her request had not connected her with my mother (the changed surnames helped). She would visit us for four days. My cousins looked too old to appreciate the game of kicking off from the Wall.

This plan would be unthinkable now. Even under what seemed like the total surveillance of that time, it was still possible to be lucky, as we were, our luck rising from human incompetence, human indifference. I carry a tracking device in my pocket. I have given away all my hiding places, casually.

*

I jabbed my meal with my fork and it wobbled, throwing off light from the lamp above us. I recognized potato, some indeterminate speckled meat, pale gravy holding it together. The rain had started. My mother looked down at the bag resting between her feet. We had a booth, and she shrunk into the corner, eyeing her sister across the table. I hoped they wouldn't laugh again, but I shouldn't have worried. My aunt, seeing how nervous the people around us made my mother, stopped asking questions and we ate in silence, my mother smiling apologetically, as if she was being ridiculous, even though she wasn't. Her arrest would have been theoretically possible. But there was something else in my aunt's face, when I think of it now, a wary amusement as she ate, that seemed private and only between them, a response to her memories: my mother, self-dramatizing, always thinking that she was the sole focus of attention.

It was hard for me to remember that Rosa was the younger one. It wasn't just her tiredness or the state of her hair or that her children were older. She was heavy with forbearance, slumped slightly over her food, didn't notice a speck of gravy on her chin.

"Wipe your mouth," my mother murmured.

"What?"

"Wipe your mouth."

She drew the napkin across her chin slowly, examined it.

"I hope your father won't let the dishes sit," she said to Marina, who didn't answer, and she put an arm around her daughter's shoulders, crumpling the napkin onto Marina's plate.

"He's not used to being alone in the house," she said, and my mother tapped the table, not interested in husbands or houses.

*

We had to put the raincoats on. My mother moved fast, as if we could make them less bright by acting quickly, but mine was twisted, my mother yanked hard at the pink sleeve, my arm flapping at it, not finding the hole. And finally we were out in the street.

"Where would you like to go?" Rosa asked. My mother thought.

"I don't know."

They laughed again. The raincoats were on: we were lit up like fireworks in our capitalist clothes.

The rain seemed to cheer everyone up. But nobody had any idea where to go. Rosa didn't know Berlin, and we didn't know this Berlin. So we set off down the same street we'd met on, and turned the more promising corner.

We walked along in the rain, and the streets grew wider, and we could see a park ahead and kept walking, not really consciously making for it; there would be nothing to do there, but the green was very vivid. I walked beside Marina. We smiled at each other from time to time, while up ahead Greta was talking to Rainer, arguing already, and the way we smiled at each other separated us from them, the ones who liked arguing, as if we were the same, watchful, not saying what we meant. I admired her hair, which was sleeked back from her forehead with a blue plastic hair band and looked very black over her coat, and I admired that she was older, looking at adulthood, though I didn't admire Greta at all, she just seemed noisy and pedantic, always trying to explain something.

We came to an intersection and paused, jostling, and a turning car threw up a curve of water from the gutter and we jumped back, Greta protesting, looking at the mud spattered over her jeans, and Marina took my hand. It was because we were crossing the street, and I was the youngest, but we stayed that way, holding hands, not talking, smiling outward, we were too shy for more than that, or I was. Perhaps it was the same for her. I haven't asked her, though we see each other as often as we can (it is so far, so expensive to fly from Vancouver), but I never remember to ask her what she was thinking, and I don't really want to, I don't want to find out she can't remember taking my hand at all, or how hard it rained, or the old actors.

We walked toward the theatre because my mother had heard there were especially beautiful stone carvings at the back entrance. The blackened stone building was eighteenth century, though much of it would have been an approximation of the eighteenth century, because much of Berlin is a clever approximation, a hybrid created after the war to disguise the effects of the bombing, younger than many North American cities. We stood in the parking lot, looking up. There were two ornate gargoyles perched above the doorway, clutching scrolls in their talons, one apparently reading aloud (open-mouthed, showing fangs), the other peering over the top of the scroll to see who approached the door.

A section of the back wall had been replaced with glass to give more light to the cafeteria, and four actors were sitting at a table in full costume. The space around them was empty, except for a little old man in an apron, who stood behind a counter at the other end where the food was served. These four were crowded near the window, and between them and the little man were rows and rows of tables, gleaming white, seeming to hover over the very clean grey linoleum, the chairs neatly pushed in. The oldest of the actors was talking as the others ate methodically, listening with the air of people who will not be surprised, even as the man became more and more animated and convinced by himself, spreading out his hands on either side of his plate. The colours of their costumes and the glare of their makeup, exaggerated for the auditorium and the lights, made me feel less self-conscious about the raincoat, and I hoped one of them would look up and notice me, but they were bent to their toilsome eating and listening and haranguing.

It must have been a period piece: ruffs and chokers and huge wigs, their faces whitened, their mouths snaked in red. They ate very carefully, tucking paper napkins under their chins, opening their lips around the fork so nothing would smear. Looking closer, they were not as old as they appeared at first, some of it was makeup, but their expressions had the same fixity, the same doggedness, as the stone faces. They were only tired, after a performance that was probably half-empty because of the weekday and the rain, and (other than the man who would not shut up) determined not to be disturbed, shepherding themselves for the evening, when there would be more people. But they seemed mysterious and melancholy in their velvets and fake pearls and diamonds, doublets slashed with yellow silk, knee breeches and mountainous lacy skirts, and I had to be pulled along by Marina, now that my mother had been satisfied about the gargoyles, and we kept walking. The rain stopped.

*

"It must be time now," Rosa said. We had circled back; we were in the same little street we'd met in. We would say goodbye here and we would go and wait and they would follow in an hour.

"What will you do for the hour?" my mother asked.

"Phone Johannes," Rosa said.

He was the reason this second part of the plan was possible. Spouses could not cross together, or if they did, they had to leave at least one of their children, insurance against defection. Maybe she had to find a phone just to say again, quickly, like it was nothing, *please buy flour* or *can you talk to Rainer's teacher.* Something that meant she remembered that no other life was possible.

Our goodbyes were perfunctory. Nobody knew how significant to be: we would see them in an hour, or not at all. My mother touched her sister's hair as if she was trying to fix it. I turned around as we went down the stairs to the U-Bahn checkpoint, thinking they would be standing, watching us, but of course they'd gone.

*

It was more than an hour, it was closer to three. We were too hot now, the sun was out. Checkpoint Charlie was full of tourists taking pictures, and a few young American soldiers who'd lived in Germany for years without learning German, competent and cheerful and bored in a different way than their counterparts on the unblemished side of the Wall, a boredom that was demanding, that placed expectations on the world.

I'd placed myself across the street from the station, while my mother and Greta went to buy some pretzels from a cart, so I saw them first. And here I wasn't shy, I screamed and whooped and jumped, embarrassing Greta. We tore the pretzels in six pieces and shared them, leaning against the fountain, staring at the sun.

*

Our apartment was large and ugly and cheap, with broadloom carpets and muddy walls that my mother had tacked lengths of fabric to, since the landlord would not allow painting. Marina would sleep in Greta's room, Rainer on the couch, and Rosa would have my room while I shared a bed with my mother. The living room had huge windows with leaded panes, the top row alternating blue and red squares that glowed on the opposite wall, and I liked to stand on a chair and pass my hand through the tinted light, one making my hand appear scalded, the other ghost-grey. But the windows also let in the cold, and Rainer was stiff and miserable the next morning with the bottomless snarling misery of teenage boys, so my mother offered that she would sleep on the couch and Greta would move in with me and Rainer with Marina, and I was terrified that Greta would tell my cousins I would wet the bed, which hadn't happened for years.

*

My mother, who had taken on as much journalism as she could scrounge after my father left, sat down at her desk by the couch after dinner, her notebook and pens marshalled beside the typewriter.

"What are you doing?" Rosa asked.

"This is due next week."

"But—"

"At night. I'll only work at night. And only for a few hours."

There was a pause.

"This is the only visit we will make," Rosa said, not angrily.

"He doesn't give me anything."

The air changed at the mention of my father, as when Rosa said she would phone her husband, both of them uneasy with these unfamiliar men. My mother had met Johannes, but she described him dismissively when I'd asked, giving the impression of someone well-meaning and not very intelligent, smiling oafishly, not getting the joke. She made him seem peripheral to Rosa's life. My mother had not, that I knew of, asked a single question about him, and I wonder now if Rosa's children noticed this, if that was part of Rainer's unhappiness, a feeling that his father was being dishonoured in some way he couldn't define, which would have carried all the ambivalence of age fifteen, wanting and not wanting to see his father as ridiculous. He scowled in the kitchen, complaining about the cold.

Rosa deliberated at the bookshelf, sat at the far end of the couch.

"I'll read until you're done," she said.

"Don't be stubborn."

"I'm not. I want to read."

She opened the book. I could hear typing as I lay in bed beside Greta and it was still going when I finally fell asleep and they did that every night, Rosa on the couch, my mother typing, the rest of us pretending to sleep until we slept. In the morning both of them looked as if they hadn't gone to bed, though they got through the days, which were good. We went to museums. We had picnics. My mother was extravagant, showering them with food, insisting they come shopping with us so they could see the grocery aisles, five different kinds of pickles, jams, the bakeries and the cured meats and the slabs of cheese from France and the wine from Italy. We walked along the wide streets where the big department stores were, stores my mother claimed to hate, but there was a cautious pride under her contempt as she gestured at the mannequins behind the glass windows, the smaller windows of the jewellery stores where the gold and silver lay on black velvet. And Rosa smiled obligingly but, I could see from my mother's face as she filled the cart with more and more food, not enough.

I don't know what would have been enough for my mother. The lavishness was a bid for something she thought Rosa could give her, or ought to give her. An admission that her life was right, that it had been worth what it had cost Rosa and the husband and the dead parents and Rainer and Marina, the way they would never have been allowed to forget what she had done, not for a second, they were punished, in small ways, to make sure they would not forget. My mother wanted Rosa to forgive her all that, as if that was a reasonable expectation, but my mother was not a reasonable person, she was a determined and unreasonable one, she could not live with conditions as they were, and I have huge admiration for that. She just didn't understand that she couldn't expect everyone else to agree with her, not with their own lives and their own rightness to maintain.

*

I saw Marina last year. She lives in Berlin with her husband; they have no children. Rainer does, but his marriage is not happy, Marina says (he lives near the town where he and Marina grew up and where their parents lived till they died and my mother is dead too, we are not a long-lived family). I visited with my wife, who is an American-born academic and conversant with the way that history is repurposed and made less real by being publicly memorialized, and she dutifully followed the line that marks where the Wall was, taking photos on her phone, touching the inscription that pays tribute to the last man shot trying to cross, only a month before the Wall came down, only a year after that visit. But she was tired and stayed at the Airbnb while I went out with Marina, who was still quiet but drank with surprising persistence, and we got drunk and stood, swaying toward each other, under the clock at one in the morning as if we had defeated middle age and we both, at the same moment, remembered standing in that exact spot together, looking up at the clock, and Marina giggled and wiped her mouth.

"We had no idea," she said, and kept on giggling. "It was almost over, and we had no idea."

And we stood for a while, looking into the street, the memory feeling vital enough that neither of us could think of what to say next.

*

The night before they left, I got up to use the bathroom. They were sitting side by side on the couch. I heard a sniffling and thought Rosa was crying, it was such a small flurry of sound, but it was my mother.

"How could you think that?"

Rosa's voice bewildered, as though a household object had exploded in her hands.

My mother didn't answer.

Rosa stood up, saw me.

"Go back to bed," she said shortly, sounding for the first time like she had the upper hand, and I wanted my mother to say it too, but she didn't care that I was there at all, she barely saw me, too involved in her own defeat.

Of course, she had hoped that Rosa would stay, beguiled by the prospect of grocery aisles, of a larger life for her children, the husband really a side note, who could be outgrown, thrown over. I don't think my mother understood love, as something real and inarguable, or understood that Rosa could feel loyalty to someone my mother remembered as a fool, and even if he was a fool, that was not the point for Rosa, the point was the habit of love, to love and to be tied to her promises. My mother wasn't naive; she knew it would break Rosa's heart, but that was something a person could live with, and she would know, she'd broken her own. She wasn't afraid of broken hearts, only of being wrong, of finding that Rosa did not want what she wanted her to want, could refuse the thing she offered her, could, herself, have choice.

*

Greta moved over for me, flinging the blanket aside.

"What took you so long?"

"They're still up."

"Tomorrow night we get our beds back," she said, turning over. I itemized the room, which was a trick Greta taught me for when I couldn't sleep. The open closet door. The framed photographs. The rug under the window, the window. Beyond the window, the street. All the streets, the whole city of streets. I lay awake, straining to hear, down the hall, the voices going on and on, so softly that I couldn't tell if they were talking, arguing, or if it was just the sound of other voices from somewhere else.

Chris Bailey

////////////////////

WE'VE CHERISHED
NOTHING

The weather waited to turn as I sailed toward the mouth of North Lake Harbour. Wooden piers streaked with gull shit made up the run. Sandstone cliffs over beaches on either side. Clouds full and heavy. My father's boat free of fish save a feed of mackerel for him. He was stepping out of the fishing industry and had me stepping in, trying his boots on for size. Could this be what I want, what he wants for me? The captain's chair he broke in from years of lobstering and all the rest. Deck scrubbed clean of blood, stained by the rust of the boom and hauler left in too long after spring. Windows I hated to clean as a youngster.

I didn't know what I was doing. With that boat or my life. I got in my Saturn and drove twenty minutes to Souris to meet Jacob Arsenault for our weekly drink at the Black Rafter. We grew up together on Elmira Road. He had gone to the army and come back a few times and had bought a house in Souris. Small-town life agreed with him. Back then I wrote poems and stories about women I had loved or could love and about places I had never been. A desire for something more. I showed these to no one outside a few friends made at UPEI and spoke of writing only when drunk. A leaving was in my heart. I was putting something behind me in one way or another. Like the fear of turning into my brothers or my father for no reason other than I wanted to be someone else. I clung to Jacob's friendship. A drink in a dark room. Bad country music. A shared past.

*

"You're late," Jacob said. He nodded toward the bartender, a woman we went to school with. "Melissa here wasn't sure you'd show. But who bets against the regularity of Clark Prosper?"

The stool I pulled out had cracked leather patched with duct tape. Every part of this place, save the liquor and maybe the wings and some workers and patrons, was older than us. Neon sign in the window flashing OPEN. Flattering dimness of bar light around us.

"You're saying I'm predictable."

"No, you live a life right full of excitement."

"And the life you live?"

"One of faith. You'll land, and Melissa here'll look good, and someone'll ask for that 'Chicken Fried' song, and you'll tell me how you're making out with the fleet, how Claire's doing."

Claire Penny and I had been together since grade ten. A lot changes in seven years. A lot stays the same. Her father died when we were in high school, and her mother, Erica, married the town's undertaker. Claire didn't want to leave Souris, so we didn't. She put her nursing degree to use at the Colville Manor, and I fished with my father and dug potatoes for Black Pond. We rented an apartment on Paquet Avenue where we paid too much for what little we had.

I asked Melissa for a shot of whisky and a Schooner.

"Cheapest stuff you got," I said.

"Forever a man of taste."

She poured the shot and took a beer from the fridge. The understanding between us that I'd settle up before leaving. Jacob went the other way. Paid for each drink as it came. He always paid cash. Money spent must always pass through his hands.

"It's strange being on the water without Dad," I said. "But what's the alternative? To ask for help is a weakness. A sign I'm not ready, and then what. The work he did to get that fleet in the eighties and then having to sell it outside the family because I'm not the man he is."

"None of us will be the men our fathers are," Jacob said. "Is it a burden or a gift, you think?"

"Claire thinks I should take over the fleet. I said, What if I gotta go west to pay for it? She said, So what? Distance, I said, doesn't make anything easy on anyone."

"She's not the type to be missing. When I got back from Ontario and everyone was here, even Jeff Whalen, the prick, I said to Claire, It's good to see you. She said nothing. No welcome back, nothing. Like I never left."

He enjoyed this memory of my girlfriend. She never made Jacob feel out of place, not even when he drank too much and ripped fence posts off decks along Main Street. She was most always calm. Relaxed. Claire was relaxed with other men. If she caught me looking the wrong direction, there was hell. I'm a man who, if I'm sitting idle and there's movement in the corner of my eye, I look. Sometimes it's nothing. A bit of dust. But sometimes there's a woman attached to that movement and in Claire's mind a comparison that is never good. If I went west, she'd find another man in another cardinal direction and head that way. Sometimes all that's needed is a reason.

When Jacob liked something, he kept at it till he grew tired or something else took him away. The gym was calling him lately, and it showed. One year he got into gardening and learned to balance pH levels in soil. I never understood how Jacob had the patience for this but thought these were details I could use in stories or something. He relished our hometown, its people. I was more concerned with what lay beyond the chalk horizon on the waters we fished. Possibility. All kinds.

We worked our way through our beers. I did my shot. Some places water down the cheap stuff to make it last. When Melissa went to the back for a phone-in order of wings, Jacob spoke about a porn star he'd seen on the computer.

"East Coast girl," he said. "She hasn't done much, but I plan on seeing everything she does do."

"What was it you said about women wrestlers on TV back in high school?"

"Oh, Christ. I was loaded drunk at one of the Savoies'. I think it was Nick I said this to: I'd hate to see what crawls on them, but I'd love to find out."

Laughter. A man who corked for Richard Charlie Ivan out of North Lake waited to order a vodka lime. Melissa, coming from the back, asked if we could go for another. I remembered Jacob had once said something similar about her. His eyes on her. The cliché of a knowing glance, a look that can speak. Was this a look I gave Claire anymore, or Claire me? Intimate. A knowing of what can happen if that look was reciprocated.

"I'm gonna head 'er," I said.

"You're taking off?"

"Well, you know Dad. Boat's still in his name."

Jacob knows Noah Prosper. He fished lobster with us one season, and they got along. He respected my father the way men respect fathers who don't own them. He still lands lobster gear for Dad. The year before this, Jacob's father, Zachariah, had a scare. His heart. I took Jacob to the Queen E. He said holy fuck the entire way and thanked me when I put the car in park.

"Back in Ontario they cheersed everything." The way Jacob said this, it sounded like *cherished*. "We've cheersed nothing. Not you getting the boat or that ring on Claire's finger. You think I didn't hear about that? Two more beers, Melissa."

"What're we cheersing to?"

"If Claire ain't knocked up, she will be soon, so how about hard cocks and handsome men?"

"Jesus Christ."

"Well then. To the works of the Lord. To the long nothing before and the solemn nothing after."

*

Months can pass without speaking to someone. Touch is easily lost. This is what happened between me and Jacob Arsenault. He returned to his childhood home up the road from my parents' place after buying it from his mother and selling his spot in Souris. Put up a new woodshed, a new garage. Kept the yard very neat. The rumour mill said he was seeing a local girl he shouldn't be seeing. Bad blood could be boiling. He did this, and I made a break for school in Toronto to try a life where the air was less salt and more exhaust and filled with languages I'd never heard. Claire became a memory tinged with regret, and Jane, whose path I crossed before on one of my rare ventures off-Island, was a happy accident in the process of happening with a yet-to-be-broken promise of a future. On nights I missed PEI, I thought of Jacob. What did he think that first Friday alone when I got on a plane and thought I could make a go of it? A few months after I left, his father passed. Zachariah not even fifty. I didn't attend the funeral. A trait shared with my father: I do not go to a funeral if I know the deceased.

*

Christmas break. Evening in Elmira, PEI. In Toronto, I'd been living in a slum near Queen and Lansdowne. While I was in Hamilton for a night in November, my apartment had been broken into, my mattress stolen, and my toilet clogged with shit and toilet paper.

When I returned home, my parents' kitchen had changed little. The white walls had yellowed, the blue lower half was faded, and the oilcloth floor was scuffed by the metal legs of my father's chair. The table freshly refinished by my younger brother, Marcus, a carpenter living in Covehead. In front of me on the kitchen table: my computer, my master's thesis. A novel set in North Lake and Souris looking at masculinity in rural areas. Writing this while wanting to write a story based on murder ballads and an unsolved murder from a century ago.

My mother was in the living room decorating the tree. She usually did this with one of our girlfriends or sisters. I was her only child without someone to point to and declare my own. Jane was, in many ways that counted, married to another man, and what we had we kept between us and a few friends. But this is not about Jane. The star doesn't go on the tree until Christmas Eve.

A hand on my shoulder. My mother's voice: "Someone's here."

I took my earphones out. Warren Zevon howled at no one in particular. The phone rang.

My mother sighed, "It's your uncle." Meaning her sister's ex-husband, making his yuletide call. "I'll take this in the bedroom," she said. "He'll be drunker than seven fucking billy goats."

The inside door opened. A slam to get it shut. Footsteps on stairs whose carpet needed replacing. Jacob was thinner than I remembered, but sober.

"Figured you were home," he said. "Thought I'd come see how things are."

"How you been holding up?"

Jacob hung his coat off the back of the chair across the table. My mother's place. His back to the window, the sink, the dishwasher, and the stove.

"Tree's looking good," he said.

"Not my doing."

He nodded as though I'd said something that required consideration. Then: "Claire's pregnant."

He said this, and I thought of Jane's daughter. How I wished we'd met earlier so she'd be mine and not the offspring of some dial tone I had, so far, avoided seeing outside of a photograph on the wall of their stairway. I asked that she take it down while I was there. She said she wouldn't change her house for me. I didn't know which of us was less considerate.

I said to Jacob, "Also not my doing."

"Did I suggest otherwise, ya old bait bag."

"Your tone implied something. Your tone was an implication."

"What the fuck're you at here?" He pointed to the computer, and I told him about my novel, about how I wanted to pose a series of what-if questions on my family and the place that's held us, the occupation that's kept a roof overhead. He tried to pay attention. If an astronaut synchronizes two clocks, takes one with him, and flies away from Earth then returns, the clock with him will hold a different time than the one left behind. Time and experience are relative things. Once, I set my watch along with Jacob's. Now the faces disagreed.

"I thought you were supposed to make shit up."

"The best lies sound like the truth."

"You ever think of it," Jacob said, "having kids with Claire?"

Claire said she wanted to name a daughter after a sci-fi character on TV. I do not care for sci-fi or fantasy. A fantasy should be almost attainable, like the idea of home. Little ones underfoot. Claire cross, for they'd been after her for something and were told no before asking me, me picking away in the workshop. Lobster traps, herring nets. Or maybe I'd take up cabinetry, maybe become an electrician. Have a hand in constructing small parts of the world. A practical pursuit.

"I'm sure she's told you all about it."

"Now look who's suggesting."

"Want a beer?" I said.

"Still put them where we used to?"

Outside, the new motion sensor my father put up in summer came on. Artificial light remained long enough for eyes to adjust. Flakes of snow spiralled earthward. Frost-hard ground. Windmill blades thrummed in the dark. We walked to a case of Schooner in the snowbank by the downstairs living room window.

"When I was away for the army in high school," Jacob said, "and came back, the clock in your rig, that Grand Am, was still six minutes fast. And off by an hour."

"Something done twice a year is easy to forget."

"And the beer here. You haven't changed any, have you?"

"I'd like to think not."

"But you know better."

"I hope I do."

Jacob took a swig. Not long ago we'd all tie one on in the basement. Jacob and me. Marcus. The Stewart boys. Mix liquor drinks and pound beer and get Mom or Dad to take us to Souris. Jacob'd mix his drinks right stiff. Fill a tall water glass three-quarters full of rum, enough pop for colour. Have someone try it. They'd grimace, and Jacob would say, *Now you know what I'm dealing with.* No real silences between us. Any were short, relaxed. Possibly happy. We thought we knew then. We knew fuck all. Young, thinking our hearts had been worked over so many times they were hardened. As though the heart were made of bone and would become stronger in the places that were broken.

"How long you and Claire been together?" I said.

Cold air in pine trees that separated the north end of the house from the long lane that ran east-west and hooked around to the backyard. When winter hits and the temperature dips, the wind doesn't howl. It's a shrill, frigid thing. My father says an increase in deaths follows wind like that. Check the obituaries. The wind hauls around from the northeast and carries people away.

Jacob: "I said I'd take her to Halifax. Get her sorted. Do it here, everyone knows."

A mouthful of beer not as cold as expected.

"In Ontario they drink Labatt 50 like we drink Schooner," I said.

"She said she would know and I would know and that's two people too many."

"There are some decisions we have no hand in. Our hands

don't fit the decision, or the decision don't fit our hands. Like gloves on setting day."

"She said she wants to keep it."

Elmira is on maps of Canada despite the Island being so small. Did Jacob know this? The railroad that bankrupted us into Confederation put it on the map. We were the last stop on this end. My family was part of the construction. We helped settle the road back when it was Portage. Sentenced to transportation to the colonies for thievery when the jails were full. A leaving has always been in my blood. A man changed the name after a street in New York for the sound.

"Yeah, no Schooner at all in Ontario," I said. "They're missing out."

"I'll drink to that," Jacob said. "Cheers."

*

Three years before this: Jacob and Claire sit talking in a living room. Pair of picture windows behind them. Jacob and Claire bright against the night outside. A party in Little Pond, the Campbell place. I go to fetch another drink and get caught up talking to one of the Mooneys in the kitchen. He says he wishes we spoke more in high school. I tell him he once said at lunch, A real man puts lots of salt on his fries.

"You're sure that was me," he says.

I move toward the crowded hall that connects the kitchen and living room. Bottle of beer in one hand. A soft voice says my name. I stop, and a MacDonald I was too scared to speak to in high school pulls my face toward hers. She kisses me.

We used to consider a moment ninety seconds. Now it is a snap of the fingers. Three minutes used to hold two moments.

My surprise plain as Brianna's smile as she takes my free hand and slides it down the front of her pants. Pulse of her breath in my ear. "We should get out of here, yeah?"

Her hair smells of coconut. Taste of her mouth: vodka, melon. I turn my head. Through a part in people, I see the living room. Jacob in my seat. Claire leans into him, her hand on his leg. No, that is not specific enough. His thigh, his inner thigh. Her wrist hooked around. The look they share. Two moments. Three minutes. My realization: Claire and I are each holding out for something we can't put words to. It could be New Year's, and all Jacob and Claire would need is the countdown. All Brianna Mac-Donald needs is me.

I never know what I need until the moment is happening or gone. I am always too late. Is there anything worse?

*

I got my thesis to my supervisor but couldn't afford to stay in Ontario to edit in person. A plane took me to the Island. Dad took me home. Spring, and lobster season around the corner.

On April 17 the boat returned to the water. Traps waited on the wharf. Snow melted into the sun. My parents' lane is three hundred feet long and made of red dirt, sand, and stones taken from the beach. The boat hauler backed up this entire length to the boat building's open doors. My father took a sledgehammer to the creosote blocking under the bow. My father is shorter than me and has led a life harder than I will ever know. No quit in him. His hands are stronger than mine and will be like that until he dies.

I removed the wooden props from the starboard side, walked bow to stern. Dad went portside and hammered more creosote.

Whine of the winch. Cement dust clouds. Pale light from a frigid spring sun. How easily the boat slid onto this piece of equipment. You see a boat that large move out of water and something ought to go wrong. There is land beneath us. The sea is three minutes away if you do the speed limit. Gravity should have a stronger hold on things. Rumbling, knocking, and screeching. Over all this, my father's voice said words I couldn't hear.

The boat hauler, yelling: "All the young fellas have around here is crushed dreams."

While I did this, Jacob was likely at home. Mowing the lawn, cutting firewood. Reading books on fatherhood before giving up to watch YouTube videos on diaper changing, baby proofing. Him in my head more than I liked. Claire pregnant. Her wanting to keep the child. Jacob was not the only one who stayed on the Island to go this route. The MacAulays on Steeles Lane. The Cairn boys in St Peters. They stayed and fished, picked up another trade, content with what they had.

Jane and I weren't speaking. There had been a scare. She was sick and got tests done and said, "I'm not pregnant. At least we know that. If I was, it wouldn't be anyone's but yours."

No doubt until then. Mentioning no other possibilities opened the door to possibilities. For a moment, I was almost a father. It was her choice to stop speaking. It always is.

*

Winter turned to summer in mid-June. Snow had fallen a week and a half before Jacob turned up. Catches were down, but the wind had settled. Looked to be fine weather till the gear hit the landwash.

I sat on the front step, looking across potato fields to what was once my grandfather's house and now belonged to a cousin I don't speak to. The stones of the driveway under Jacob's tires. Him in shorts and a T-shirt climbing out of his big GMC.

"You haven't been around," I said.

"I been to the Rafter every Friday since the season started. You're the one not around." He spit in the dirt. Stuffed his hands in his pockets, took them out, and folded his arms across his chest. "I got a coffee in the truck if you want. You look like orange baked shit."

I was sunburned from the last two days on the water. The backs of my ears were peeling. Too hot to work in an oil coat or a sweater. Down to the T-shirt, sometimes less. My skin would darken, yet my hands would remain pale as though I were still wearing my gloves. A fisherman's tan. You always look ready to do bait.

I said, "How's Claire making out?"

"You'd have to ask her."

"Jacob," I said, "what did you do?"

"She calls when she knows I'm not home. Leaves messages that're just quiet. I call back, she don't pick up. I don't know," he said. Then: "I love her."

I looked at him. The diminished shoulders, the loss of hair. Beard greying. Nails rimmed with grease. Tired face, stooped body. Oil stain on his shirt. Flecks of bleach on sneakers knocking on five years old. He once told me he wore sneakers a size too small so he wouldn't stand still when there was work to do. We all need reasons to keep moving. A shiver went through him with a gust of northwest wind. Northwest wind can bring rain at any time. Jacob pointed to the old apple tree we used to climb as children.

"What happened there?" he said.

"Lightning. Same storm near got Dad when he was walking from the building. Hit the ground in front of him, he said, right in front of his eyes. The earth smoked, and then boom. The tree. It's only half-dead, and the fruit it grows, you don't want to eat."

*

Landing day. Lobster gear left to dry on the wharf. Traps not fit for another season had their heads cut and were given a burial at sea. The hottest day of the season. All the work done, and Jacob and me at the kitchen table with a feed of burgers and fries.

I hadn't told him about Jane. How to explain? Her older by more than a decade, married to a high school sweetheart with money. Even secure things fall apart. Jacob asked what I thought of love, and I remembered: he loved Claire. She wanted to keep the baby. He had a hesitation: an expression of doubt as good as cheating. Cheating with what is expected of you.

"I used to think love was a natural formation," I said. "A river cut through the landscape. Something strong enough to wear through mountains."

"Rivers dry up. Or there's runoff," he said, "from farms and shit. Everything dies."

"You're not wrong."

"And you've been in love."

"I've dipped my toes."

"Never dove right in?"

The move to Ontario. My pick of schools, and the one I chose because I'd met this woman and she would be close.

"You know about fishermen," I said. "So few of us know how to swim."

He chewed on a burger. He laced the bun with cayenne powder, saying he liked the heat. No. I need the heat. That is what he said.

Jacob: "You talk to Claire?"

"By now she's forgotten the sound of my voice."

On my parents' wall, the clock ticked beside a Lions Club calendar. Day boxes filled with birthdays. There used to be anniversaries on there, small hearts next to them. Deaths with black crosses. Now only births and holidays.

Jacob said, "Come by the house later."

"Of course, I want to see what you did with the place."

*

Everything appeared the same as when Jacob's father was alive, but fresher.

Point of contention with Jane: things must be modern. You wait long enough, things come back around. But a lack of patience in Jane. I am not one to decorate or keep with trends. I dress like my father dressed when I was young. Jane keeps up with music, fashion, home decor. Claire much the same, though she wanted to do it the way women in their twenties often do by having signs around the house with live and laugh and love painted on them. Jacob said no to this.

He brought me through the porch to the basement. Warned me about the steps.

"Test one before you put weight on. I never got around to replacing these yet. Never did stairs before."

"They're supposed to be difficult, aren't they?"

"Pot meet kettle, eh wha?"

The basement was the only thing Jacob had really done over. Click flooring save for around the furnace and where wood was piled against the west wall. His father's old weight machine. A white heavy-bag streaked with the rust of dried blood. The bedroom Zachariah roughed in for Jacob, finished and waiting for a coat of paint.

"I thought this'd be the nursery, then realized, shit. That's fucking dumb of me."

"Claire excited?"

"She isn't living here," he said. "She'd come up, put in a night. Play house. But when she saw this, the nursery upstairs. She freaked. A child she's ready for. But commitment. A family. She went back to the spot she's renting in Rollo Bay."

"She's not with her mother?"

"Clark, you don't know? Erica died of cancer last year," he said. "You're lucky, you still got both your folks. It was hard on Claire. The loss, then the baby. She wouldn't talk about it. She carried it in her shoulders. Her neck gets right stiff."

I wanted to tell Jacob about Jane's pregnancy scare. That she wasn't sure she could ever leave her husband and if she did, it wouldn't be for me. How my father thought he had cancer, and the doctors lost the biopsy. Secrets loaded across sore shoulders. A thing his father said when he taught catechism, that he was happy being bald because it saved time in the shower. The thumbs-up Zachariah flashed when he saw me in church before a niece's baptism. Upstairs, the phone rang. Jacob even kept the wall phone going.

He said, "Could be Claire," and looked at the floor. Hands on his hips. Sighed. Sunlight from the porch window making his face resemble a man's whose funeral I chose not to attend, and never forgave myself. Jacob turned toward the stairs.

Lynn Coady

THE MONEY

"Why do you say yes to everything?" asked Helen, peering backward into the bathroom mirror. Her back looked as if she had been attacked by giant leeches. Like she'd been running for her life and they fell upon her, attaching their suckers to her spine, her shoulder blades, leaving large, perfectly circular hickeys. And she had just lain there face down, as if paralyzed, and let it happen. That part of it was true, actually.

Ernestine had told her that cupping was her new thing. She had been reading up on it, she said, and Helen's body and its particular needs had popped into her mind. Helen couldn't help it—she liked hearing about popping into Ernestine's mind. It made her feel cared for. That was the reason Helen had transitioned from taking Ernestine's yoga class Saturday mornings to coming in Wednesdays as well for a bodywork practice called redirective therapy. Ernestine said, one Saturday, as Helen unrolled her mat, "You know, I have been thinking about that wonky shoulder of yours. Make an appointment—I might have a trick that can help." Helen, who had a chronic hip thing but hadn't even known about the wonky shoulder, said yes.

Ernestine flounced into class in neon-pink tights and oversized tops with proclamations on them like *JOYFUL* or interrogations like *WHAT are you GRATEFUL for TODAY?* And the tops were always elaborately spangled, which you didn't often see with athletic wear, but apparently Ernestine possessed some kind of crafting device that allowed her to bedazzle all her clothes.

For most of her life, Helen had avoided flakery. When her physio first advised she try yoga, she went out of her way to find a class that defied every possible cliché. She found one in midtown that was run out of a kick-boxing club by a former junior hockey player named Gary with a perspiring face. He called it "kick-ass yoga," and he always opened class by shouting: *"Who here is ready to get their ass kicked?!"* And the participants were supposed to scream back at him: *"Sir, yes, sir!"* Helen thought this was great until she noticed that every class, when Gary would cue them into happy baby pose, he'd make the same joke, which was: *"Or, as I like to call it, happy husband pose!"* None of the women lying on their backs and hanging on to their feet ever laughed at this. But Gary kept making his joke.

So Helen started looking around for other classes. Ernestine was flaky, but her flakiness was so extreme and insistent that it struck Helen as honest in some objective way. It didn't feel trendy, like a vibe Ernestine had picked up from social media. It seemed essential and unselfconscious, like she had soaked it up in the womb. Whenever she came bounding into the studio on Saturday mornings, it felt like someone had thrown open a set of heavy curtains to let in the daylight—the proverbial ray of sunshine.

And it wasn't like Ernestine didn't know how she came across. She was often apologetic about what she called her "intuition." Every once in a while, while pulling and twisting Helen's limbs this way and that, she'd let something slip about Helen's "energies," which Ernestine indicated she was "picking up on." Then she'd chuckle self-deprecatingly and say, "Sorry if that sounded a little wavy-gravy." But Helen didn't mind. Yoga people were supposed to be that way. Gary had been fun for a couple of classes, but Ernestine was a far better teacher, her classes more meditative and uplifting. And, as for the bodywork, Helen always left Ernestine's table feeling better, lighter. And that other thing—cared for. Ernestine would pull Helen's arm one way and then the other, across her body, then above her head, murmuring to herself as if deep in contemplation. She'd place a hand on Helen's hip, let it sit for a moment, then shift it, gently but decisively, to one side, and exclaim, "That's the money!" It made Helen feel understood in a way that she didn't even comprehend herself.

The cupping bothered her, though. The furious, identical circles emblazoned across her back, like she'd been branded. Ernestine had said, "I just wanna try something out on you, okay?" And Helen had said yes. Yes, because she was there on the table, blissed out, feeling Ernestine's hands radiating warmth and compassion into her muscles, listening to Ernestine's murmurs and cooing. And saying no would have ruined it.

It seemed to Helen that she didn't used to be such a pushover. During corpse pose at the end of her classes, Ernestine would play music that sounded like wind chimes, over which she'd utter a stream of platitudes that Helen just tried to ignore, because if she didn't, she thought she might snicker. But, once, Ernestine had murmured something about how important it was to "hold yourself in kindness," and Helen, who had been drifting content-edly up until that point, had thought, *How inane,* and then burst into tears. She sat up, and Ernestine was at her side, enveloping her, ushering her swiftly to the back room, where her massage table lived.

"Yoga brings up so much," Ernestine told her, rubbing her back. "And, Helen, you hold on to so much. Can I say that? You carry so much."

*

A woman named Dana, whom Helen didn't know, reached out to Helen through her university email address. The message was brief and uninformative, asking only if they could set a time to speak on the phone. Helen scanned and then deleted it, because at the bottom of the message Dana identified herself as "Assistant to Nicola Rasmussen," which to Helen's mind was like identify-ing yourself as assistant to the ocean—or Santa Claus.

Then Dana left two or three voice mail messages, also through the university, which were easy enough to ignore. "If she calls again, just tell her to fuck off," Helen told the secretary. "It's an angry student or something."

The secretary was aghast.

"No, no," Helen amended. "I mean it's someone trying to prank me. She says she works for Nicola Rasmussen."

The secretary blinked at the famous name, then laughed. "It could be legit! Maybe she wants to star in a movie about your life!"

Helen grinned and looked down at her own chest. The secre-tary grinned back. They were both thinking the word the whole world associated with that name, which was *tits.*

"Yeah...I can't see it," said Helen.

"Poetic licence!" chuckled the secretary. "The magic of Hollywood."

Helen tried to imagine a movie about her life starring Nicola Rasmussen: Corpse Pose *is a lush cinematic feast about a large-breasted woman with noticeably hard nipples crying at yoga.*

But, the next day, Nicola called Helen on her cellphone.

*

In her films Nicola Rasmussen played women you couldn't trust. She joked about it in interviews—these were the only roles anyone would give her. Nobody saw her as a faithful wife or devoted mother or a frazzled lady scientist peering into a microscope, frantically searching for ways to save humankind.

She started out famous in a basic sort of way, for being stunning and young. But she "exploded onto the scene," as the saying went, because of the nipple business. A-list actresses didn't usually show their breasts in those days, but Nicola Rasmussen not only showed her breasts onscreen, she *did* things with them, like smoosh them together or cup one breast in one hand and the chin of some man in the other, whom she would then draw slowly to her. But the real detonative moment happened when Nicola's breasts were completely covered—albeit by a sheer material. She caressed, and then flicked, her left nipple with one manicured finger, making it harden in real time, right there on camera, on the big screen. She became an instant object of cultural loathing and celebration as a result, and that had never quite gone away. It had been decades ago, but when her name came up, people still found it funny to call her *Nippla*.

"I've been trying my hand at poetry," said Nicola Rasmussen when Helen spoke to her on the phone.

"Okay," said Helen. "Wow!"

"I think I might eventually have something."

"I see. Huh! Like…a book?"

"Well, Helen. This is why I reached out to you. Only you can tell me if I've got a book on my hands."

Nicola Rasmussen had somehow got a hold of Helen's twenty-two-year-old sophomore poetry collection. The book had gone nowhere and done nothing other than provide a line on her CV, which may or may not have helped Helen get the job she currently had. Helen had garnered a lot more attention for her first story collection but understood now how much of that had come from the fact that she'd been a twentysomething woman with an intriguing author photo. Her boyfriend had taken the picture at two in the morning at a hookah bar. Helen had her head thrown back and was releasing a stream of fragrant smoke into the air above her. Her fingers looked extra-long and poetic, twined around the pipe, fingernails painted black. Massive earrings, shitloads of eyeliner. She'd looked decadent and squalid, like a lady poet should. *Wow,* people used to say, when they flipped the book over and beheld Helen's expanse of exposed white neck. Her publisher, Melanie, who was also her publicist because she ran the whole (now defunct) publishing imprint as a one-woman show, had told her the photo hinted at a story of some kind, like a Hopper painting, and that's what people responded to. They bought the book hoping to know more of Helen's story.

"I'll bet 50 percent of your sales came out of that author's photo alone," Melanie had said.

"Huh," said Helen. "Three whole books!" She was cynical and impish and dark back then. She certainly didn't do yoga. She took long, intense walks that sometimes lasted four or five hours, during which time she would smoke several cigarettes. But by the time she'd published her second book, the one that had so captivated Nicola Rasmussen, she'd had to quit smoking because it triggered her migraines. And the issue with her hip came about from walking for hours in bad shoes.

*

Ernestine came racing into the studio wearing a tights-and-bra set that was covered with rainbows. She whipped off her bedazzled top (which today read *Grace*) so everyone could admire the outfit.

"Running a yoga studio is not always easy," she told them. "But there are perks! I get outfits like these offered at a discount!"

Helen thought it was the kind of pattern that might have been sitting in the discount bin anyway, but of course it looked natural and right on Ernestine, who turned around and raised her muscled arms and flexed her extraordinary buttocks, making the rainbows shimmer.

"I am really trying to focus on this kind of thing lately," Ernestine confided to the class. "Things that delight me, that give me joy. Little things. It doesn't have to be a material thing, it doesn't have to be something you buy. But if that's what gives you joy, what the heck! Focus on it! Don't focus on the furnace!"

The furnace in the studio kept shutting down in the middle of class and had been doing so throughout the winter months. Ernestine had started encouraging students to "bring lots of layers," which Helen and the other diehards had obediently done. Some even wore fingerless gloves. Ernestine herself had started bringing a woollen cap with teddy bear ears to class for the very bad mornings when the furnace had shut off at some point during the night and the studio felt like a walk-in freezer.

But Ernestine always put on a happy face. She cultivated gratitude and joy all winter long. "You've heard of hot yoga?" she'd declare to her bundled attendees. "Well, today we're doing cold yoga!" And then she'd pull a pair of spangled sweatpants on over her tights.

Then, in the spring, Ernestine became more ebullient than ever because she had found a yoga boyfriend. Helen knew from their conversations during bodywork that Ernestine was divorced, that her ex was a bad man—bad in ways she didn't get into but that Helen could guess at, having a bad ex of her own. Ernestine hinted that custody arrangements regarding her little girl were an ongoing trial because of this man's stubborn selfishness. Ernestine often talked about the travails of being a "single mom and small business owner"—how demanding the two roles were, how easy it would be to get overwhelmed if not for her regime of fitness and wellness and cultivating joy.

But, once the boyfriend had been acquired, Helen realized that Ernestine had in fact been putting on a brave face through much of the winter. She talked a good game, speaking of her gratitude and her health-giving routines and her vast love for her daughter and her work and for Helen and all the diehards who showed up for yoga on Saturday mornings. But to compare Ernestine then to Ernestine now—it was like she'd been uttering her winter-long affirmations through gritted teeth. Because now, in the springtime of her yoga boyfriend, Ernestine actually glowed, she beamed, bouncing from mat to mat to give instructions during class, sometimes impulsively embracing Helen and the others as they balanced and strained, planting a nurturing smooch on a random shoulder or the back of someone's head once she was finished adjusting their postures.

She had met the boyfriend on some kind of retreat, and Helen had yet to catch his name. He was long-haired with a Christlike centre parting and beard, always smiling gently, showing wonderful teeth. As a couple, they gave off a giddy air of all-consuming sexual infatuation. Helen found it disconcerting to be in the studio with them. The boyfriend would join the Saturday morning classes—he and Ernestine tumbling into the room like puppies, pawing and nipping at each other. Sometimes, when everyone was seated in a cross-legged position, Ernestine would rise like a sleepwalker, go over to her boyfriend, and wrap her arms and legs around his shirtless torso in a full-bodied embrace.

"I'll be honest with you. I had a pretty hard winter," Ernestine confessed one day in the treatment studio as she guided one of Helen's legs straight into the air and pushed it back toward her head.

"I wouldn't have known," said Helen. "You always seem so positive."

"That's because there's no reason not to be positive," murmured Ernestine.

"Was it the furnace?"

"Yes, the furnace. I was so relieved when the weather finally warmed up. I don't know what I'll do next winter, but that's a worry for down the road. And my daughter, you know, she's a tween now…"

Ernestine went quiet for a few moments, becoming lost in Helen's quadriceps. Helen felt them loosen, and then everything else seemed to loosen along with them. Her eyelids fluttered, and her mouth fell open.

"She wants *stuff!*" exclaimed Ernestine. "Like, out of the blue. Her father took her snowboarding at Christmas. Now all she talks about is snowboarding next year. She wants all the gear. And she doesn't want to go sledding anymore, which I think is so sad, because I love sledding! You don't have to be a kid to love sledding. But she says it's lame."

Ernestine fell silent, and Helen blinked at the ceiling, dozy. "But now things are looking up," she ventured.

"Exactly," said Ernestine. "And that's my point. No matter how hard things get, the most unbelievable joy is always around the corner. You just can't lose faith. Faith is like an ember—you have to blow on it! You can't let it fade!"

*

A day later, Helen heard herself repeating the ember thing into the phone to Nicola Rasmussen. She was so nervous and, after an hour and twenty minutes, was struggling to find something to say that seemed like the words of a serious and deep-thinking person. You'd think a line of actual poetry might've popped into her head, maybe a snippet of Mary Oliver—always a crowd-pleaser. Or any one of the authors she'd spent the last decade reading and talking to students about. But no. She quoted Ernestine.

"What does that *mean?*" Nicola Rasmussen demanded. "How am I supposed to *blow* on it?"

They sat and talked another two hours as a patch of afternoon sunlight slid from the upper corner of the wall into a warm, square puddle at Helen's feet. What threw Helen wasn't that Nicola wanted to talk for so long—it was more that all she wanted to talk about was death. Helen didn't know what she had expected going into this, their first official "work" call, but it hadn't been that. Nicola had not yet sent Helen any of her writing to read. At the outset, Nicola asked Helen to consult with her about her poems—to perhaps become her editor if Helen thought there was a book there—but added that she wanted to have "a good talk" with Helen first to explain what it was she was trying to achieve. Helen said that sounded okay by her, so they booked this second call, which at first seemed like it, too, might be businesslike. Nicola picked up precisely where they left off, bypassing small talk, and explained to Helen that her poems were about her mother, "who I adored. Who I worshipped my whole life."

An empty notebook page stared up at Helen from the table, so she wrote on it: NICOLA'S MOM. "I think that sounds lovely," said Helen. She had a sudden memory of a magazine cover that featured Nicola—back in the late nineties, one or two years after the nipple furor. Nicola had faded into the background during that period, as it was widely felt she should, but this cover—likely timed to promote a film—had been some publicist's notion of a cheeky nod to the controversy. NICOLA RASMUSSEN: SUPER-NOVA OF SEX, read the headline. She'd been wearing a gown that looked to be made of disco balls and stood with her head thrown back the way Helen's head had been thrown back in her hookah photo, arms extended, backlit in such a way that her golden body seemed to exude light. Both nipples were prominent.

"It wasn't lovely," said Nicola, "because my mother died from Alzheimer's in a nursing home, and she didn't recognize anybody for two years before her death. Every day she would wake up and look around in horror, not recognizing anyone or anything, terrified, thinking she had been abandoned by everyone who loved her."

"Oh my god," said Helen.

"And I'd come to see her and I'd say: 'Mommy, it's me, Nicki.' And if I had just said to her, 'Hi, Mrs Rasmussen, I'm Doris or whatever, your designated visitor today,' that would have been less traumatizing for her, but instead she'd stare at me and start screaming, 'What have you done with Nicki? Where's my daughter Nicki?' Then she'd just start screaming my name: 'NICKI! NICOLA!! NICKI!!' While I'm right there sitting in front of her and there's nothing I can do to console her, to convince her I'm there, because as far as she's concerned, I'm one of the horrible strangers who is keeping her captive and torturing her by pretending to be her daughter. And then she just died one afternoon. I'd brought her some muffins, and she threw a fit and shoved them off the plate onto the floor, and she just died, thinking and feeling all those things. Calling my name at the same time as she was screaming at me to get away from her."

"Oh my god," said Helen again.

"So I'm trying to write about all that," said Nicola. "That's what I need help with."

Helen's plan for the summer otherwise mainly involved researching a paper that would, ideally, get her accepted to a conference in Barcelona next year. But all she really needed for that was an abstract, so she told Nicola she would help however she could. Then she dug out her old reading copy of her second collection, bulging with old yellow Post-its. It had been published so long ago that she found it hard to remember how she'd been as a person then, what her life had felt like. She took a look at the pages she had always chosen to read in public and read a few out loud to herself, trying to spark old synapses, remind herself of their writing, and then, hopefully, detect whatever the thematic and emotional currents were that had sparked with Nicola.

She was relieved to find that she liked the poems—they weren't naive and callow, didn't have any of the qualities for which she had typically berated herself when she was young. It was the work of a person obsessed with fleeting moments and impressions, who spent hours trying to resurrect them on a page. Helen found she could kind of admire that person, how tireless she had been. The way she'd decided that this weird project—attempting to capture the ineffable and then fixing those attempts onto a piece of paper like a specimen of insect—was so important it should take up all her time and mental energy.

Then again, that person didn't have much better to do. That person didn't yet have a perpetually aching hip or a crippling course load or aging parents. She hadn't yet met the person she would move in with and, eight years later, file a restraining order against. Really, she didn't know how good she had it all those years ago, dawdling over her PhD, losing days in the library, student loans a worry for down the road—a future *worry* for this person, this Helen, to deal with. She hadn't even suffered much by way of loss at that point, except for the family dog being hit by a car when she was fourteen—which was, admittedly, awful. And, of course, the death of grandparents. But everybody lost their grandparents. In Helen's intro poetry class, she was regularly besieged by dead grandparent poems.

*

Ernestine wrapped her hands around Helen's ankles and gently pulled. Helen loved everything about the exercise—the feeling of space it created in her hip sockets, the feeling of Ernestine's strong, warm hands wrapped around her lower legs. Helen had a brief fantasy of levitating above the earth. Drifting helplessly upward into god knew what. Ernestine taking hold of her ankles just in time, beaming up at her, gently guiding her feet back toward the ground.

Then Ernestine released her ankles and moved midway up the table to push down with either hand on Helen's hips.

"Oh boy," said Helen.

"That's the money," Ernestine agreed.

There was a spell of humidity that summer, and the studio was stifling even for morning classes. Ernestine arrived to class carrying what looked like a large pickle jar filled with yellowy sludge. To Helen, perspiring on her mat, it looked like humidity in a jar. Ernestine explained that the sludge was bone broth and unscrewed the jar lid and took intermittent sips as she set up her mat at the front of the room. "It's so good for you," she told them.

Helen noticed that Ernestine hadn't bounded into the room the way she usually did. A woman with a thick black ponytail— someone Helen felt companionable toward because they always seemed to set up their mats alongside each other—must've noticed Ernestine's subdued energy too. The ponytail woman asked if Ernestine was feeling under the weather.

"It's a low-energy day," said Ernestine. "We all have them! That's your body saying: *Pamper me! Baby me!*" She sipped her yellow muck. "So we're going to have a gentle, low-key practice today."

Someone else asked where Ernestine's boyfriend was today. No one felt shy about asking these kinds of questions because Ernestine overshared as a matter of course. She had told them about her ex-husband's erectile dysfunction and her daughter's sexual precociousness and the incontinence issues she'd had to deal with after the daughter's birth. "I'm the queen of TMI!" Ernestine would declare. But, this being a low-energy day, she merely waved her hand. "He's at his cabin this weekend." Helen knew that the boyfriend's cabin three hours outside the city was not a place he just went to unwind and be in nature every once in a while—some middle-class urbanite's cabin. The boyfriend had built the cabin himself. He lived in it full-time—or had done until he met Ernestine.

"It's all part of self-care," Ernestine explained with respect to the missing boyfriend. "Sometimes you need a little space." She raised the jar, toasting them like she was hoisting a pint of Guinness, then shoved it against the wall, causing the muck within to slosh. "You need 'me time'," she continued, scratching the side of her neck. "To focus inward." That was when Helen noticed the large patch of flaky red skin creeping up from Ernestine's collarbone—the scratching had caused it to glow brighter.

*

Writing poetry was also about focusing inward, which was maybe why Helen had done so little of it over the last couple of years. She joked about that during her calls with Nicola, which, now that classes had resumed, took place on Wednesday afternoons, when Helen didn't have to teach. But Nicola, it turned out, had no patience for such jokes.

"Helen, I hate it when women beat up on themselves."

"Oh, I'm just kidding," said Helen.

"I used to be self-deprecating all the time," said Nicola. "I thought it made me cute and relatable. I'd say, *Oh I'm such an idiot. Oh I don't know what I'm talking about.* And then I started to notice that no one was arguing with me. They'd just smile and nod as if to say, *Yup—assumption confirmed.*"

Helen started to protest that she wasn't being self-deprecating, exactly, she was just admitting to a certain fearfulness that had begun to make sitting down and thinking about anything that wasn't right in front of her—exams to be marked, grades to be submitted, taxes to be filed—feel like too much of a heavy lift. It wasn't self-deprecation, she wanted to explain, it was self-care. It was *letting go,* like Ernestine was always encouraging her to do, be it bad thoughts or muscle tension. Nicola thought Helen had been berating herself for not writing poetry anymore, but really Helen was just acknowledging that she didn't want to.

Because imagine being Helen as she was back then, writing the poems that made up her second collection—just sitting around wallowing in all that contemplation. *Now let's think about dying. Let's think about the War on Terror and the Highway of Tears and the serial killer with the pig farm. Let's think about cruelty and indifference and the essential impossibility of connecting meaningfully with another human being. Let's spend the prime of our lives doing that.*

Helen didn't get around to saying any of this, however, because Nicola was now narrating a memory of some acting teacher who used to SCREAM at Nicola whenever she gave any indication of feminine self-effacement.

"She'd SCREAM at me if I cast my eyes downward, and she'd SCREAM at me if I smiled too much, and she'd SCREAM at me if I giggled nervously, and you can imagine I was doing a hell of a lot of nervous giggling around that lady."

"What would she say?" asked Helen.

"She didn't say anything, she screamed."

"She'd just scream in your face?"

"Yes," said Nicola. "She would scream in my face."

Helen always felt relieved when Nicola wanted to talk about something other than her own poetry. But she always came back around to the poems, speaking of some as if they were already written and of others as if they were still in her head. Helen couldn't always tell which was the case, she only knew that Nicola talked about them incessantly but still hadn't sent Helen anything to read. The best part of the calls was when one of Nicola's long, grim tangents would unexpectedly feature a twinkling glint of Hollywood lore. Once, Nicola had been talking about losing one of her best friends to AIDS, rushing to his bedside but not being allowed to see him and having to comfort his boyfriend outside the hospital because the boyfriend wasn't allowed to see him either, and the boyfriend ended up killing himself shortly after Nicola's friend had died. The call had strayed over the two-hour mark again, and Helen was lying on the floor of her kitchen watching the patch of sunlight make its slow diagonal crawl across the wall when suddenly Nicola pivoted and started griping about a man she happened to be sleeping with during that period, an Oscar-winning director, someone whose films Helen had seen. Helen sat up, electrified, and Nicola treated her to a twenty-minute exposé of the famous director's multi-layered sexual dysfunction and emotional impairment.

Helen kept hoping something like that would happen again, but the aspects of Nicola's life that were most interesting to Helen seemed least interesting to Nicola. "I have nobody else to talk to about this stuff," she'd say as she wrapped up an anecdote about a conflict with the nurses at her mother's long-term care home. They had apparently taken Nicola's mother's call button away because she pressed it incessantly. So Nicola kept finding her mother, in this posh institution for which Nicola had paid through the nose, in various states of neglect—soiled or thirsty, her skin gouged from where she had scratched herself with nails that hadn't been trimmed or even cleaned. One time, Nicola arrived and her mother casually handed her a turd like it was a keepsake pebble from the beach.

"You're the only one who wants to hear about it," she told Helen.

*

Helen arrived for bodywork again, and they began, as they always did, with Helen standing, facing Ernestine, a few feet of distance between them, so that Ernestine could assess Helen's body.

"You're all out of whack," she said after a moment. "It's like someone sort of picked you up off the ground by your right shoulder and kind of dangled and shook you for a bit, and now the right half of your body is higher than your left."

Helen lay down on her stomach, and Ernestine lightly placed her hands on Helen's shoulders.

"Aw!" Ernestine exclaimed, as though someone had let her down.

"Oh no," said Helen. "What did I do now?" She chuckled as Ernestine pushed more firmly on her shoulders and leaned over to whisper.

"Helen, you didn't do anything wrong. You know that, right?"

Helen stopped chuckling because a lump had manifested in her throat.

"You're feeling low today. You've got a lot on you. Sometimes we stop being in tune with our bodies. Our brain decides it doesn't need that connection, that it can just operate independently. And the brain sort of leaves the body behind—and then everything falls apart!"

Helen started to relax, and the lump lessened.

"You're someone who is very in her head," said Ernestine, who was now sort of wobbling Helen's hamstrings.

"Yeah. Not great in here," said Helen.

"Especially today," murmured Ernestine.

How did Ernestine know? Helen hadn't arrived red-eyed or blowing her nose, hadn't been dragging her feet. Helen, as far as she knew, was the same as always—except for, apparently, her body being wildly out of alignment. But Helen's younger sister, Wendy, had called the night before, not long after a marathon call with Nicola. And Helen knew she had to take the call this time. Wendy was angry Helen had not visited over the summer. And she'd been emailing all month about wanting to speak on the phone and making it clear what she wanted to discuss—that their father had started peeing in his chair and was refusing to talk about it.

At first Helen told herself, in the name of self-care, that she should delay this conversation, because it felt big and she had her hands full with her job and this absorbing new project working on poetry with famous movie star Nicola Rasmussen. But then the calls with Nicola started hitting Helen in the same way her sister's emails were hitting her, like a hard finger poking her in the windpipe—a thing her ex used to do when poking her in the shoulder didn't do the job. The calls with Nicola started to feel like counterparts to Wendy's emails, somehow, as if Nicola and Wendy, from their opposite poles of Helen's life, were in touch, in cahoots, working together to nudge Helen toward the same pit.

On the phone, Wendy told Helen that their father would silently get up, change his pants, put some towels down in the chair when he returned, and sit back down. It was more domestic labour than he had ever performed in his life and the total extent of his acknowledgement of what was going on. "Remember," said Wendy to Helen, "when you went off to school? And I joked how my greatest nightmare was being left behind to look after Mom and Dad when they got old and senile?"

"Yes," said Helen.

"Well, guess fucking what?" said Wendy.

"How is Mom?" Helen had asked after a moment.

"Mom," said Wendy, "is a whole other conversation."

"Can I suggest an exercise for you, Helen?" said Ernestine, after Helen had dressed and was lacing up her shoes. Helen braced herself, because Ernestine's exercises mostly required holding her body in unnatural positions for excruciating amounts of time.

But, instead, Ernestine asked, "Do you ever write?"

Helen secured her shoelace with a double knot and straightened up. "Do I *write?*"

"Like, journalling," said Ernestine. "Or inspirational thoughts? Or poetry?"

"Sometimes," said Helen.

"It can be so therapeutic," said Ernestine. "I was feeling anxious the other day. And I said: *I'm just going to write down all the things that are making me anxious!* And you wouldn't believe how open my hips felt afterwards. So I'm going to share with you what I did. Try writing, like, a dialogue. Get your favourite pen and some nice paper—I have paper that smells like strawberries. And first, you write what's bothering you, whatever's at the heart of your anxiety. Just get it all down on your nice paper. Then you reply to yourself as love."

"I reply as what?"

"As love. Just love. If love was a person, what would love say? How would love respond to you?"

Helen stood a moment. "Okay," she said.

*

HELEN:

I think I have systematically shut myself off from all the people I've ever cared about, and anyone I might have the potential to care about, because I would rather not feel pain. I've tried pain voluntarily the way you watch horror movies to try out fear but then when you feel actual fear, you're like, Yikes, no thank you, and that is how it's been re: pain, both psychic and physical. When I say I tried pain voluntarily, what I mean is I feel like I have courted it somehow in my writing when I was younger, and even though at the time I thought I was doing the MOST IMPORTANT AND MEANINGFUL THING IN THE WORLD, *now I think that maybe I was being ignorant and careless, like a teenager who drinks and drives because she believes she is immortal. And then I think what if the thing I have devoted my adult life and a good portion of my youth to actually amounts to a kind of pathetic dabbling, what if it wasn't daring or bravely artistic at all but yet another way of shutting myself off from people while telling myself I'm very busy doing the* MOST IMPORTANT AND MEANINGFUL THING IN THE WORLD? *And instead of embracing actual relationships and human feelings, I was embracing bullshit chimeras and counterfeit grief without realizing I didn't have to bother because the real thing was just around the corner?*

LOVE: *Wow.*

Helen looked at the page. She put her pen down, shook the cramp out of her hand, and picked the pen up again.

But that was all that Love could think to say.

*

September passed, and Nicola emailed to say she was coming to town at the end of October. She had a friend who was acting in a one-man show, and she was going to get tickets and buy Helen dinner and then take her to the play.

For the first time, Helen wished she had told someone about what she'd been doing all these months—so that she could now announce that Nicola Rasmussen was taking her to dinner and a show without sounding unhinged. Nicola's fame was of the sort that caused people to unravel—to imagine she was their antagonist, or their lover, or that she was sending them coded messages in her movies. It was literally a maddening level of fame.

Helen had a game plan for the meeting. She would insist that Nicola finally show Helen some of her poems. It had been months of Wednesday phone calls, and at the end of each call Nicola would say, *I'll send you something by the weekend,* and she never did. At one point, midway through one of Nicola's long, awful memories of her mother, Helen blurted: "I would really encourage you to get this down on paper. I mean, if this is the stuff you really want to write about. But you know what? It's okay if it's not."

Nicola seemed blindsided. "Of course it's what I want to write. Why else would I be here?"

"It just seems like a fraught topic for you," said Helen. "You know, writing doesn't always have to be therapy."

"Oh, I've done therapy, believe me," said Nicola.

"But that's not what your work has to be, is what I'm saying," said Helen.

Nicola paused, which was unusual. She hardly ever paused. "This is my subject matter," she insisted. "It's painful. But I have to confront it."

"But what if you let go of that?" Helen was aware on some level that these words would be taken as heresy. But they were almost into hour three of this particular call, she was starving, and she had nothing in the house. She had planned to order noodles, and now noodles, glistening with soy sauce and sesame oil, were all she could think about. "Writing can be play," she ventured, thinking about noodles. "Really, it is play. The idea that it's anything more...maybe that's what—"

"Poetry is the most serious thing in the world to me," Nicola said in the booming stage actor's voice she hauled out whenever she felt that Helen needed correcting. "*Deadly* serious." The words travelled from Nicola's diaphragm into Helen's ear and silenced her—silenced her because they'd made her angry.

If it's so serious, she thought, *why don't you try actually writing some?*

But, ever since childhood, words would desert Helen when she got angry—if she felt any kind of strong emotion, really.

*

It was a sunny and beautiful autumn day, but it stopped feeling that way once Ernestine arrived. She was wearing a slouchy pale-pink top that read *LOVE & LIGHT*. She also wore her knitted cap with the teddy bear ears and kept it on as she unrolled her mat at the front of the room. But it wasn't cold in the studio, and it wasn't a cold day outside either.

"Hi," said Ernestine, without making eye contact with anyone. Usually, she swept her beaming gaze around the room the moment she arrived.

She plopped down on her mat and adjusted her body into a cross-legged position. Helen was bothered by her posture. Ernestine looked off-kilter today—one of her knees sat slightly higher than the other. Then again, Helen wasn't one to talk—she was sitting with all her weight on one butt cheek because the opposite hip was killing her. Normally, Ernestine would notice something like that and ask her about it—maybe run and get Helen a bolster from the shelf in the corner.

Everyone watched Ernestine in silence. She sighed. She'd brought her backpack to the mat with her and now unzipped and started rifling through it. "Some mornings are easier than others, guys," she said into the backpack.

A couple of women said quietly how true that was.

Ernestine pulled out a tube of something and then yanked off her *LOVE & LIGHT* sweatshirt. The blotch of red that Helen had previously noticed on Ernestine's neck had crept toward the opposite collarbone and was encroaching onto her chest.

The woman with the black ponytail gasped.

"It's eczema," Ernestine told them. "Kind of out of control right now. It happens when I'm under stress."

She began to slather lotion from the tube onto her blotches. There were blotches on her arms and elbows too, and Helen saw, as Ernestine rubbed her hands together, that her fingers looked as if they had been dipped in boiling water.

"We don't have to do this," Helen heard herself saying. Everyone turned to her. Helen knew she had spoken too loud for a yoga studio—she had spoken like an affronted Nicola, from her diaphragm. Ernestine looked at Helen, scratched her neck, then realized what she was doing and made herself stop.

"We could all just take it easy today," said Helen. A few women on nearby mats began to nod. "We could just—lie back. Do corpse pose."

"Oh Helen," said Ernestine. "If I lie back now, I might never get up again."

She tried to laugh—a grinding, squeaky sound, like a rusted bike chain.

*

Helen sat in the hotel restaurant for twenty minutes as the waiter kept returning to smile and fill up her water glass. Finally, she got a text from Nicola: *Where are you? I thought you were here?*

I am here, wrote Helen. *Are you here?*

Yes, I'm here!

I can't see you. Where are you?

In the corner by the fake fireplace.

Helen looked around. There was no fake fireplace. She texted this to Nicola, wondering if her nerves and general apprehension had sent her into some kind of fugue state. They had confirmed it was the right hotel, in the right part of town. So it was here or nowhere. But maybe it was nowhere. Maybe, thought Helen, the last few months had been an elaborate catfish and her initial assumption, that a disgruntled student was playing a prank on her, had been correct all along. It was an apprehension that had never quite gone away during their weeks together on the phone.

Or what if Helen was, in fact, the thing she'd been worried people would assume of her if she ever mentioned Nicola? One of the maddened? That almost seemed more likely to Helen now, as she sat alone, with the waiter shooting her pitying smiles every time he passed her table. What if Helen had beheld Nicola's face in some old movie on late night TV last spring and something about her glossy early nineties perfection had caused Helen to lose her grip?

In the basement, texted Nicola.

At the bottom of the stairs was the entrance to a pub called the Bulldog, and Nicola had found herself a secluded and fireplace-adjacent corner within. The gas fireplace generated real, if overly uniform, flames. Flames like soldiers—side by side, identical, obedient to the twisting of a knob. Nicola was twisting that knob as Helen sat down, making the flames swell then shrink.

"They told me I could fiddle with the fireplace as much as I want," she told Helen. "I'm always too hot or too cold."

They sat and smiled at each other. Helen realized she was starving. "I'm so hungry," she told Nicola. They ordered food.

It was difficult to sit across from Nicola and not think about the way she looked. Helen couldn't imagine it as anything but an inconvenience. How it must have been in the way her whole life, tripping Nicola up, like having one leg longer than the other. They chatted about the city as they ate—Nicola had lived here in her twenties—and then the school where Helen taught—Nicola had attended a year of an undergraduate program in drama before realizing the best thing she could do for her acting career was to leave Canada as soon as was humanly possible. Helen leaned forward, thinking this comment might lead into a few glamorous stories of twentysomething Nicola taking Hollywood by storm, but instead Nicola started talking about a sound poet she'd met the following year in New York who didn't wash as a rule and never wrote anything down and also refused to allow anyone to make audio or video recordings of his work. He always said he wanted to appear and then disappear without leaving a trace, which Nicola said was ironic, because you could go into a room he'd exited hours ago and still smell him there. Nicola said she had followed him around Berlin for the better part of a year, but the sound poet was elusive—"That was his whole thing! In art and life! Being elusive." So she never really got anywhere with him. On the upside, she did end up developing a deep appreciation for the city and its arts scene at the time.

A waiter in a Union Jack waistcoat noiselessly removed their plates as Nicola plunged into a rhapsodic memory of Berlin in the late eighties. But Helen had made a deal with herself that she would say what she planned to say as soon as they were finished eating. "At this point," she interrupted, "I'd really love to see some of your work."

"At this point?" repeated Nicola. "You mean right now?"

"No, no," said Helen. "I just mean—soon."

"Of course," said Nicola. "I'm planning to send you something early next week."

"Okay," said Helen. "Then maybe we should postpone our next call until after I've taken a look?"

Nicola paused. She looked at her the way Ernestine had looked at her when Helen suggested they all just lie back in corpse pose for the duration of their ninety-minute yoga class.

"But why would we do that? I find our calls so fruitful."

"Because I feel like we're not really getting anywhere," said Helen.

Nicola sat back in her chair but held Helen's eye. "Well," she said, "I'm actually glad to hear you say that."

"You are?"

"Yes. And I'm wondering why you think that is."

"Because," said Helen, "you won't show me anything."

"But why is that, Helen?"

Helen frowned.

"For months you've been listening to me bare my soul," said Nicola. "I've told you all about my heartbreak with my mother, what I went through with my family…I don't think there's anything about me you don't know at this point."

Helen was nodding. Was Nicola commiserating with her? "I know!" she said.

"And so," said Nicola, "why aren't we at a place where I can trust you yet?"

Helen sat blinking. Nicola explained that a thirty-year acting career allowed a person to develop a razor-sharp intuition for how others are feeling. She was especially good, she said, at intuiting "resistance."

It seemed like an Ernestine thing to say. *I'm feeling some resistance,* she'd whisper, wobbling a knuckle into a knot of fascia. *Breathe through it, Helen.*

"But the more I open myself up to you," said Nicola, "the more you seem to close yourself off."

Helen could feel the language centres of her brain beginning to flicker, like a modem about to go offline. "I sat there," she said at last. "On the phone with you. For months. Listening."

"And yet I've somehow never felt that you were *with me,*" said Nicola. "Why is that, Helen?"

*

An early cold snap had occurred, and the treatment room was freezing. Even though Ernestine always began each session by swathing her in a heated sheet, Helen found it impossible to relax. The warmth of the sheet couldn't penetrate the morning chill.

"Sorry, Helen," said Ernestine. "I can't use a space heater in here because I've already got one running in the studio space for my next class. If I use two at once, it blows the fuse."

Ernestine worked on Helen in silence for a while. She was wearing her hat with the teddy bear ears again, and now Helen knew why she had barely taken it off in the last few weeks. She'd yanked it off briefly to scratch her head not long after Helen arrived, and Helen had seen a patch of bare scalp.

After several minutes of silent, chilly bodywork—during which, every time Ernestine manoeuvred one of Helen's limbs out from underneath the sheet, she would shiver—Helen asked Ernestine how things were going.

"Well, I've finally had a diagnosis from *Doctor Gerry*," she said. "Which I think explains why I've been feeling so poorly the past couple of months."

Ernestine had said "Doctor Gerry" with emphasis, as if Helen would know who he, or she, was.

"Toxins," she continued. "They're in everything. Nickel, in particular. Oh my gosh. You wouldn't believe how bad nickel is for you."

"Is nickel in a lot of stuff?"

"So much stuff…" Ernestine murmured. She fell silent for a moment as she shifted Helen's hips to one side, extended her top leg, and started moving it up and down like a lever. "Anyway," she resumed. "Gerry has me on a treatment program now."

A moment later, Ernestine stopped in the middle of levering Helen's leg. She straightened and sighed. "Are we ever going to fix this hip of yours, Helen?"

The truth was, Helen was planning on going back to physio. She'd obtained a doctor's prescription so that her insurance would cover it and had vowed that this time she would do the exercises they gave her every day, no matter how tedious and agonizing. Right now, however, it seemed important for Helen to reassure Ernestine in the sort of way Ernestine would respond to.

"I just think we have to have faith," said Helen. "And keep a positive outlook. And be, you know, open."

"You're so right," said Ernestine, resuming. "You're so wise and even-keeled, Helen. I always get this, like, calm vibe from you. Some days you get loaded down with stuff, sure—we all get loaded down. Oh boy, do I ever. But with you, nothing penetrates too deep."

When Ernestine left her to get dressed, Helen threw aside the sheet, and her skin cinched tight with goosebumps. She couldn't believe Ernestine hadn't fixed the furnace. And now, apparently, the furnace guy was "booked up for months." There was no way Helen could keep doing this. And there was no way she would spend another winter doing yoga in fingerless gloves and a puffer jacket.

*

It hadn't occurred to Helen to ask what the play was when Nicola invited her. She only knew it was a one-man show starring an old friend of Nicola's, some elderly theatre stalwart whom Helen had never heard of. When they got to the venue, however, she saw it was going to be Beckett. The atmosphere between her and Nicola was already not good, they'd barely spoken during the short walk to the theatre, and now dread settled between Helen's eyes like a headache. She should have, she realized, anticipated this. Every Beckett play she'd ever sat through had felt to Helen like being crouched inside someone else's bad dream, and what had her hours on the phone with Nicola been like if not that? A filthy, ancient man sat in his chaotic study, listening to recordings of himself. Every once in a while, he'd lurch centre stage and have a banana, standing completely still with the banana sticking out of his mouth for what felt like an eternity, before he resumed lurching around and ate it. Something about the fact that he did this more than once panicked and infuriated Helen, made her want to shout: *Are you kidding me with the fucking banana again?* She really did have a headache now. She imagined walking out. She wondered if that might be the best and easiest way to bring this whole Nicola Rasmussen interlude to a close. Would she ever hear from Nicola again? Would assistant Dana with the impeccable email etiquette reach out the following week to confirm their Wednesday time, as she had done without fail every Monday since the spring?

Instead, she absented herself by focusing on the tape recorder as the old man played and rewound the audio. He was using an ancient reel-to-reel machine like the one Helen's father had brought home in the seventies. One of the first recordings Helen's parents made was of her mother saying, "Jesus Christ, how much did that cost, Ray?" It had been high-tech and extravagant—just the kind of gadget her father always liked. The very next recording they made was of Helen, their first-born. Helen the toddler had discovered singing right around that time, and it was all she wanted to do. When she got a little older, one of her favourite things was to ask her parents to haul out the massive tape recorder and play the tapes of her singing as a toddler. She'd sit listening to her toddler self warbling away, getting the words wrong, making up gibberish to the tune of "Big Rock Candy Mountain." Older-child Helen would listen to younger-child Helen, feeling wise and affectionate and superior. The funniest thing was that sometimes toddler Helen would exclaim: *"I want the girl to sing it now! I want to hear the girl!"* Which meant she wanted her mother to rewind the tape so that toddler Helen could listen to herself. Sometimes, she even asked to hear "the girl" sing a song before Helen herself had sung it. Eventually, her mother had to stop everything to explain to Helen that she, Helen, was the singer on the tape. Of course, this made no sense to the toddler, the two-Helen thing, but she just paused and then launched into another song. Older-child Helen had loved that about the toddler, that she'd decided, in that pause, she didn't care. The tape recorder was uncanny and miraculous—so what? So was everything in childhood. So what if there were two of her now—the one who sang in the machine and the one who sat outside and listened?

Catriona Wright

///////////////////

MAKING FACES

Amanda learned by watching YouTube tutorials of young women sitting in their pastel bedrooms, their faces bright and glowing, as they wielded their arsenals of beautifying implements. The palettes with their circles of shimmer, satin, matte powders. Fluffy brushes, slanted brushes, stiff bristled. Sponges and liquid liners. She ordered her own materials and practised in the bathroom mirror—the bathroom was the only room in the apartment that locked—her laptop balanced on the edge of the tub. She paused the videos, listened, tried again. She took selfies before destroying her artistry with pre-moistened wipes. She repeated the secret vocabulary to herself like a spell: buttery, blendable, crease, waterline, fall out. Every evening, for five minutes, she was beautiful.

*

Nobody had warned her a miscarriage could mean contractions, so much blood, days of pain. She knew, in a vague, incredulous way, that miscarriages were common, but after what she went through it seemed impossible. All these women, everywhere, on buses, at the gym, laughing in the grocery store, all these women cooking and cleaning and fucking, all carrying the memory of their creations emptying out of them. Had they also been compelled to touch the greyish flesh, the clots of blood, looking for a face? For months afterward, she stopped sleeping, purple bags beneath her eyes. She learned to erase these shadows with concealer then re-create them, sculpted and refined, right-side-up.

A few times, maybe three, she'd almost sent Alex a photo of herself done up with a full face, hoping he'd be intrigued enough to reply. That one time with the emerald shimmer, the dramatic cat-eye swoop of liner, the feathery lashes, that was the time she'd come closest. But in the end she deleted it. She didn't want to tamper with their time together, which she imagined existed in his mind as a pale-pink room, clean, uncluttered, girlish. Surely, in his version, blood never streamed down the walls.

*

The first time Alex took Amanda to his condo, she marvelled at its cleanliness. The white walls and huge windows and framed jazz concert posters seemed so adult and expensive. The sleek black leather couch, the marble kitchen island, the well-groomed monstera plant in a concrete pot. It looked staged, right out of a magazine, so unlike her great-aunt Gertrude's apartment where every surface was covered in books or papers or old copies of the *New Yorker,* where dust clouded the patterns in the Persian rugs, where the houseplants all had sinister personalities, the branches jutting out to snag sweaters, the leaves oozing toxic sap.

"What do you think?" Alex asked. "I just finished decorating. I was going for the minimalist thing."

"It's so organized," Amanda said. "But in a non-threatening way."

Alex laughed. "Like me, right?"

Amanda nodded, blushing. It was true she'd never met anyone like Alex, so self-assured and driven yet somehow also naive. One night, her sister, Eileen, high on something, had stolen Amanda's phone and swiped right on his profile. When he responded with "Are you my missing semicolon?" Eileen quipped back, "Depends. How big is your dangling modifier?" Eileen must have assumed, based on the pickup line, that he was a copy editor like Amanda, but after some confusion he explained it was a programming joke. "Semicolons are ever-present in code. They provide structure and clarity, like micro-commitments."

Eileen, bored, handed the phone back to Amanda. "Another tech bro."

Amanda agreed, pretending to be disgusted, and without telling Eileen or anyone else, set up a time to meet him.

He'd spent their entire date enthusing about his start-up, explaining the intricacies of interface design, how he wanted to help people interact with the world in intuitive ways, open them up to possibilities. He'd asked her questions about her career aspirations, which she struggled to answer, redirecting the conversation back to him. She knew her friends would have rolled their eyes—only late capitalist apologists believed in "careers"—but Amanda found his optimism refreshing, if alien.

When Alex said, "Television," in his loud, firm voice, a slit opened in the ceiling and a flat screen descended. Later, when he said, "Bedroom," she felt similarly compelled to obey. She followed him, delighted by the upholstered headboard and heap of plump pillows. From his side table, he produced a smooth, sage-coloured silicone oblong and clicked on an invisible button.

It purred reassuringly, promising a tidy orgasm. That first night it was the only thing that touched her.

*

Eileen knocked on the bathroom door.

"Are you almost done masturbating? I need to piss."

"One minute." Amanda tapped the brush on the edge of the sink to dislodge excess product. A touch of burgundy on the outer lids to give her autumnal look extra dimension.

Eileen rattled the handle.

"One minute." Left eye complete, she turned her attention to her right.

Louder, more insistent knocks. Stomping feet. "I can feel a UTI coming on."

"Fine." Amanda opened the door. Eileen rushed in, her pants already down, sat on the toilet, and, with a satisfied sigh, let out a gushing rush of urine.

The sisters had been living together for two years, ever since their great-aunt Gertrude passed away and left them her apartment. There were still traces of Gertrude everywhere. The medicine cabinet overflowed with expired heart medication, hotel-sized shampoos and conditioners, rose-shaped soaps. On the counter, a crystal perfume bottle, the fragrance now a musty layer of amber gel at the bottom, the tasselled spray bulb too stiff to squeeze.

Amanda, hoping Eileen wouldn't notice her face, hastily gathered her materials, looking away.

No such luck.

"What's with your face?" Eileen said, wiping herself. Their mother rarely wore makeup, at most a hint of lipstick at a wedding or a dab of concealer for a particularly belligerent zit. "You know those companies are evil, right? Animal testing, toxins, palm oil harvesting, and rainforest deforestation . . ." She zipped up her pants and swayed toward the sink. She was either coming up or coming down.

"I know," Amanda said, not wanting to hear it. "These brands are sustainable, though."

"Sustainable?" Eileen washed her hands, shaking her head and laughing. "What a crock of greenwashing bullshit. You're seriously stupider than I thought if you believe that."

Amanda needed to shift the focus of the conversation if she wanted to avoid another fight. "You used to wear makeup, back when you worked at the firm."

With no clean towels available, Eileen wiped her hands on the back of her pants.

"I only wore it because my boss was a misogynistic patriarchal trust fund asshole who said it was unprofessional not to. How about a little blush? A little mascara? And I was too brainwashed to argue. I went straight to the cosmetics counter after work and they covered me in slime. Did I tell you how he always sat me with the secretaries and paralegals at the Christmas gala?"

"Tell me again," Amanda said, gently leading Eileen out of the washroom, toward the couch in the living room.

*

The sisters took turns sleeping on the large green couch, which was more comfortable and forgiving than Gertrude's lumpy bed with its paisley sheets and stained yellow skirt. It was the preferred location for naps and blackouts. Months ago, in the moments after Amanda had peed on a stick and seen the two blue lines—her old life and her new one side by side—she'd lain down on that couch, sinking into the cushions, clutching her stomach, panicking. Her body hadn't felt any different. Her breasts weren't swollen and she didn't feel nauseated and she definitely wasn't glowing. There must be some mistake.

Alex had broken up with her so kindly and efficiently she'd only realized what happened hours later, walking home from his condo, dazed. The whole relationship felt like a pleasant misunderstanding, destined to be corrected eventually, yet here it remained in the form of two blue lines. Had she ever loved him? It didn't matter. He didn't have time for a baby because he was too busy making the internet feel familiar.

Could she raise a baby on her own? She'd been accused all her life of being unemotional and secretive—surely those were the worst possible traits a mother could possess. And she didn't experience pangs of maternal longing when she saw onesies with woodland animal prints. Plastic in the ocean, deforestation, pandemics, widening inequality, so many reasons not to burden someone else with existing. The planet was already full. Besides, Gertrude's apartment was no place for a baby. A death trap of rickety bookcases and choking-hazard tchotchkes, lead paint and leaks, haunted by two spinsters, three if you counted Great-Aunt Gertrude.

She lay there for a long time, watching the sun set through the blinds, slashes of orange and pink illuminating the dust, reflecting off the glass cabinet doors. Two blue lines. Parallel. A proofreading mark. Or else a lane, narrowing her path. Giving her a new direction.

*

After Eileen had tired herself out ranting about her vile former boss and fallen asleep on the couch, Amanda returned to the bathroom to finish her look. A pop of yellow in the inner corners of her eyes and a sweep of muted terracotta on her cheekbones. She looked like a harvest spirit, a promise of lush abundance, until she blinked and turned into a scarecrow, a lifeless decoy drooping amid warted squash, a crow unstitching her smile.

What did others see when they looked at her? For the first time in months she logged on to Reddit—she'd opened an account for lurking on miscarriage subreddits but never actually posted—and clicked through the makeup options until she found TodaysFace. She took a dozen photos from different angles, uploaded the one that made her look thin and confident, and waited. Moments later, someone named *trashpanda* wrote *Obsessed with these fall vibes and your eyebrows. What palette did you use?*

After that, Amanda devoted herself to developing her skills. On breaks from copy-editing reports, she read reviews of the latest cosmetic releases and articles about trends. She watched hours of YouTube tutorials. She ordered specialized products. Setting sprays, primers, loose pigments, mixing mediums. Her hand got steadier and her winged liner more aerodynamic.

She posted selfies every few days, waiting, excited and anxious, for people to upvote or downvote or comment. "Love the blending, girl!" said *sapphireprincess* and "What do you use on your skin? Luminous," said *makeupaddict*. Each compliment calmed her, if only for a moment, assuring her she wasn't deluded or alone. There were other women who spent hours scrutinizing their faces in the mirror, refining their technique, who encouraged each other to achieve their goals, recommending the perfect bronze eyeshadow to complete a halo eye or offering tips on how to achieve a dewy glow. She wondered if any of them actually wore makeup outside or if, like her, they protected these faces for people who could understand them.

*

When Amanda found out that Great-Aunt Gertrude had left them the apartment in her will, she'd immediately felt guilty. For years, Amanda had been scared of ending up like her. She hated when her mother said she had Gertrude's eyes or ears or smile. In family lore, Gertrude served the role of cautionary tale, living alone in the big city, barely scraping by. Apparently she'd had a brief, disastrous marriage to a successful painter in her youth, and after years of trying to paint herself, she'd accepted an administrative position at a nearby design college. No one ever explicitly told Amanda that Gertrude's life was sad, but every mention of her was suffused with pity.

For Christmas, Gertrude gave the sisters age-inappropriate gifts, like *The Diary of Anaïs Nin* or a partially used anti-aging skin cream. She was outspoken and prickly and had strong political convictions. When she was drunk, which was often, she would lecture them about the unacknowledged brilliance of female artists they'd never heard of. It was hard to believe that Gertrude was their grandmother's sister. Francine, their sweet, quietly competent, no-nonsense grandmother, the expert baker and de-escalator of family conflicts, who taught them how to make the world's flakiest pie crust and how to get period stains out of underwear.

Their whole family would visit Gertrude once or twice a year. She would insist she was going to cook some outrageous feast, often involving quail, even inquiring about food allergies and preferences, only to end up ordering from Swiss Chalet. Amanda and Eileen would be enlisted to clean the greasy puddles of auburn sauce off the chipped dishes while the adults laughed and argued in the living room. During this ritual, Eileen would whisper made-up stories about Gertrude. She was a thousand years old. She astral-projected into former lovers' bedrooms and sucked their life force out of them (Eileen added a spooky half whistle as a sound effect). If you glanced at her quickly, before she realized it, there was only a smooth blankness where a face should be.

*

One morning Amanda's phone wouldn't unlock. *No face detected,* it said. Then: *Face not a match.* Probably some tweak to the facial recognition software. She had to use her password instead. She image-searched "baby" and scrolled through the chubby, wide-eyed, open-mouthed pictures. Babies on their tummies. Babies gazing into their mother's eyes. Babies strapped to fathers. Babies yawning, crying, grabbing their toes. After clicking on a thumbnail of a particularly cute one—cheeks covered in icing and sprinkles, chubby fingers clutching a silver cupcake wrapper—she somehow found herself on a web page called Baby Face Predictor, where you could upload a photo of yourself and a partner—there were a variety of stock celebrity photos to choose from—to see what the algorithm thought your child would look like.

Without thinking, she uploaded a bare-faced picture of herself and scrolled through her gallery for one of Alex. There he was, smiling at her over his shoulder while he prepared food on his stove, probably a keto cauliflower stir-fry from a meal kit. She chose "Boy" from the options, watched the loading wheel spin, and waited, at once expectant and ashamed by her expectations. It was a game an engineer had probably whipped up on a lunch break. The baby appeared onscreen, smiling, a round, expressive nose (Alex's), thin lips (hers), squinting blue eyes (Alex's), straight black hair (neither of theirs). She stared at him for a long time, indulging in the fantasy of the baby's soft skin and bunched-up knees, until Eileen's wheezing snores wrenched her back to reality. She shouldn't be doing this to herself, it wasn't healthy or helpful. She clicked on the Tinder app icon, a stylized flame.

*

When she stepped into her date's condo, she paused, confused. There must be some mistake. This was Alex's condo, the same white walls and windows, the clean lines and kitchen island. After a moment, she detected the deviations—as though she was playing one of those "spot the difference" children's games. The posters were for microbreweries, not jazz concerts. The leather on the couch was caramel-coloured, not black. The monstera plant was a fern, possibly fake.

"Great place," Amanda said. "Very minimal."

"Thanks," Evan said. "I've been getting into interior design lately. I'm saving up for an Eames chair."

"Cool," Amanda said. Her body conveyed her smoothly to the couch.

Evan made her a Manhattan with expensive maraschino cherries, their glossy red skin so dark, almost black, clots at the bottom of her glass. She popped one into her mouth, the thick syrup coating her tongue. She felt at ease, relaxed, as though she'd performed this date so many times she'd memorized the moves. Evan handed her another drink, stronger this time, while summarizing an article he'd read about artificial intelligence, the uncanny valley, how people look for faces everywhere.

He wasn't as smart as Alex or as attractive. His eyes were too far apart. She got out her phone and checked for comments on her latest post, a departure for her, green-and-gold eyes with purple ombré lips. Nothing yet. Should she delete it? She guiltily glanced up to see if he'd noticed her staring at her phone, but he seemed content, and slightly drunk.

"Engineers want to make robots that look human but not too human, you know?" he said.

Without answering, she finished her drink and he handed her another.

"Television," she commanded at the ceiling. "Television."

"I don't have one," Evan said, apparently unfazed by her outburst. "We could watch Netflix on my laptop."

Amanda giggled, now thoroughly tipsy. She knew she wouldn't see Evan again, there'd be no point, and they didn't have any friends in common, so she decided to tell him. It would be like yelling it into a hole in the ground. Or telling it to an Alex alternate.

"I had a miscarriage." Her self-assurance vanished. Waves of pain in her lower back and thighs, sticky fluid dribbling then gushing, a cold toilet seat, thinking it was over and hobbling to the bed, only for the cramping to return, blood and tissue trailing behind her as she rushed back to the bathroom. Her voice wavered, cracked. "Six months ago."

Evan inched closer to her, wrapping his arms around her, stroking her hair. He smelled like baby powder and musk. "We can take it slow."

"Thank you." Amanda sank into his arms, overcome by an unexpected surge of relief, her eyes wet with tears, her body shaking. Maybe not every messy, bleeding thing needed to be hidden under the floorboards.

"And don't worry," Evan said. "A quarter of pregnancies end in miscarriage."

Amanda stiffened, pulling away.

"My sister told me that," he continued, oblivious. "She had three and now she has a healthy baby. You'll be a great mom one day."

Amanda nodded, her eyelids heavy. Two blue lines, bars trapping her inside, alone. "I'm going to call a Lyft."

*

Halfway up the flight of stairs, she heard it. Carole King's heart-broken nasal crooning accompanied by Eileen's off-key butchering of the lyrics and the thumps and scrapes of furniture being moved. When she opened the door, she was greeted by a swarm of dust and noise. She went over to the record player and lifted its arm, which got Eileen's attention.

"Darling, I'm home," Eileen said, directing her huge pupils at Amanda.

Scanning the room, Amanda saw that Eileen must have been cleaning for hours. There were garbage bags full of papers, and boxes labelled *Nope* and *Maybe* and *Feeling Lucky*. The air stunk of cloying orange-scented cleaning spray. The green couch had been moved to the middle of the living room, and Eileen was on her hands and knees in the couch-shaped patch of dust that had accumulated beneath it.

"What are you doing?" Amanda said.

"Guess." Eileen laughed. She lifted a massive dust bunny by its hair and shook it at her until it fell apart. Then, in an instant, she was on her feet. "I need to show you what I found! You'll never believe it."

She dashed into the bedroom and returned with a dark oil painting in a gilded frame. "It says *Self-Portrait* in the corner there."

Amanda leaned in and saw the title in white paint along with a signature. Gertrude.

"I found it in the back of the closet," Eileen said. "I guess Gertrude was actually talented."

Amanda stared at the painting, unsettled. The figure was a kind of chimera, part woman, part frog, all done in moody ochres and dark greens. She recognized Gertrude's arched eyebrows and smirk, a certain amphibian inscrutability, which was only now legible to her. High cheekbones, crooked nose. She was ugly, raw, and utterly familiar.

"She looks like you," Eileen said, and maybe because she was exhausted, Amanda didn't object. The portrait *did* look like her, just not a version of her she'd ever seen before. The curve of the nose, the hint of cold-bloodedness she'd always suspected herself of. A vulnerable tilt of the head she'd glimpsed in the mirror but never quite captured in a photo. The threat of a tongue darting out.

Gertrude/Amanda's freckled neck gradually shaded into chartreuse shoulders, delicate dapples of gold. The blending was subtle, the lines exquisite and balanced. Amanda imagined posting it on TodaysFace. *Gorgeous. Mona Lisa meets Kermit vibes. Gothic frog mother fantasy.* Her womb was open, transparent; instead of amniotic fluid, green swamp water, clouded with mud and algae, and a tadpole–baby hybrid floating there, content, body curled around an umbilical lily pad stem.

Amanda closed her eyes, her chest tightening.

"I meant that as a compliment," Eileen said. "She looks like a badass."

"Can I show you something?" Amanda said, choking the words out.

She opened her phone and showed Amanda her baby, the algorithm-generated one with the blue eyes and flushed skin. The one who lived in her phone.

Eileen frowned. "What am I looking at here?"

"It's mine," Amanda said, then corrected herself. "Or it would have been. Remember how I slept for a week back in June and blamed it on a hangover? I miscarried."

Eileen took a deep breath, her face rapidly cycling through expressions. "Wait. Does that baby exist?"

"No," Amanda said, annoyed. Why couldn't her sister keep up? "This baby is a prediction from an app. You upload your picture and the guy's picture and it spits out an idea of what your child might look like."

Eileen considered this, confused, as though ransacking her mind for the meaning of the word *miscarriage,* and having found it, launched into a frenzied interrogation. "Who's the guy? Are you okay? Why didn't you tell me? It's fine. I know why you didn't tell me. I'm a fucking mess. Are you okay? Did I already ask that? A miscarriage! I haven't had sex in years. Not since my boss at the firm, but you know all that. Are you okay?"

"I'm fine. It was intense. But I'm fine. The guy's name is Alex. He doesn't know," Amanda said, feeling calmer in the face of her sister's panic. Then, surprising herself, "But I'm going to tell him. I just need to figure out how."

Eileen nodded. "You don't owe him shit."

"I know, but I owe myself." Amanda's attention returned to her body, specifically to her bladder, which was threatening to burst. "One minute," she said, hurrying toward the bathroom. She didn't bother shutting the door as she peed, closing her eyes, enjoying the release, a brief moment of calm and resolve. She was going to tell Alex. Let him carry some of this pain with her.

In the living room, Eileen, a new ring of white highlighting her left nostril, threw Amanda's phone on the couch, as though it had scalded her. "So I maybe did something you might not like."

"What?" Amanda said, her tongue thick and heavy in her mouth. Trust her sister to ruin a cathartic moment.

"Hear me out. I know you, you know? And you say you're going to do something and then maybe you don't do it and you regret it and I wanted to speed up the process."

Amanda lunged for her phone, which immediately began to beep and vibrate with incoming messages from Alex: *Are you serious???? That's not funny. I assume this is a weird joke? If so, haha. Seriously. I'm worried about you.* The phone rang. She panicked and hung up, turning off the volume so she'd have a moment to think.

Her sister had texted Alex the photo of the baby along with the message: *Congratulations Dada! Meet your son Reginald!*

"What the fuck, Eileen?" Amanda said. What was Alex thinking? She imagined the pink coils of his brain throbbing and short-circuiting. His life was so regimented and easy and here she was splashing buckets of shit and baby spit up all over his marble kitchen island. "I open up to you and less than a minute later you pull this? And you wonder why I don't tell you things!"

"You don't tell me things because you're a repressed, uptight asshole."

"I don't tell you things because you're a judgmental, self-righteous addict." She'd never said anything like that to her sister before. Even in the raw satisfaction of it, she knew she'd feel guilty later, ashamed.

"I'm a bitch," Eileen said, shrugging and returning to her dusting. "But you want to talk to him, so you should. I'm helping you."

Amanda sighed. It was too late to turn back. "But what should I say?"

"Up to you," Eileen said, grinding her jaw. "I wouldn't fucking bother, but that's me."

Amanda answered the next call and locked herself in the bathroom, which she now noticed was sparkling, clean, uncluttered. She explained to Alex about Baby Face Predictor and the miscarriage. He calmed down and said kind, supportive things about how brave she was, how sorry he was, how amazing that app was, seriously, the baby looked just like him. She agreed to go over to his place for coffee the next day. She promised herself she wouldn't leave anything out, not even the aching, horrible parts.

"But why Reginald?" Amanda said later that night, sitting on the vacuumed couch as Eileen continued to whir around the apartment, scrubbing and polishing.

"Why not? I like the name Reginald. In fact, I call dibs."

"Dibs?"

"When you fall in love with some boring guy and move out and get married and have a kid, you can't call the kid Reginald. Because by then I'll be clean and I'll have enough money for a sperm bank baby or a dog. I haven't decided which. Either way, I get Reginald. Promise." Staring into each other's eyes, they hooked their pinkie fingers together and shook on it.

In the morning, Amanda put on makeup, nothing too extreme—concealer, mascara, taupe eyeliner, a swipe of peach blush—just enough so Alex could detect a difference, a slight, persistent unfamiliarity. Holding her breath, she tiptoed past Eileen, who was splayed and snoring on the couch, and went downstairs.

While waiting for the bus to Alex's condo, she watched a small drama unfold. A toddler in a Spiderman T-shirt was having a meltdown, something to do with wanting to play longer in the park. His face was scrunched, his fists balled, a wall of fury. The mother crouched down to his eye level, her expression taking on some of the boy's anguish (his tense mouth and furrowed brows), yet somehow remaining calm, as though she had already moved through and past the upset and was encouraging him to do the same. She spoke in soothing tones, her face smoothing out slowly. He mirrored her, then went even further, a faint smile creeping into his lips. She mirrored him and smiled more broadly. She stood up and, squeezing his hand, they continued on their way.

Marcel Goh

THE VIGIL

I realize now, looking back, just how unusual it had been for my family to have entrusted three children with the overnight watch of a corpse.

It was the third night of the wake, held on the open-air void deck beneath the Jurong housing block where Ah Gong had lived and where Ah Ma would continue to live by herself. Six round tables, each covered with a white plastic sheet and accompanied by flimsy red chairs, were arranged around the slabs of bleached concrete that supported fifteen more storeys of concrete above us. During the day, people who had known our grandfather sat at these tables to play mah-jong and eat shelled peanuts. Off to the side was a rectangular table with gas burners on it. Every evening a catering man simmered vats of soup and curry on them.

At the opposite end of the void deck stood a white tent that housed Ah Gong's shiny wooden coffin. In front of it was a portrait, tinted reddish like many colour photos of that time, from when he'd been young and skinny. People went into this tent to stare and gasp and weep and nod and declare how peaceful Ah Gong looked. These visiting people bored us children, always saying they knew us when we were *this* small, and we had to be good to our Ah Ma now that our Ah Gong was gone. To escape this, we spent much of the daytime upstairs sleeping, and so didn't get over our jet lag.

Things were different at night, however. The deserted, fluorescently lit void deck became electric with menacing possibility. The two previous nights we'd performed this vigil with our parents, but we had proven ourselves trustworthy and they didn't find the job quite as glamorous as we did, so now it was just us—stalwart defenders of order and tranquility, aged ten, nine, and six.

Being the eldest, I was technically the boss, but my sister was a militaristic, commanding child, which made me mostly a figurehead. This was in the days before she fully accepted a female identity, when she wore her hair short and insisted on being called Jo. Little Roland was our lackey: at that age he was still loyal, stupid, and affectionate, more of a cute durian-headed pet or work beast to us than an actual person.

To pass the time we made up games and feasted on the endless supply of snacks. One was called Taste Your Testbuds. It had originally been called Test Your Tastebuds, but Roland had said it wrong once and the name stuck. You closed your eyes and someone fed you a fruit Mento and you had to say what colour it was. We stopped playing when our tongues stung from the acid and we got too good, even Roland guessing correctly more than half the time.

In our next game the goal was to get a ball of rolled-up Ferrero Rocher foil into an overturned cup in the fewest hits possible. It was aptly named Golf. As clubs we used the bendy straws from boxes of Vitasoy and Yeo's Lemon Barley Drink. I went first, and at each hole my score was considered par against which my siblings' points were calculated. On the score sheet we all sported the surname Woods. The courses became more and more inventive as the night went on. In one we went into the stairwell and chipped the ball down two flights of stairs; in another we teed off from the top of Ah Gong's coffin.

This game kept us entertained well past three o'clock. We'd been told that one of the adults would be down around six.

Our father was Ah Gong's first-born, so the funeral's logistical burdens fell to him, and he and my mother had quickly overcome their jet lag from sheer exhaustion. This was the first time we got some inkling of what had made him and my mother leave Singapore. It wasn't the search for economic opportunity, as with previous generations. Like many in the modern wave, they'd both had stable corporate jobs when they moved five years before. They threw their careers away to live in the wastelands of Canada, where my father was unemployed for a whole year. A reckless thing to do at the best of times but unspeakably irresponsible when you had young mouths to feed. At least, that is what our grandfather thought. To my father, the austerity was worth it in return for emancipation from rigid Singapore society, and it was clear, watching him organize Ah Gong's funeral, that he never possessed the filial piety demanded of a Straits Chinese son.

We'd left the very night we learned of Ah Gong's stroke, and had arrived in time to see him alive but unconscious in the hospital. Our uncle hadn't been so fortunate. He had also left Singapore as soon as he could. At that time he was working in Japan and had only been able to take off work a day after the stroke. Ah Gong had died in the hospital unattended, while our parents were fetching him from the airport. My father's aunts, whose proper names to us were Big Gu Por, 2 Gu Por, and 3 Gu Por, were convinced that the hospital had unplugged Ah Gong while our parents were away.

Even if that were true, so what? was my father's defence. He would have been a vegetable the rest of his life. Anyone should be glad to die in such a merciful way. In the Gu Pors' eyes this was an unforgivable thing to express. The Gu Pors terrified us—with their fierce scowls and incisive cackles, they were like three malevolent witches, always appearing together, conducting loud seances in unintelligible Hokkien, and ratting us out to our parents and grandparents. They were eternally judgmental of the generation below them, and their proclamations were treated as gospel by all the extended family except our father. Because we so feared the Gu Pors, we always saw him in a heroic light for standing up to them, but with age we came to realize that many of the skirmishes were a result of unbridled insolence on his part. One episode was because he'd omitted the Gu Pors' names from the newspaper obituary; another had been triggered by his saying he hoped all three of them died together in a freak accident, because he couldn't afford to keep flying home for funerals.

As far as we knew he didn't cry over Ah Gong's death, but our mother certainly did. She'd lived with my father's family in the months around when I was born, while she and my father saved up for their own place, and she told us how great a man Ah Gong had been. Ah Gong had grown up poor, and had had terrible luck in business, so he worked in his last years as a taxi driver. He got up at five every morning and never left for work before boiling eggs and making kaya toast for everyone, setting each individual place at the table and covering it all with a plastic dome to keep the flies at bay. It was the little things, my mother said, that were most telling of a man's character.

Was this all it took to be considered a great man: providing for one's relatives, adhering to a routine? More or less, according to the ancient creed that governed our family. I suppose that Ah Gong was at least noble in the sense of an inert gas: predictable, steadfast, incorruptible. In a colonial twist, these Confucian traits were seen as symptoms of Ah Gong's unwavering duty to God—the Christian one, that is. A friend had converted him as a young man, and he gradually converted his siblings and cousins. Even his mother, who for many years had held firm against Christianization, pledged herself to Jesus on her deathbed. So in the Gu Pors' eyes, Ah Gong had saved our whole clan from hellfire, and this fact made it all the more outrageous that his own son, my father, had lost touch with God, married a heathen, and was now making a fiasco of his father's memorial ceremonies.

I can only imagine the Gu Pors' reaction if they knew that we unwashed children were the sole protectors of their baby brother's dead body that night. By four o'clock a strong breeze had picked up, which made our foil ball zip around uncontrollably. We'd grown tired of Golf anyway and decided to take our job as guards more seriously. Roland and I filled our pockets with snacks and dragged chairs into Ah Gong's tent to get out of the wind. Jocelyn went into the shrubbery by a nearby playground and returned with small fallen tree branches.

"Why do we need sticks?" asked Roland.

"To protect Ah Gong," I said.

"From what?"

"Dunno, animals. Stray cats."

Jocelyn stood at the opening of the tent and kept watch. "Cats eat people, you know," she said matter-of-factly. "They're too small to attack us alive, but they wait for us to die so they can eat our eyeballs. Can you imagine that, Rolo? A cat munching Ah Gong's eyeballs."

Roland was getting spooked. Another favourite game of Jocelyn's and mine was making Roland cry. We had well-defined roles: I was bigger so if it became necessary I dealt physical punishment; meanwhile Jocelyn was something of a verbal enforcer, an expert at emotional manipulation. If we made him cry in the next hour and then spent the hour after that cheering him up, that would keep all of us entertained until six o'clock.

"And you know why they have the wake for five whole days?" continued my sister. "It's to make sure Ah Gong doesn't get *buried alive*." Her eyes widened with manic vigour to emphasize this point to Roland. "So we might need the sticks for that also. If Ah Gong wakes up, Rolo, you run upstairs to get Mummy and Daddy. Me and Oliver will keep him in his box."

Roland nodded. Then he asked, "Can I see Ah Gong again?" and stood on his chair. We slid the panel to peer through the glass at our grandfather's face. He'd died overweight, but he didn't look so fat in death. He wasn't skinny like in the portrait at his feet, but he had lost some pudge nonetheless.

"His eyeballs haven't been ripped out," said Jocelyn, and walked back to her post.

Roland and I sat back down. "I'm scared," he said.

"Scared of what?" I snapped.

"Ah Gong waking up."

"If Ah Gong wakes up, it's a good thing. It means he's alive."

"Scary though."

"You shouldn't be scared of Ah Gong waking up," said Jocelyn. "You should be scared of animals coming to eat Ah Gong. Or hungry ghosts."

"Ghosts? I don't want to hear about ghosts!" Roland covered his ears.

"No, we have to be ready," she said. "Mummy says there are ghosts everywhere in Singapore."

Unlike my father, my mother was raised under the deeply superstitious Singaporean brand of Buddhism. She never so much as cut across a lawn in Singapore without muttering apology to any ghost she might have trampled. At night, she said, ghosts were more daring, and you were liable to see or hear them anywhere, not just on unpaved territory. When we asked her if she'd personally seen any, she said no, but that was only because she was a Tiger. Ghosts were afraid of Tigers, but the rest of us had to be vigilant. She also believed in reincarnation and other mystical things, so any unnatural goings-on could be messages from our dead ancestors.

A flash of light illuminated the void deck, followed by a deafening peal of thunder. Roland jerked upright and clutched his stick until his knuckles turned white. He clambered onto his chair to make sure the thunder hadn't woken Ah Gong, then walked over to join Jocelyn at the entrance of the tent and scan the surroundings. It began to rain.

For Roland's benefit Jocelyn recited a lecture she'd gotten from our mother: "If you hear a noise behind you at night, don't just turn your head. They want to trick you, eat your third eye." She placed her index finger on the centre of his forehead and he crossed his eyes to look up at it. "But they can't do it if you turn your whole body around. Your shoulders are like your headlamps. It scares them away. Understand?"

He swallowed and nodded.

Satisfied, she turned back to look outside the tent and gave a shriek, startling both me and my brother. Roland yelled and swivelled his head around wildly, and I jumped to my feet.

"You okay? What is it?" I asked.

"Sorry, sorry," said Jocelyn. "It was just a rat."

"Oh," I said, relieved. "Still, if he comes into the tent, we have to get him."

We paced around, newly aware of the fragility of our grandfather's safety. The rain was coming down loud outside.

A moth flapped into the tent and circled a few times around the light bulb. It was the biggest moth I'd ever seen, light reddish-grey with black splotches on its wings. We stared at it, mesmerized. It spiralled downwards and landed on the corner of the coffin.

Roland leapt into action. He bashed his stick against the coffin with fervid brutality, missing the moth several times before finally landing a hit. The moth fell to the ground writhing and my brother struck it until it was still. We squatted around the mangled corpse of the moth. What an obese moth.

"Wait, Jo, what if—" I said.

She'd had the same idea. "What if this was Ah Gong reincarnated?" she said.

"What's that mean?" asked Roland.

"Reincarnation is when you die and in your next life you become an animal."

Roland was horrified. He started to wail.

"Ah Gong came to visit us and you killed him, Rolo, how can you be so bad!" said Jocelyn.

"I didn't mean to! I didn't know!" Roland dropped his stick and looked at us for some kind of forgiveness. He sobbed, tears and snot running down his face.

We let Roland cry for a while then felt bad. A part of me really did believe that Ah Gong could come back as a moth. I sat and pondered the violent misunderstanding that had occurred. My sister went into consolation mode. She hugged Roland tight and shushed him over and over and said it was okay.

"Ah Gong is a Christian," I said. "He doesn't believe in reincarnation, so maybe the moth wasn't him."

Once my brother calmed down, we surveyed the damage to the coffin. There were gashes in the wood where he had hit it. We would think of some excuse later. We decided that whether or not it was Ah Gong incarnate, the moth deserved a funeral.

Jocelyn wanted it to be a Viking funeral. She cut a corner off a plastic tablecloth, placed it over our Golf score sheet, and folded them together into a paper boat that was waterproof on one side. We secured loose ends with some tape we found, then tore strips of newspaper and stuffed them into the boat. Still breathing erratically, Roland picked up the moth and placed it on the pile and for extra fuel we broke some wood chips off the murder weapon, stacked even more ruffled paper on top of the moth, and added some Mentos wrappers to boot.

We grabbed a lighter from beside the gas burners and walked out toward the open gutter that ran along the side of the housing block. We draped plastic sheeting over the boat to keep it dry. The gutter was a foot wide and about eighteen inches deep. A decent river had formed at the bottom. Big monsoon rain poured down and we were getting soaked. No doubt we'd get a scolding later.

I set the boat down beside the gutter. Roland diligently held the plastic sheet over her hands while Jocelyn clicked the lighter a few times. Nothing happened.

"You have to hold that switch down while you squeeze the trigger," I said.

"Okay, I got it," she said. "I figured it out." A little flame emerged from the end of the barrel. She pressed it into the tangle of paper and the flame growled into life, hissing whenever it met a raindrop on the boat's hull. She and I lowered it into the gutter, where miraculously it stayed upright. The mass of glowing orange floated down the stream of rainwater.

The three of us stood silent. I don't know what my siblings thought of, but I thought of Ah Gong. With juvenile agnosticism I imagined him up there with Jesus or in that formless limbo between incarnations. I wondered if he could see us from wherever he was. We'd left Singapore so early in life that I never really got to know him. In my memory he was jolly, his laughter loud and booming, and I wasn't allowed to sit on his armchair by the television unless he was also sitting in it and I was on his lap and he was telling me in his choppy English, "Don't forget, Oliver, you are Hokkien boy. Like your father, like me." But I don't actually remember his deep voice or his thunderous laughter, only that they were that way, and now and then when I contemplate what Ah Gong could have meant by telling me I was a Hokkien boy, I think of the impact he had had on all his relatives except his own sons, of his failure to pass down his ideal of how one should care for and honour one's own.

We stood in the rain and blinked water from our eyes, watching the moth's funeral longship get smaller until it rounded a corner, into a culvert under the main road and out of sight.

CONTRIBUTORS' BIOGRAPHIES

CHRIS BAILEY is a writer, graphic designer, and commercial fisherman from Prince Edward Island. He holds an MFA from the University of Guelph, and is a past recipient of the Milton Acorn award for poetry. His work has appeared in *Brick, The Fiddlehead, Grain,* and elsewhere. Chris's illustration *Fisherman's Repose* was a winner of the BMO 1st Art! Award in 2022. His debut poetry collection, *What Your Hands Have Done,* is available from Nightwood Editions. His second collection, *Forecast: Pretty Bleak,* is forthcoming from McClelland & Stewart in spring 2025.

CHRISTINE BIRBALSINGH is a second-generation mixed-race writer who may or may not have been to couples' therapy. She has been published in several journals, including *The Malahat Review* and *The Antigonish Review.*

CODY CAETANO lives in Toronto. His first book, a memoir called *Half-Bads in White Regalia*, received the 2023 Indigenous Voices Award for Best Published Prose.

KATE CAYLEY has published two short story collections and three collections of poetry, and her plays have been performed in Canada, the US, and the UK. She has won the Trillium Book Award, an O. Henry Prize, and the Mitchell Prize for Faith and Poetry, and been a finalist for the Governor General's Award for Fiction, among other awards. She is a frequent writing collaborator with immersive company Zuppa Theatre, most recently on *The Archive of Missing Things* and *This Is Nowhere*. Her writing has appeared previously in *Best Canadian Stories,* and also in *Best Canadian Poetry, Brick, Electric Literature, Geist, Joyland, The New Quarterly,* and *North American Review.* She lives in Toronto.

LYNN COADY is the author of seven acclaimed works of fiction, including her short story collection *Hellgoing,* which won the Scotiabank Giller Prize in 2013, and her novel *The Antagonist,* shortlisted for the same prize in 2011. Coady's work has been published in Canada, the US, the UK, Germany, France, and Holland. Her most recent novel, *Watching You Without Me,* was published by Knopf US in 2020. Author Johnathan Lethem called it "witty and endearing . . . like a Lorrie Moore book suffering a Patricia Highsmith fever dream." Coady lives and writes in Nova Scotia.

CAITLIN GALWAY is the author of the novel *Bonavere Howl,* and the forthcoming short story collection *A Song for Wildcats.*

Her work has appeared in EVENT, Gloria Vanderbilt's *Carter V. Cooper Anthology*, House of Anansi's *The Broken Social Scene Story Project* (selected by Feist), *The Ex-Puritan* as the 2020 Morton Prize winner (selected by Pasha Malla), *Riddle Fence* as the 2011 Short Fiction Contest winner, and CBC Books as the Stranger than Fiction Prize winner (selected by Heather O'Neill).

MARCEL GOH was born in Singapore, moved to Canada at the age of five, and spent most of his childhood in Leduc, Alberta. He is a co-founder and editor of the magazine *Ahoy Literary*. His short stories have appeared in *Ricepaper, The Prairie Journal,* and *Existere*. He resides in Montreal, where he is currently pursuing a PhD in mathematics at McGill University.

BETH GOOBIE hails from Treaty 6 territory, Saskatoon. She grew up in Guelph, then attended the University of Winnipeg and the Mennonite Brethren Bible College concurrently, graduating in 1983. After her first year, she worked as the college summer janitor, but did NOT secretly copy the campus keys. In fact, this idea as story didn't coalesce for twenty-odd years. It was then approximately twenty more years before a protagonist showed up to carry the plot.

MARK ANTHONY JARMAN is the author of *Touch Anywhere to Begin, Czech Techno, Knife Party at the Hotel Europa, 19 Knives,* and the travel book *Ireland's Eye*. He has published in journals across Europe, Asia, and North America. A graduate of the Iowa Writers' Workshop, he edits fiction for *The Fiddlehead,* and he co-edits a brand new magazine, *Camel. Burn Man,* his selected stories, was an editors' choice with the *New York Times*.

SAAD OMAR KHAN was born in the United Arab Emirates to Pakistani parents and lived in the Philippines, Hong Kong, and South Korea before immigrating to Canada. He is a graduate of the University of Toronto and the London School of Economics and has completed a certificate in creative writing from the School of Continuing Studies (University of Toronto), where he was a finalist for the Random House Creative Writing Award (2010 and 2011) and for the Marina Nemat Award (2012). In 2019, he was longlisted for the Guernica Prize for Literary Fiction. His short fiction has appeared in *The Ampersand Review, Descant, Augur Magazine,* and other publications. Saad's debut novel *Drinking the Ocean* will be published by Buckrider Books/ Wolsak & Wynn in 2025. He lives outside Toronto and is working on his second novel. His website is: www.saadomarkhan.com.

CHELSEA PETERS is a writer and editor from Treaty 1 territory. A graduate of the MFA program at UBC's School of Creative Writing, her poetry and short fiction have appeared in *The Fiddlehead, This Magazine,* PRISM *international, Contemporary Verse 2,* and *The Dalhousie Review.*

KAWAI SHEN is a writer based in Ontario.

LIZ STEWART is a fiction writer from Minto, Manitoba. She recently completed a Bachelor of Arts in Writing at the University of Victoria, and now lives with her girlfriend in a car somewhere. She is the winner of the *This Side of West* 2021 Prose and Poetry Contest, and her work has been published in *Plenitude Magazine,* CAMAS, and *carte blanche.*

GLENNA TURNBULL's short fiction has appeared in *PRISM international, Riddle Fence, The New Quarterly, Cliterature, Luna Station Quarterly,* and, once upon a time, in *Room.* She was shortlisted for the *TNQ* Peter Hinchcliffe award and earned an honourable mention. She was also shortlisted for *EVENT's* Let Your Hair Down speculative fiction contest, and in 2023 won *PRISM's* Jacob Zilber Short Fiction prize. Her non-fiction has appeared in *HomeMakers, Reflex, the Same,* and *Okanagan Life* and been read on CBC radio. She put herself through university by taking one course per semester while raising two boys as a self-employed single parent. She graduated from UBC Okanagan at the age of fifty with a BA majoring in English and creative writing. Glenna had a weekly column called Arts Seen that ran for more than a decade. She currently works as a freelance writer, photographer, and stained glass artist and lives in Kelowna, British Columbia, with her two dogs and grown children. Her story "Because We Buy Oat Milk" came spilling out of her one morning as she sat drinking coffee, listening to the CBC news, and worrying about the state of our planet. Her debut novel, *Finding Sally's Cove*, is forthcoming with Breakwater Books.

CATRIONA WRIGHT is a writer, editor, and teacher. Her most recent poetry collection, *Continuity Errors,* was published by Coach House Books in 2023. She is also the author of the poetry collection *Table Manners* and the short story collection *Difficult People.* Her writing has appeared in *The American Poetry Review, The Walrus, Grain, The New Quarterly,* and elsewhere.

CLEA YOUNG's stories have been included in *The Journey Prize Stories* three times, and she was twice shortlisted for the award.

Her work has also been twice longlisted for the CBC Short Story Prize. Young's debut collection, *Teardown,* was published by Freehand Books in 2016. Her second collection, *Welcome to the Neighbourhood,* is forthcoming with House of Anansi Press in spring 2025.

NOTABLE STORIES

Caroline Adderson, "Homing," forthcoming in *A Way to Be Happy* (Biblioasis, 2024)

Jamaluddin Aram, "Let Hope Divert Them," *The New Quarterly* 165

Ben Berman Ghan, "Spectres of Bibliotecha," *The /tɛmz/ Review* 22

David Huebert, "The Business of Salvation," *Geist* 124

Robert McGill, "The Thunberg Pledge," *Prairie Fire* 43.3

Deepa Rajagopalan, "Cake," *The Malahat Review* 222

Mary W. Walters, "A Change in the Climate," *Prairie Fire* 44.1

PUBLICATIONS CONSULTED
FOR THE 2025 EDITION

For the 2025 edition of *Best Canadian Stories*, the following publications were consulted:

The Ampersand Review, The Antigonish Review, Border Crossings, Broken Pencil, Canadian Notes & Queries, Canthius, The Capilano Review, carte blanche, Catapult, The Dalhousie Review, Electric Literature, EVENT, *The Ex-Puritan, Exile Quarterly, The Fiddlehead, filling Station, FreeFall, Geist, Grain, Granta, Hamilton Arts & Letters, Hazlitt, Horseshoe, The Humber Literary Review, Leaf Magazine, long con magazine, Maisonneuve, The Malahat Review, Maple Tree Literary Supplement, McSweeney's Quarterly, The Nashwaak Review, The New Quarterly, The Newfoundland Quarterly, Open Minds Quarterly, Parentheses Journal, The Paris Review, Peach Magazine, Plenitude, Prairie Fire,* PRISM *international, The Quarantine Review, Queen's Quarterly, Qwerty Magazine, Ricepaper Magazine, Riddle Fence, Room, subTerrain, The / tℇmz / Review,* THIS *Magazine, Typescript, untethered, The Walrus, The Windsor Review, Yolk*

ACKNOWLEDGEMENTS

"We've Cherished Nothing" by Chris Bailey first appeared in *Brick*. Reprinted with permission of the author.

"Couples' Therapy" by Christine Birbalsingh first appeared in *The Malahat Review*. Reprinted with permission of the author.

"Miigwetch Rex" by Cody Caetano first appeared in *The Ex-Puritan*. Reprinted with permission of the author.

"A Day" by Kate Cayley first appeared in *The New Quarterly*. Reprinted with permission of the author.

"The Money" by Lynn Coady first appeared in *The Walrus*. Reprinted with permission of the author.

"Heatstroke" by Caitlin Galway first appeared in EVENT. Reprinted with permission of the author.

"The Vigil" by Marcel Goh first appeared in *Ricepaper Magazine*. Reprinted with permission of the author.

"Dark Rainbow" by Beth Goobie first appeared in *Prairie Fire*. Reprinted with permission of the author.

"That Petrol Emotion" by Mark Anthony Jarman first appeared in *The Malahat Review*. Reprinted with permission of the author.

"The Paper Birch" by Saad Omar Khan first appeared in *The Ampersand Review*. Reprinted with permission of the author.

"Mudlark" by Chelsea Peters first appeared in *The Fiddlehead*. Reprinted with permission of the author.

"The Hanged Man" by Kawai Shen first appeared in *The Malahat Review*. Reprinted with permission of the author.

"Funny Story" by Liz Stewart first appeared in *carte blanche*. Reprinted with permission of the author.

"Because We Buy Oat Milk" by Glenna Turnbull first appeared in PRISM *international*. Reprinted with permission of the author.

"Making Faces" by Catriona Wright first appeared in PRISM *international*. Reprinted with permission of the author.

"Nest" by Clea Young first appeared in *The New Quarterly*. Reprinted with permission of the author.

EDITOR'S BIOGRAPHY

STEVEN W. BEATTIE, a writer in Stratford, Ontario, spent twelve and a half years as Review Editor at *Quill & Quire,* Canada's magazine of the publishing trade industry. His writing and criticism have appeared in the *Globe and Mail,* the *Toronto Star,* the *National Post, The Walrus, Canadian Notes & Queries,* and elsewhere. He maintains the literary website *That Shakespearean Rag.*

Printed in the USA
CPSIA information can be obtained
at www.ICGtesting.com
JSHW020745251024
72355JS00001B/1

9 781771 966344